FREE

By:

Connie Racine

iUniverse, Inc.
New York   Bloomington

FREE

Copyright © 2009, Connie Racine

All rights reserved. No part of this book may be used or reproduced by any means, graphic, electronic, or mechanical, including photocopying, recording, taping or by any information storage retrieval system without the written permission of the publisher except in the case of brief quotations embodied in critical articles and reviews.

iUniverse books may be ordered through booksellers or by contacting:

iUniverse
1663 Liberty Drive
Bloomington, IN 47403
www.iuniverse.com
1-800-Authors (1-800-288-4677)

Because of the dynamic nature of the Internet, any Web addresses or links contained in this book may have changed since publication and may no longer be valid. The views expressed in this work are solely those of the author and do not necessarily reflect the views of the publisher, and the publisher hereby disclaims any responsibility for them.

ISBN: 978-1-4401-3444-9 (sc)
ISBN: 978-1-4401-3445-6 (e-book)

Printed in the United States of America

iUniverse rev. date: 4/10/2009

Dedication

To my Mother, Catharine Racine, who taught me how to survive with her strength and perseverance. To my Father, Victor Racine, who taught me that I could do or be whatever my heart desired with his patience and acceptance with all things. Finally, to my children, Cody, Harlee-Jean and Keirstyn. They are my life and the air that I breathe.

My heartfelt thanks go out to my sisters, Catharine and Brenda, and to my best friend, Pam, for their constant support, advice and encouragement. Also, I would like to thank Erin Brown for her wonderful job of editing the manuscript. I know her work was cut out for her, and she did an amazing job!

Chapter One

It was getting difficult to crouch with the growing bulge in my belly. I had been there for almost two hours, and I desperately had to go to the bathroom and to stretch my legs.

Goddamned, bastard. Even with the door closed and a pile of clothes around my head, I heard the television blaring; I could still make out the disgusting sound of lusty gulps and hard swallowing, followed by wet belches. The reek of beer and his pungent body odor wafted its way into the closet. I closed my eyes and imagined him wiping his mouth with the back of his hand, letting the drips of beer and saliva roll carelessly onto the front of his shirt and pants. It didn't matter that it looked like he pissed himself. All that mattered was the fact that he had a brand new case of beer every other day.

As I always did, I wondered how the hell I got into this place, and how the hell I was going to get out of it. This is not the life I wanted for my baby. This was not the life we deserved. This was certainly not the life that anyone knew I had. Although, I'm sure my mother had her suspicions. And, most certainly, not the life that *I* thought I was going to have.

We had been happy once, David and I. There was a time when I believed I was deeply in love with him and that my life was going to be good. But then again, fifteen year old girls could be like that, falling in love every other week. David and I used to be close and connected. We laughed together. We shared dreams of a future filled with happiness and contentment. My life was complete with him in it. He *was* my life, and I thought I was his. Of course, I am no longer fifteen.

Another half hour went by. More bottles clanking, more disgusting burps. But it was slowing down. Soon I would be able to get up and lie down. I knew that once he crashed, I would get at least six to eight hours of blissful peace and quiet. I would be able to lift my hands to my belly and feel the swell that encumbered the sweet life that was to become my future. I prayed everyday that God would not allow anything to happen to *this* baby.

In the last three years, the back of the closet had become my refuge. It stank of cat urine, sweat and stale vomit. *I* could reach to the back of the closet, but he couldn't, and the last time he went on a drinking binge he tried desperately to crawl in after me. He only succeeded in slamming my foot repeatedly on the floor, because that's all he could reach, leaving me with several splinters.

David was so drunk that night that he couldn't dodge my injured foot before it shot up and caught him in the jaw. His sweaty head snapped back, hit the door jam, and left him unconscious for the next half hour. My sudden surge of courage was strictly a result of the fact that he was so drunk, I knew he wouldn't remember. The next morning, when he asked how he got the bump, I told him that he had banged his head on the coffee table, trying to grab my cat.

He was always trying to get my cat. For whatever reason, the cat meowed incessantly when he was drunk. It *was* extremely annoying, but I cheered the kitty on for the sheer enjoyment of knowing it drove him crazy.

Concentrating on the present, however, I pressed my ear to the wall and listened. I hadn't heard any movement for some time now, so I thought it was safe to leave my refuge. Willing my toes to wiggle, the feeling came back after a few moments and I felt that my legs wouldn't give out on me when I put my full weight on them.

God, this was getting hard. I didn't know how much longer I could endure hiding in a closet to get away from David's violence, while he went from a happy drunk, to a lethal weapon. The transition took place in the course of about half a case of beer. Hiding in the closet was becoming more and more difficult. My belly was large enough that it was getting tricky to bend over. Most of my time was consumed by the needs of a drunken sod, dodging slaps and punches.

For some time now, I knew I had to get out. *Duh! Why are you still here?* I thought to myself. But, I also knew that to escape, I would have to be prepared to kill him…before he killed me.

He had come close to doing it a few times. I needed to protect this one, precious, innocent life. I had failed to do so twice before, and the nightmares that plagued me burned in my mind almost nightly.

I still can't believe that I have to worry about that. He wanted children, badly. *We* wanted children. I was very young, seventeen, in fact, when I was expecting our first child. It was a happy time. That is, until the death of my father.

The bundle growing in my belly delivered an unpleasant flurry of kicks to my bladder, reminding me that I had to pee. I didn't know if the strength of a kick could determine how strong a baby would be, but I believed this child would survive. I had to. And I prayed.

I had never gotten this far into pregnancy before, and I was finally able to distinguish between a foot and an elbow, or a little bum and a head. I could feel the fierceness of the blows, as if frantic to get out, or the gentle fluid movement of a stretch. Sometimes I could even feel quick, little jumps, as if the bouncing bundle hibernating within had the hiccups. I cherished the curve of my belly, and the soft, tender roundness of my breasts.

This child had been an unexpected gift. After the last time, the doctor told me I would never conceive another. He said that there was too much damage, too much scar tissue from two previous miscarriages.

My second miscarriage took place upon realizing too late that David wasn't nearly as drunk as I had thought. Regardless, I couldn't hold my bladder for much longer and there was no room in the closet for any kind of movement to relieve myself in a cup or bowl. So I crept out, moving as slowly and quietly as I could. It was dark, and the only light available was what the television gave off.

As I poked had my head around the open door, I was startled to see that he wasn't on the couch or the floor. I remember slowly scanning the room, seeing the usual mess of beer bottles and cigarette butts. The stink of beer belches still clung to the smoke in the air. But there was no David.

Where the hell was he? He couldn't have gone out, because I would have heard him. I felt the pit of my stomach clench. The hair on my entire body seemed to be standing on end and although I had to go to the bathroom so badly I thought I would burst, fear kept me rooted to the spot. If I close my eyes and listened carefully, I can still hear and feel what I felt and heard that last time.

God, how many times had I felt his presence before he came at me? How many times had I smelled his stench while bracing myself for the blow? This last time though, he had a different plan. I stood there as quietly as I could, my palms sweaty, my eyes wide. I remembered for the millionth time that I couldn't have taken a breath for the lump of fear in my throat.

From where I stood in the bedroom doorway, I could see into the family room on the left and the kitchen to the right. A bathroom opened off the kitchen near the apartment door, and another bedroom loomed in front of me.

Although David wasn't the swiftest of the bunch, he was very cunning, and I realized with a sudden start where he must've been lurking, waiting for me to come out. Before I could turn around, I felt hot breath on the back of my neck.

"Aren't you the tricky little bitch?" he snarled.

My blood ran like ice through my veins, and I remember, I had let my bladder go. The blow came so quick, and violent, that I heard a deafening ring shriek through my ears as a bone crushing smash landed on the back of my head, throwing me forward and leaving me with the immediate need to vomit. There was a searing, white-hot pain that started at my crown and branched its way down to the small of my back. Oh God! I knew I was going down, and without the agility that was mine before pregnancy, I could do nothing to save myself from falling onto my belly. My hands were outstretched, but it was no use.

The vise-grip clench in my lower abdomen was agonizing. How many times I had replayed this in my head, I don't know. It was always the same; *'God please don't let me lose this baby. I need this baby.'* But I somehow knew it was already too late, and I also knew that David was just beginning. I couldn't move. In the back of my mind, I was screaming, pleading, and begging, but I can't say for sure that I was saying anything aloud, or that I even could. At first, I thought that I might be paralyzed, but then I wouldn't have been able to kick up my heels, and smash them into David's back, because this time he had straddle me and was sitting on my back.

That just pissed him off even more, and he crudely flipped me over onto my back. I was finally able to vocalize my anguish at this point in our little party, and by the time I was finished screeching, David was so infuriated that he took his hands from his ears, balled them into fists, and landed a flurry of blows that bludgeoned my face. I vividly remember each blow as if it just happened yesterday.

He wrapped his hands around my neck and squeezed. His hands were powerful and thick, easily crushing my throat and not letting any air in or out. David's hot breath was on my face, and drool and sweat were dripping into my eyes and mouth. I lay there wondering why I always saw different colored spots when I was about to pass out. Odd, that I would think of that, just then.

Every sense, feeling and thought vanished from me, and I also noticed a sticky, hot, wet puddle oozing between my legs, and I knew that it was everything that I was living for. It was my sweet baby. I remember letting myself go then, and welcomed sweet blackness and then the light.

I dreamt. This is what I remember from those years ago.

There was a kitten wandering around in the forest, stepping carefully around little patches of thick, green grass, making its way to where I lay. Soft droplets of water trickled down my face, and the fresh sent of rain clung in the early dawn air. I lied there, blissfully content, with my baby cradled on my chest, gently snoring and suckling in her sleep.

Her tiny bum fit neatly in the palm of my hand, and the fuzz of soft brown curls brushed my breasts whenever there was a breeze. We were both naked, but surprisingly warm, with our bodies at one with the earth. There was a peace that engulfed our surroundings, leaving me with the sense that we were probably in Heaven.

We had to be in Heaven. How else could this perfect little creature be with me? I looked down to examine her. As if on cue, she stretched lazily, reaching her pudgy little fists up over her head. Her tiny fingers opened and closed several times before resting, once again, against my body.

Gently, I lifted my hand to feel the softness of her hair, and drew my finger down her back, causing tiny little goose bumps to rise on her body. She opened her mouth in protest, and mewed much like the little kitten that had finally made it to our side. Just as quickly as she fussed, though, she fell back into blissful sleep, pursing her perfect lips into a tiny rosebud.

I turned my head to look at the kitten, which was now standing on my chest, intently gazing at me. It bent its head and touched my lips with its pink, wet nose. I laughed, shaking my belly, and the baby, causing the kitten to jump back and land in a crouch. The kitty had a purpose though, because it stepped back up and licked my lips again.

Gazing up at the kitten, I became entranced with its eyes. They were pools of gold and green, and had flecks of blue. The pupils constricted as it returned my gaze, transfixing me. Reflexively, I put my hands more protectively on the baby, slowly entangling my fingers in her hair. Something wasn't quite right. Slowly, but surely, an uneasy queasiness gripped me in the pit of my stomach.

I couldn't tear my eyes away from the kitten's mesmerizing gaze. It was opening its mouth over and over again, but nothing was coming out. Not at first anyway. After a few minutes, the kitten wasn't meowing anymore. It started to talk. It said my name. How? I must be dreaming. If we were in Heaven, then maybe animals could talk. But that didn't explain the dread I began to feel.

The weight on my chest where the kitty stood was rapidly increasing. I looked down on the baby's sleeping face, and then back to the animal. I was startled to see that the kitten's eyes were glowing red. Its mouth was contorted into a sneer and fangs sprang out with fresh blood dripping down onto my chest. Where was the blood coming from?

My hands shot up and hit the cat off my chest. Again, it jumped back into a crouch, but it was now growling at me, and I could see that the fangs were growing into long, pointy spikes. So, maybe we weren't in Heaven after all.

The baby woke then and let out a piercing screech. I bolted up and gripped her fiercely to my breast, frantically looking around for something to keep the demon kitty away. It was slowly creeping forward, growling and snarling, causing the blood and spit to froth out of its mouth and nose. The blood was filling its eyes now, too.

I backed up to the tree we were laying beside, and hoisted the baby up onto my shoulder. She was wailing frantically, and her tiny fist was getting tangled in my hair. It was getting cold and a wind had picked up, swirling leaves around our heads, and chilling us to the bone. Could we be in Hell instead?

How could any of this be happening?

The cat was fast approaching, and seemingly growing in size with every step. The sky was turning black and everything around us was dying. The baby continued her frenzy, wildly flailing about.

The demon kitty was circling us. Almost the size of a cougar now, its movements were sure and purposeful. Again, it opened its mouth, and I hear, not a meow or growl, but my name. I heard my name! With every step, it said my name.

"Kathryn." It said. "Kathryn." Its voice sounded like David's, but with a low rumbling thunder behind it.

I closed my eyes and slid back down the tree. The baby was still on my shoulder, but a little less frantic now. She was just whimpering quietly. With my free hand, I continued to grope for a stick to hit the cat with. There was nothing but the mushy leaves at my feet.

Suddenly, the ground gave way and the baby and I were falling. There were leaves and dirt raining down with us and I couldn't see anything but blackness below. As we fell, the demon cat was standing above at the edge of the hole. There was a sneer on its face and it was laughing.

I clutched the baby to my body as we tumbled through the darkness, but couldn't keep her in my grip. Invisible hands were pulling my arms away from her. I began screaming, frantically trying to hold on, clawing at dirt and unseen hands.

I looked up again to glimpse the cat, but instead saw David crouching at the edge of the hole, where the demon cat had just been standing.

"Kathryn. You bitch! You will not get away from me!" He bellowed down the hole. "Kathryn! Kathryn! You are mine!"

Over and over he screamed my name. Over and over I tried to keep my baby girl in my arms. We were still falling. Eternally falling into an abyss. The invisible hands finally managed to pull my arms free from her, and she fell away from me. I watched in horror as she fell out of my sight, deep down into the black hole. I finally stopped falling and seemed to hover where I was, David still laughing above me. It was an evil, spine tingling laugh. When I looked up, he had grown horns and his eyes were oily pools of black. There was steam coming off his body, and I could see that the tree the baby and I had been under was now dead.

"Noooo!" I screamed, over and over.

My entire body was tearing apart from the anguish of losing my daughter. How could God do this to me? How could He let me hold her, feel her, and smell her, to then rip her from my arms, body and heart? I wanted to die. I wanted to fall into the abyss with her. I wanted to protect her, and nourish her. I could not live without her.

*But, she was gone. Oh, God. Oh, **God**; she was gone.*

Only the Devil could cause this much destruction. Was she at the bottom of the hole, broken and dead? Or, had she disintegrated into the mucky, hot earth?

"Oh God! Oh God! Oh God!" I kept saying it over and over.

The being that was once David was still bellowing. I closed my eyes and willed myself to let go. But I couldn't let go because it was saying my name over and over.

"Kathryn. Kathryn, open your eyes." It said.

This time, though, it wasn't David's voice I heard. It was a woman's. Gently, and slowly, sounding every syllable with care. Soothingly, she crooned my name. An angel maybe?

I remember after the miscarriage awakening to a voice in unfamiliar surroundings.

"Open your eyes, Kathryn. You can do it." She encouraged. "You must try, darling."

Darling?

"Kathryn, Darling. Come back to me. Open your eyes." Gentle as ever, my mother tried to coax me back.

No! *No, mother. I can't come back. My baby is gone.*

"Kathryn baby, come back to me. Darling, I need you." She said again. "You must try to wake up."

I did love my mother, and she did need me. Ever since my father passed away, she had become, for the most part, a normal mother. Except for the fact that my mother still believed David was a sweet, loving husband. He was very persuasive and led her to believe that my occasional, *visible* bruises were due to clumsiness on my part. "If she would just watch where she was going," he would say. Well, he couldn't talk his way out of his finger marks around my neck.

I squeezed my eyes tight, and willed my mother to go away.

Quite against my will though, my eyes struggled to free themselves from the squeeze. It seemed an impossible task to keep them shut, even though they felt like they were stuck together with super glue. I wasn't even sure that I was using the muscles I needed to be using to keep them shut. My whole head felt as if an elephant had stepped on it.

Just leave me alone, mother. Let me be with my baby. Hear me, mother. Let me go. Your wonderful son-in-law killed his child, I thought bitterly.

"Kathryn, wake up. You can do it, darling." She said. She was the only one who ever called me "darling." It was my father's nickname for me. When he passed away, she adopted it for herself, thinking it would soothe me somehow. It didn't. It sent chills down my spine every time she said it.

My mother wasn't what you would call a *modern* mother. She still believed that you stayed with your man, no matter what. She had stayed with my father, no matter what. They had married young, and my mother had a daughter at age fifteen. My sister only lived to be eight, though. She died when my father slammed into a wall with his pick-up. My sister flew through the windsheild and died instantly. Her name was Emilia.

My father had been smashed, drunk. It was unusual for him to be that drunk, because before the accident, he hardly drank at all, except for special occasions. After the accident, however, was a different story. One would think that killing your own child would be cause enough to never drink again. One would think. Not for my Dad, though. He began to drink *more*. Almost daily, in fact.

I remember the day we lost Emilia. My parents came home from the hospital crying and yelling at each other. Mom was wailing, "Why? Why?" and my father kept asking her to forgive him. I remember the moment clearly when the light flickered out in her eyes, and she stopped yelling and crying. She simply walked up to Emilia's room and stayed there for a long, long time.

I was only four, but I knew that something was very wrong, because a few days later, we all dressed in our Sunday best to go to church, and everyone was crying and talking about Emilia. I remember tugging at Mom's shirt, asking when Emilia was coming home. She ignored me mostly, and as I think on it now, I'm sure she just couldn't face me. Not just because of the trauma of telling me that Emilia was dead, but also because my sister and I looked almost exactly alike.

Mom couldn't ignore Dad, though. I honestly think he stayed drunk for the rest of his days.

At home, after Emilia's funeral, I was sitting under the kitchen table, peering out quietly from my hiding spot. I knew my mother couldn't see me, and I felt terribly alone without my sister, for it was beginning to dawn on me that she wasn't coming home.   Mom would not get to mourn her child. Dad was needing her. The day was over.

Before we lost Emilia, I thought our lives were normal. My sister and I played outside as late as possible every day. Mom baked cookies and pies, and we had friends over all the time.

After the accident, the desire to get away from Dad was stronger than my guilt for leaving Mom alone with him, so the older I got, the later I stayed out. Mom never said anything about it, so I assumed what any kid would assume. My mom was cool. She let me stay out as late as I wanted. She would have never done that when Emilia was alive. But then again, people change when faced with the trauma such as loosing a child.

That was our life, growing up. I remember feeling dread and guilt when I moved out, leaving my mother alone with him. I was deathly afraid that whenever I came home for a visit, which I have to admit wasn't often, my father would kill my mother before I saw her again. Some of these feelings were selfish too, because I knew that I would be expected to take my mother's place and come home to take care of him.

Long before we all thought he would, dad passed away first. It was one of the most bizzarre experiences of my life.

It was right before David and I got married. Literally. My mother had found a small church that would marry us, even though I was only seventeen and five months pregnant with my first child. A boy. *My son. Nicolas.*

David and I were standing at the altar waiting for the

priest, Father Tony, to get organized. He was very old, shaky, and painfully slow. The priest wore glasses that were as thick as the bottoms of the old pop bottles that we used to get at Al's Corner Store. You know, before all the corner stores became 7-Elevens. Nice, family run stores.

After an eternity, Father Tony finally made his way over to us, and slowly, very slowly, opened his book to where he wanted to begin. Because his glasses were so thick, when he looked up at us, his eyes resembled large, turtle eyes. The priest was clearly oblivious to how comical he looked and blinked several times, as the simple act of blinking made his resemblance to a turtle more prominent.

Anyway, my father and David had shared a twelve pack that morning while preparing for the wedding, and were a little tipsy, and hadn't yet looked at Father Tony. Well, David took one look at him and broke out laughing hysterically. After David started laughing, my father joined in. There weren't any other guests besides my mother, the organ player, and the two teenage twins, a brother and sister, who were standing up for David and I. *They* broke out laughing, followed by my mother.

Father Tony and I just stood there dumbfounded, looking at each other. Although he *did* look funny, the last thing I wanted to do was laugh. My father wanted this wedding, and my mother did whatever he said. Whatever my thoughts were, didn't matter to either one of them. David was eight years older than me, and even that didn't matter. I was getting married, and I truly felt like my life was over, that I was forever trapped. I did love David, but that didn't mean I wanted to marry him.

The laughter continued, and my father got up from the pew and came over to David, probably to slap his back in comradery. Instead, he staggered into me, broke out laughing again, and promptly fell forward onto his face with a resounding *thud.*

The priest gasped, my mother yelped, David laughed louder, and I continued to stand there, speechless. After a few moments, I found the courage to kneel down beside my father to see if he was OK. When I reached his side, I could see a small puddle of blood gathering around his face. I thought he must have broken his nose. Upon closer inspection, I noticed that he wasn't breathing.

I snatched my hand back from his face, and dug my finger between the folds in his bulging neck to find a pulse. No matter how much I searched, I couldn't find one. David had finally stopped laughing, and after a few minutes, pushed me aside with more aggression than was neccesary, and dropped to his knees beside my father.

"Are you stupid? Call a fucking ambulance!" He screamed at me. He didn't have to tell me twice. I turned toward Father Tony, who was already turning to show me the way. He then turned back to utter a few words of prayer in my father's direction.

When I got back to the chapel, David and the organists' son had managed to roll my father onto his back. There was a bloody mess on the floor, but it was easy to see that no more blood was coming out of his nose. By this time, my mother had sat down on the the first pew, and was just staring at the floor. She didn't seem to move or breathe, but just sat there with her eyes closed.

David, on the other hand, was still sitting on the

floor beside my father, blubbering like a baby. He was also *blabbering* like a baby, saying things like how good of a man my father was. Maybe he had had more to drink than I originally thought. It was revolting watching him like that, with snot running down his lip, mixing with drool from his mouth. It was a sight I had never seen before, and it left me feeling queasy. David had also never yelled at me like that before. He was usually loving, even when he was drinking. His outburst should have set off alarm bells in me, but I can be slow on the uptake, and chalked up his bizarr behavior once again to his being more drunk than I initially thought.

David and my father had been friends for years. David had actually apprenticed under my father at the machine shop where they worked. My father had always talked about him, and I was surprised when I met him at how good-looking a man he was. I was fifteen and David was twenty two when my father invited him to come over for a barbeque. He was of medium height and build, with long black hair, and slightly round features. Not movie star good-looking, but good-looking nonetheless.

He came over that Sunday afternoon to celebrate his graduation from college. David didn't have any family and had spent his life in foster homes after his mother died of a crack overdose when he was just four. Apperently, she didn't have any family either, and David knew absolutely nothing about his father, or whether he had any living relatives.

My mother had me cooking and baking throughout the day for "our guest." Being only fifteen, when I first saw him, I developed an immediate crush. Also because I was fourteen, I was very, very shy and giddy. It didn't help at all that I was pie-eyed because my mother would let me have wine sometimes on special occasions.

My parents didn't mind that David was obviously trying to get my attention.. *I* certainly couldn't see a problem. At least not at that time. What fifteen year old girl didn't want to boast to her friends that she had a twenty two year old boyfriend?

By the time dinner was over, my father had all but given David permission to do what he pleased with me. He even joked about having me married off as soon as possible, so he could have one less mouth to feed.

At the time, I didn't complain much. I really did like David, and the thought that he might take me away from my parents' home gave me a thrill. So by the end of the night, ignoring uneasy glances from my mother, I was sitting on David's lap, tipsy like everyone else, and flushed with a tingling sensation between my legs, as David ran his fingers gently up and down my thigh.

For the next year, aside from the occasional heated petting and necking sessions, David was pretty much a gentleman with me. He treated me with respect and gentleness. He didn't pressure me in any way about having sex with him. And I didn't offer. I was terrified to have sex. My father was very pleased with the relationship and thought that if he and my mother could have children and get married at fifteen, his daughter could as well. David, on the other hand wasn't keen on getting hitched until he could work as a licenced millright for a few years, and definitely not before I was eighteen.

But that didn't mean he was willing to wait until we got married to be able to sleep with me. So on the day I turned sixteen, David took me out for dinner, a walk in the park, and back to his place so he could "break my cherry." Of course the first time hurt like hell and I was scared shitless, but after a few times, I was into it, and truly thought that I was in love with David. My father even stopped belittling me in front of him, and I believed that David would save my life.

Soon after I started having sex with David, I discovered that I was pregnant. My mother was not thrilled. My father seemed indifferent and David just kept walking around shaking his head and rubbing his forehead in exasperation. It wasn't too long though, before he resigned himself to the fact that we were having a baby, and decided that we should get married and live together. And that leads us to the chapel and our wedding day.

My mother was still sitting on the bench in the first pew, her back ramrod straight. Father Tony was praying over my father's body, and David was wimpering like a small child who just dropped an ice cream cone. I didn't know what to do. I was panicked, but not over my father's death. I felt somewhat detached about that.

Minutes later, the ambulance arrived, followed by the coroner. By the time they finished their duties and left with my father's body, David had calmed down. Now he just sat there on the floor at the altar, staring off. My mother still hadn't said anything, but she at least seemed a little more animated. The priest, the organist and her children stood back to give us a few moments of silence.

By this time, I had made my way toward David and put a comforting arm around his shoulders. He accepted this act of affection and leaned closer to cuddle me. We jumped in unison when my mother finally spoke.

"I think we should have the wedding. Your father

would be upset if his money was wasted," she said matter-of-factly.

"Mom, Daddy just died. *Here!*" I looked from my mother to David.

He looked up at me and shrugged his shoulders, clearly not knowing what to do.

"I think maybe your mother might have a point, Kathryn. I know your Dad worked overtime to pay for our wedding, and I'm not going to disrespect his generosity," he said.

"I can't get married now. Wouldn't it be like an omen, or something?" I looked over to where my father's body had lain. The priest had, by that time, covered the area with a sheet, but little spots of blood were seaping through. I was incredulous.

She was getting agitated now. "No. No, I think you should go through with the wedding. Now."

"The priest is here, Kathryn. Let's just get married, and go home." David looked at me pleadingly. Having heard the reference that David had made to him, Father Tony ambled over, Bible still in hand. His pop-bottle glasses were perched high on the bridge of his nose.

"We could do the short ceremony, dear. It won't take long." The priest was *clearly* uneasy and wanted us to leave one way or another. "We could say a lovely prayer for your father."

Not knowing what else to do, I accepted, and Father Tony whizzed us through our marriage ceremony and said a small prayer for my Dad. The organist's twins, our witnesses, hastily signed the marriage certificate, and scurried away like we had the plague. The organist offered her condolences and congratulations then followed her children out. After uttering a word or two to my mother, Father Tony excused himself to leave. He shook David's hand, congratulated us, and bid us farewell.

"Well. You kids should go on the home." Mom's usual matter-of-factness seemed to have returned.

"Mom. You can't be serious! Don't you need me to help you with some arrangements? All of this is so bizarre." For a lack of a better expression, I was truly shocked and creeped out. I had this sick, unnatural feeling in the pit of my stomach. It was as if we were in the Twilight Zone, and I was dreaming. Just to make sure though, I pinched myself. No. I *was* awake. I looked from my mother to David. Back and forth.

They were both wearing the same expression of impatience with me. Weren't they shocked? My father *just died.* I *just got married.* There seemed to be no way out of this, so I followed them out of the chapel to go home with my new husband, despite offers to go help my mother at the hospital.

When David and I got home, needless to say, the mood was less than light and happy. He was very moody. I couldn't blame him, though. He and my Dad had been good friends. The buzz he had earlier from slugging back a few with my father had worn off as well. I didn't know what to say to him. He was clearly more upset than I was. I felt comforted that maybe my sister was up there to greet our father, and although I felt grief, the shocking reality of the situation hadn't hit me yet.

"Would you like me to make some supper for you?" I asked.

"No. I can't eat just now. You can get me a beer,

instead." He was being quite coarse with me, and hot tears sprang to my eyes.

"Now!" he barked, because for the third time that day, I was just standing there dumbfounded. My mind was fuzzy and there were a web of emotions jumbling around inside my body, making me feel dizzy and weak. David hadn't noticed, and was getting impatient.

I jumped and hurriedly ran to the kitchen. Quickly returning with a cold beer, I placed the bottle in his hand and sat down to join him on the couch. David's mood was making me very anxious. He was sitting in a slumped position, legs apart, with his beer in hand.

Without looking at me, he put a hand on my arm, urging me off the couch. "Kneel in front of me," he demanded.

I wasn't quite sure what he wanted, but wifely duties dictated that I did as he asked, and knelt before him on the floor, resting my arms on his legs. His meaning became clear quickly enough, when he roughly grabbed my hair in both hands, and pulled my head toward his groin.

"Get to work." He said.

I sat there gaping at him for a moment, not sure if he was being serious. When he gripped my hair more firmly, however, I decided that he was deadly serious.

"David, you're pulling my hair. It hurts." Although this wasn't my favorite thing to do to him, I obliged.

David unbottoned his jeans and exposed himself. He was ready and slightly purple with anticipation. He didn't wait for me to move on him though, yanking my head forward with one hand, forcing himself with the other. I gagged and my breath caught because I wasn't ready for his forceful thrust.

He held my head with both hands and thrust again, moaning with the movement. He was shoving too deeply, and I started gagging again, and tried to push back so I could catch a breath. My nose was runny from crying and I started panicking when he wouldn't let me up.

"Don't do that!" he bellowed.

David arched his hips forward and simultaneously forced my head down. "Don't even think about biting me, or it will be the last thing you do." The threat came out in a rush, because apparently I was still pleasing him despite the fact that I couldn't breathe.

I felt desperate to push myself off of his pelvis. The more I struggled, the harder he held me down. It was a scuffle that took me by surprise. David had never been aggressive with me before. A little snippy and bossy, but never violent or hostile. I was getting more terrified by the second.

He abruptly let me go and pushed me back onto the floor. He then jumped on the floor in front of me and roughly yanked at my panties from under my dress. He ripped them off in one powerful snap of the wrist and literally thumped onto me, pressing me to the floor. He pried my legs apart with his knees and forced himself into me with a thrust that made me scream in surprise and pain. Thrusting hard and fast, he finished quickly and slumped his whole body down on mine, crushing me with his weight. He lay there so long that I tentively raised my hand and stroked his arm to get his attention.

"David?" I whispered through a phlemy throat.

"Are…are you OK?" I couldn't breathe, yet I could feel the movement of my baby under his weight.

"Ssh-ssh. Be quiet," he said. After a few minutes, he slowly rolled off me. I just laid there, my legs still open, my dress up over my waist, with the slippery fluid of David sliding out and a burning, painful sting between my legs. I could also feel chafing on my inner thighs where David's jeans had rubbed them in his frenzy.

"I'm sorry, baby." He said. "I got carried away. Get me another beer, will you?"

"OK, David."

It took a few minutes to get back to David with his beer. He grabbed it greedily and gulped it back in the way that would soon become his most disgusting, vile habit.. Well, having him drool on me while he hovered and panted in lust certainly took precedence, but the sound of guzzling beer made me feel just as sick. I had no idea who this man was, but it wasn't the man I fell in love with, and I remember wondering how I could not have known that this was who David really was.

This was the first day of my new, married life.

Chapter Two

Later on that night, I started bleeding and contracting. I tried waking David up, but he had drunk so much that he was passed out on the living room floor. So I called my mother.

She picked me up and took me to the hospital, where I gave birth to my premature, perfect little boy. I named him Nicolas. He died just a few moments after he came out. The nurses let me hold him for a while, until the heat left his tiny body. I kissed every inch of his scrunched up, perfect little face, fingers, and ears. His skin was red and raw from being born before his time. He had only weighed just a pound or two.

I sobbed into the wee spot on his tiny little neck where his ear lobe was and told him over and over, how much his mommy loved him and how sorry I was.

The grief of the entire day rushed out of me in that moment. I cried desperately for my father, David's sudden and uncharacteristic act of cruelty, and most of all, for my baby. My precious, precious, innocent baby.

When they finally pried him from my arms, I prayed that God would take me with him. I prayed that David would come and hold me and tell me it was OK. I prayed that my father, having gone up to heaven only hours before, would take my little boy and watch him grow. I prayed that my sister Emilia was up there, holding my Nicolas close, the way she did with me when we were hiding from Daddy on those few occasions that he was angry with us. Before he got like that all the time.

That was my first baby. And about a year later, my second, a girl, who I named Gabrielle, had been born on the floor of my apartment after I came out of hiding from the closet too soon. I did not get to hold her, except in my dream, where we lay in the forest, naked and warm. Where the demon cat attacked us and we fell into the abyss. Where I remember my mother trying to wake me and bring me back.

I found out later that the bleeding had been so severe that I had needed two transfusions and had been unconscious for three days. David told them all that I had fallen down the stairs while bringing up the groceries.

"You know how stubborn she is, Merideth," he said to my mother. "Instead of taking the elevator, she wanted to walk up the stairs to get some exercise."

My mother, being who she was, accepted this story, even though my whole body was covered in bruises. She believed that I fell down the stairs and then walked back up to go into the apartment, where I fell again after fainting. I had no way of knowing just how long David let me lie there before calling an ambulance. He had tricked me then. He knew that I could have only gone so long before having to releave my full bladder, so I simply could not have crouched in the closet any longer.

Chapter Three

But that was then. This is now, and none of that mattered. I was expecting my third child, and the only thing that mattered, was *this* baby. I would always mourn the loss of Nicolas and Gabrielle, but I had to focus on the present. I had every intention of killing David if I had to. I *would* free us from this trap.

David kept an electronic dead bolt on the inside of the front door. It was a digital, high tech lock David had installed to keep me inside. There were two key pads, one on the inside, and one on the outside. Only David knew the code, so I couldn't leave the apartment when he passed out.

I was not allowed to have friends over, (not that I had any), and he didn't usually have visitors, so there was little chance of someone questioning the significance of such a hi-tech lock, with an actual keypad beside the door. It simply looked like a security system, and nothing more.

As far as my mother was concerned, that's exactly what it was. She wouldn't have known any better. She just looked at me with the faintest hint of concern and dropped the subject, as she always did.

What David didn't know, was that I had been watching him in the reflection of different appliances in the kitchen for some time now, while he punched the numbers in the keypad. While I stood to do the breakfast dishes, I could see him clearly in the toaster. *Thank God for stainless steel!!*

It was a small reflection, and it took me quite some time to get the numbers right, but I persevered. Every day when he left for work, I would jump up and try a new code. The day I got the numbers correct, was the first day of impending freedom for me and my unborn baby. Now all I had to do, was bide my time, and try very hard not to piss him off.

And that, my friends, is how I came to be here. Once again, hiding in the closet, waiting for Dumbo the drunk to fall asleep. I was now ready to take my flight. I had been slowly collecting loose change from under the cushions of the couch and chair, stashing my collection in some boots in the closet by the front door.

Ever so slowly, I crawled out of the closet on my hands and knees, pushing back the memory of losing Gabrielle after crawling out of the closet too soon, and listened carefully for the telltale sign that he was unconscious. Yep. There it was. The snore. Not just any snore, but the gurgling snore that ended with sputtering and choking on saliva. Well, the little bit of saliva that didn't run down the side of his mouth, eventually drying into a crusty film.

Moved by an increasing courage growing inside me, I quietly made my way to the bathroom. I *could not* go through with my escape with such a full bladder. I was still good for time. A few seconds of urinating wouldn't matter.

Having finished my necessaries, I reached once more into the back of the closet, behind the antique sewing machine that sat on the floor to one side, and grabbed a small duffel bag. In it, I had only a few things--a couple changes of clothes and the small amount of change I had collected. And most importantly, a piece of paper with the code to the lock on it.

The only thing left to do was to get David's wallet so that I could snatch his bank card. When my father passed away, he left me a small amount of money, and David added to it every month. It was a savings account, and the only time David used it was when he bought alcohol. All other expenses were in a different account. I had to give David that. He was good with money.

The amount in the bank would not last forever, but it was enough to make my escape and start new. My only problem was how I was going to get all of it out. There was a daily limit of course, so it would take me time to collect all I could. Zig-zagging all over to mix up my trail. I would have to get the maximum out tonight, travel on a bus somewhere over night, get the maximum out first thing in the morning, get on another bus, and so forth.

I knew that he would call the police and declare that I was missing, so that meant that the most money I would be able to get out would be a few thousand dollars, before David realized the card was missing. He still had a few cases of beer left in the pantry, so he had no reason to use the card.

I had no idea where I was going, but I didn't care. I would contact my mother when I got there to let her know that I was OK and that under no circumstances would I be coming home. Ever.

I carefully placed my bag at the door and tiptoed into the living room to grab David's wallet off the coffee table. The light from the TV was enough for me to see what I was doing.

It seemed like an eternity before I finally found the card. I continuously had to look up at David to make sure he wasn't waking up. God, must have been on my side though, because I got the card and to the front door without so much as a squeak from the floorboards. The only sound was David's gurgling snores.

My heart was pounding so hard that I thought it was going to come out of my chest. My ears felt like there were large amounts of blood sloshing throught them, throbbing with every beat, and my fingers were so slick with sweat, I was afraid that I wouldn't be able to turn the knob on the door.

I hastily wiped the palms of my hands on the front of my maternity jeans and reached into the duffel bag and grasped the little piece of paper that had the code to my freedom on it. I tentively looked over my shoulder, stopped to listen, then punched in the code.

Chapter Four

Standing outside the apartment building, all I could think of was that I was free. *God, I was free.* Free at least from the stifling apartment. And I knew without a doubt that my babies were up there floating above with their angel wings, paving my way. They were helping me to escape. They were going to help me live free from the monster that I had once loved. The school girl crush was gone and I was not fifteen any more. I was a woman. A young woman, I'll admit, but still a woman, and I was going to save this baby.

David would not allow me to work, which at first I resented. He was afraid I might learn something, or meet someone, so he locked me in every day when he left for work. It wasn't long before I realized that I could actually learn a few things from T.V. talk shows and radio shows. So I became grateful for the fact that I was alone and unemployed for the time being.

When Oprah or Montel Williams helped some poor girl get out of an abusive relationship, or start her life over again, it gave me hope. I thought that if these girls could do it, I could also. So I watched. And over time, I learned. I learned that if I found the right person and paid enough money, I could buy a new identity. *Where* I could find the right person, I didn't know. But I would worry about that later. Right now, I needed to make my way down to the store at the end of the block and call a cab.

Chapter Five

Once in the convenience store, I bought a chocolate bar, some milk, and used the pay phone to call a cab. I waited for the taxi around the side of the building where it was dark, in case David woke up and found me missing. Luckily though, the cab came within a few minutes.

"To the bus station, please," I said. I was so nervous and consumed with the thought that I might get caught, that I didn't notice we had stopped until the cab driver impatiently yelled at me.

Instinctively, I flinched, and shrunk back.

"I'm not going to hit you lady. Snap out of it long enough to pay and get out," he said, clearly annoyed.

"Oh. Sorry. How much?"

"Ten bucks."

I reached into my bag and pulled out the loose change, taking several minutes to count up to ten dollars. By the time I came up with it, he was staring, or should I say, glaring at me with malevolence. My nerves were already wrought tight, and this only made them stretch further, causing me to drop half the change onto the front seat, instead of into his hand.

"Jesus Christ, lady!" he bellowed.

"Sorry," I mumbled while stumbling out of the car with my bag.

I knew that there was a bank kiosk inside the bus terminal, and that it was our bank. I went inside to the machine and took out the first of the money from David's bank account. David always used my father's name as the password for such things. He didn't know that *I* knew that. He often talked in his sleep. Especially if he drank whisky instead of beer.

"Sorry about your luck, David," I said, then walked over to the bus schedule posted on the opposite wall, to decide where I was going to go.

I wanted to pick a high tourist area, so it would be harder to find me. I wasn't geographically knowledgable, but at least I knew that my best bet would probably be Niagara Falls, Ontario. I hated leaving British Columbia, but had no choice now. I loved the little town of Kaslo that I had grown up in. All the forests, and changes in the seasons. Yes. I would miss it.

What I needed to do now, was concoct a plan that would take me zig-zagging to throw anyone off my trail. I did feel guilty about leaving Mom to deal with David, but the baby's life was more important, and I would contact her later. So with a mixture of sheer terror and excitement that I had gotten this far, I went to the ticket booth to buy my first ticket.

While waiting to board the first bus, I went to the little café that was in the station, and bought myself a sandwich and a coffee. My stomach was very upset, but

I knew that I needed strength to be able to travel for the next few days. It was going to be an exhausting trek, to say the least, and I wouldn't be able to go through with it if I was passing out from starvation.

I sat waiting in the terminal, forcing the egg salad sandwich down my throat, contemplating what my next step would be. I had been fantasizing about my escape for years. Especially since the loss of little Gabrielle, my baby girl.

I became a shell. I realized that the David I had a school girl puppy love for, was gone forever. I no longer wished for things to be different. I wished for them to end. After Gabrielle died, I stopped living. The only thing that kept me going, was the fantasy that David would stumble down the stairs and break his neck. Or that he might choke to death on some beer.

A few times a week, he would stagger into the bedroom and take me. He was always selfish, and rough. When he lay on top of me, I would turn my face to try to get away from his breath. It was so foul, and acrid from the beer. No matter how much I was able to recede into my self, there was no escape from his hot, sour breath.

I won't ever forget the feel of his heavy body, pounding me into the mattress, saliva and sweat dripping down into my eyes, nose and mouth. His breath toxic and on fire, invading my body because I couldn't hold my own breath for long periods of time. Every time his heavy body crushed down into mine, it took the little bits of air in my lungs, and squeezed it out in a gasp, forcing me to take another breath. Every time I opened my mouth to take a breath, his saliva and sweat dripped in slimy strings down my throat, that tasted like a mixture of bile and rancid beer.

He would often punch the side of my head to get me to look up at him. I wouldn't, nor could I. I would rather suffer the blows, than look up into those glazed over, greasy eyes. If I didn't look, then I could shrink inside myself, and pretend it was a nightmare. Just a few more seconds, and it would be over. He would flop down on me, roll off, and fall asleep.

I always got up to shower, and scrub his scum off of me. I sometimes got sick, and I always cried. It pissed me off to cry, and it made me feel weak. Like he was somehow getting the best of me. But, who was I kidding. He had already gotten the best of me. He stole my life, and he stole *me*. As always, sex with David left me defeated, and internally scarred. It left me with a profound sense of aloness.

When my sister Emilia, died, I was very, very lonely. My best friend on the planet was gone. I was only four, but I remember her clearly. I remember that she was so good to me. She gave me the kisses and hugs that we didn't get from our mother. She read me stories, and made my hair pretty.

Emilia played tea-party with me. She dressed me up in her clothes, because our Mother wouldn't allow us to play with hers. Although Emilia's clothes were tattered, and worn, I truly felt like a princess when she dressed me up. She seemed like such a grown up to me.

I desperately missed the way she smelled, after a bath. I missed the way she would hold me if I had a nightmare. My heart ached without her presence. I often wished it was me who had died in the accident, but then would feel guilty, because then she would have been left without *me,* to deal with our parents. And, I didn't want her to feel lonely like this.

I had decided at an early age, that Emilia was definitely better off in Heaven with God, than here on the Earth with Demons and Monsters. In a way, I also knew that Nicolas and Gabrielle were far better off in Heaven with God. I could give them the love of my entire being, but I could not at that time, ensure their safety. But, this left me constricted, and so alone that I sometimes forgot that God might love me too.

Then, by some small miracle, I became pregnant again. At first, I was very resentful of it. I didn't think I was going to keep this one either, and I prayed day and night for the strength to not hope. I contemplated having an abortion. I cried, and pleaded for God to not allow this to happen again. But, despite all my efforts, the baby conitnued to grow.

As the baby continued to grow, and week after week went by, I began to realize that I wanted this baby. I began to feel a little flicker of hope, and small slivers of light began to fleck through my daily life. As bleak as my exsistance was, I was falling in love with the idea of this miracle inside of me.

After a few months, I began to feel the fluttering of movement in my lower abdomen. Just an occassional flutter. But, enough to give me a little courage. And, with a little courage, came a little life. And, with a little life, came a fighting chance. The one and only chance. The chance to change my existence, and fight for the life of my baby. To the death. But, it wouldn't be the baby's death, nor mine. It would be David's.

So. When the flicker of hope, became a string of hope, I started taking actions. I began to eat more, and when David was gone to work, I would do Pilates to strengthen myself. It came on in the morning on one of those cable networks. I watched David's every move, very, very carefully. I kept notes, and hid them in between the mattress and the boxspring of our bed.

It took a couple of months, but what I came to learn was very valuable. I learned that it was his third day of drinking, that he was the least likely to wake. I learned to disassociate myself when he came at me. I learned to turn my back effectively, so that every time he hit me, it would be the back of my body, instead of on the front where my hands would instinctively go to protect this little strange creature.

The Pilates helped me to be able to hide the growing bulk a great deal. My muscles were elongated, and I was standing taller, which made my middle appear smaller. This gave me some time. The time I needed to get some change out of the cushions, and the code to the lock. (I still can't believe he had a key pad to open the door.) The time to plan my escape.

And now, after all the planning, all of the work, here I was, on the bus to somewhere, with David hopefully still asleep for a few more hours, and my ray of hope, courage, and resolve, growing with every mile on the road.

Chapter Six

I woke on the second bus, on the third day, not quite sure where I was. I looked out the window and noticed we were driving through a small town. So far, I had been lucky and was able to continue to get money from the bank machines I had tried along the way. I knew the police would be able to track where I had used the card, but I kept my faith in God, that He would help me. The police might be able to see where I used the card, but they had no idea where I was going.

If I knew David like I thought I did, he would have already called the police to report me missing. What I didn't know, was exactly how long he would have waited before he called the police. I hoped that it would have been at least a few hours, to give me a little more time.

I desperately needed a shower and a change of clothes. At the last stop, I had gone into a little shop and purchased some toiletries and hair dye. Mom's best friend was a hair stylist, and I remembered her telling my mother that coloring hair was perfectly fine while pregnant. There was just no guarantee that the pregnancy wouldn't alter how the color may turn out. I shrugged my shoulder, and took the box I had in my hand to the cashier. I wasn't going for a drastic makeover, but just enough of a change that I wouldn't be recognized right away.

My plan was to ride the bus until evening and then get a room for the night in a motel. I was exhausted, and my back ached from sleeping on the buses. My nerves were shot, and I still wasn't nearly far enough away to feel safe, but I desperately needed a long, hot bath, a pizza, and a good night's sleep.

We arrived at the station fairly quickly, and I once again thanked God for helping me to get this far. If I had nothing else in me, I still had my faith. There was a time when I questioned it or maybe lost it all together, but my faith was now back in full force, urging me on to a new life of freedom with the baby.

It wasn't dark yet, but the sun was on its way down. The scenery surrounding the little town was breathtaking. There were some rolling hills in the distance, and it created the illusion that this little town was the only spot of civilization on the planet. I couldn't help but to take a few moments to just sit on a bench outside the bus stop, take some slow and easy breaths, and marvel at the wonder of nature.

The breeze was slightly cool, and it felt like small whispers of a feathery touch as it surrounded me. I wondered if my children in heaven were blowing gentle kisses on me, as encouragement to go on with my plan. I certainly felt positive. I couldn't remember the last time I sat, simply watching the sun filter behind the gently, swaying leaves of a tree. It was something that Emilia and I used to do.

The thought of my sister Emilia snapped me back to reality. It was time to get up and find a motel. The town was so small that I decided to walk through it. It couldn't be that difficult to find a motel.

Across the street from where I had been sitting, I noticed a small bank, tucked neatly between two little shops. I realized it would be foolish to pinpoint my location now, so I would have to wait to use the ATM until morning, just before my bus was leaving.

Turning right for no other reason than it was in the direction of the setting sun, I started walking slowly down the street. After a few moments, I came upon a little drugstore and went inside. I thought I should purchase a few cosmetics. David would not allow me to wear make-up, so I figured it would help with the subtle changes I was making.

When I reached the counter to pay for my purchases, I asked the clerk to direct me to the local motel and the nearest pizza place. She was a portly woman in her late fifties. Kindly, with a warm smile and a comforting presence, she directed me back in the same direction I had been traveling, down another few blocks.

I stopped dead in my tracks as I walked out the drugstore. There, not ten feet away, were two police officers. I swore under my breath and internally panicked! Both officers were looking right at me! The taller one, made a move toward me, looking as if he were about to ask me a question.

I froze. I could *NOT* go back home! I *would not* go home! Before the police officer could say anything though, I forced my feet to move forward, lowering my gaze and headed in the direction the lady in the store had suggested I go.

Good. They didn't follow, and I didn't look back to see if they were watching. Maybe I was just being really paranoid, and sighed in frustration. Half a block later, I was standing in the lobby of the little motel.

Once registered under an assumed name, I entered the dim, quiet room and breathed a sigh of relief. The man at the front counter offered to order my pizza and deliver it to me when it arrived. In the meantime, I set my duffel bag on the bed, and began taking out the things that I would need.

The hair dye, a small pair of scissors, a comb, blowdryer, brush, toothbrush, and toothpaste. I would dye my hair first and then practice applying make-up before my bath.

The extent of my knowledge about applying make-up was playing with my mother's when I was little. Even on my wedding day, I only wore lipstick. To help me along, I had purchased a fashion magazine at the drugstore to see what the latest look was. Judging from the pictures, the trend was pretty natural looking. Perfect.

I went into the bathroom and sat on the edge of the tub to read the instructions on the box of hair dye. It seemed easy enough. Mix, apply, time it, and wash off.

After spreading out the supplies, I stopped what I was doing to have a good look at myself in the mirror. It had been quite some time since I looked myself over in such detail. It could be worse, I thought, considering some of the things I had been through.

I had a picture of myself holding Nicolas in those few moments that he live. In the picture, I had a somewhat healthy flush in my cheeks, which still had the subtle roundness of a cherubish child, as I had only been but a girl of seventeen. But staring back at me in the mirror was a timid-looking creature, with fine bone structure and petite features. My cheekbones were slightly high, and my eyes were large and slanted a little, like cat's eyes.

My mother was of Irish descent, and I had inherited those genes. My eyes were a light, hazel green, and my skin was cream colored. Upon examining myself, I realized that my skin was, in fact, quite transluscent. I could see the small, barely visible veins snaking their way here and there, on the insides of my arms, and around my temples.

Back to the mirror, I next studied my hair. It was very long, and swept down in soft waves. The color was a light, golden brown, but I was going to change it to the color of my childhood, which was strawberry blonde. I thought it would bring out the color of my eyes. I just hoped that it didn't make me look more pale.

Before coloring my hair, I took the scissors from their case, and cut my waist length hair, up to my breasts. Not too short, yet long enough to pull back in a ponytail, or barrettes, if I chose. My head felt very light by the time I was done. I had to admit, I liked the new length--it would be easier to apply the color now, as well as being more practical.

The pizza finally arrived while the color was on my hair, and I sat down in ecstasy to devour a few pieces. I hadn't realized how hungry I was until I smelled the pizza and my mouth started to water. I sipped my Coke after eating, washed the color out of my hair, and started a steaming bubble bath.

While the bath was filling, I undressed, and finished looking myself over. I leaned in as close as I could to study the 2 inch scar that led from the corner of my left eye to just below my hairline. That was the result of one of David's tantrums, when he flung a full beer at the wall where I was standing. The bottle smashed into little pieces after it hit my head, with the fragments flying all over the place, covering me in beer and broken glass.

I knew that the scar could be used as an identifiable feature, but as much as I tried, I could not cover it with the make-up.

Looking down, my eyes fixed on my breasts. The veins were more visible there. Blue lines running down, forming a web, leading to my very dark nipples, which had grown even larger because of the pregnancy. I brought my fingers to my nipples to feel the soft skin, tracing the blue weblike patterns.

The tender touch made me feel calm and relaxed. My limbs felt languid as I gently slipped into the bubbles and hot water. I truly could not remember the last time I was so relaxed, and I could feel the heat of the water flushing my skin aglow.

When David was home, there was no such thing as relaxation. It was like walking around a glass house, every step possibly being the last, with the threat of shattering everything. And when the glass house shattered, which was often, it was more and more difficult to glue the pieces back together again. With every crash, the foundation became increasingly fragile. My hope was that I would be able to blow new glass into the foundation. Strong, thick glass for me and for my baby.

I slept through the night and got up just as the sun was rising. Inspired by the scenery of the setting sun the night before, I rolled out of bed and went outside to sit on the front stoop of my motel room. While watching the sunrise, I thought of what a peaceful and fearsome thing nature could be. I would think, for most people, it could be compared to the natural process of a parent peacefully loving their child, yet fiercely protecting them.

My husband had barely shed a tear when we buried our sweet, little Nicolas, just two days after we buried my father. Both funerals were delayed until I was well enough to be discharged from the hospital. I will always remember the grief that threatened to swallow me whole when Nicolas' tiny, white casket went into the earth, right beside my Daddy. That grief will stay with me forever. The memory of that tiny scrunched up face, and a head that was the size of a small peach covered with a delicate black fuzz, will *always* be at the front of my mind, glued to the inside of my eyelids.

Nicolas's fingers were only the width of cocktail straws, and his nose was not much bigger than that of a grape pit. His eyelashes were long and feathery, resting gently on his miniature cheeks, and his legs were the size of my index and middle finger pressed together. Before he let go of his struggle, I saw the rise and fall of his chest, and the faintest presence of a heart beat through his raw skin. There had been life in his delicate body. A life so brief, yet so profound, taking its rightful place in the universe.

Gabrielle's life had been so violently snuffed out that

she hadn't even had the chance to take her first breath. I did not get to see or hold her. I only remember the feel of her inside my own body, stretching and rolling in the only world she would ever know. Encumbered within, floating in the perfect warmth my body could offer her.

I did not know the color of her hair, nor if she even had any hair. I did not feel her perfect little fingers curl around mine, or that perfect smell of a newborn baby. Even had I not been unconscious for three days, I wouldn't have been able to hold her. I remembered hearing a couple of nurses gossiping in the hallway, and the whisperings of "the baby was a bloody mess. Such a waste."

At the time, I wished to be dead with them, yet I could never bring myself to do it. I thought of so many ways, so many places to do it, and who would probably find me. And yet, I couldn't leave my mother. She was a timid little mouse. She had always been so dependant on my father, and then on me. At the time of Gabrielle's death, as much as I wanted to be with my babies in heaven, I just couldn't leave her all alone. I resolved to continue living, if only until she was gone. As pathetic as her life was, I had to stay, because although we never spoke of it, we shared that life, one of sucking grief that only those who have lost so much could ever know. We were also both dead inside.

With that thought, I changed my focus and thanked God for the blessing of such a beautiful sight and went back into the motel room to gather all my things. I had practiced a few times the night before with my make-up and I was a more than pleased with end result. I had never seen myself like this before and I couldn't help but blush at my own reflection in the bathroom mirror. I had even pulled my hair up into a modern twist, leaving wavy tendrils that hung loose around my face. Even my mother wouldn't recognize me at first. Just the effect I wanted.

There was still time to explore this quaint little town on my way to the bus terminal, so I window shopped in a few spots, went into an antique store, ending up in a cute little book shop for a short while. The store was in a very old brick building, set back in a little nook near an alleyway. The alleyway was short, and led into a small residential area. I felt oddly safe here, despite my scare the night before with having seen those two police officers.

As I hopped on the next bus out of town, I marveled yet again that I had used the bank card without any problems. I knew that I could probably only make one more attempt before David was hot on my trail, if he wasn't already. I would need more to be able to provide for the baby until I figured out what I was going to do, but couldn't risk it.

I thought I might catch a train from the next major city. I had decided to go to Niagara Falls, but would only make Saskatchewan by nightfall, which meant I still had at least a few more days to travel. The sooner I found a small, furnished room to rent, the fewer chances there would be of being seen. I did not need anything fancy. Just the barest of amenities were required.

When I got to my destination, I would go shopping for the baby and myself. It was April, so I wouldn't have to buy too much. I was due in about fourteen weeks, so by the time the baby came, it would be warmer, and summer clothes were less expensive than winter clothes. I didn't need much of anything. I had my pre-pregnancy jeans and sneakers, so I only needed some sandals, summery tops, and a couple pairs of shorts when the time came.

I would stock up on diapers, wipes, breast pads, and other necessary baby things. The excitement in my belly was growing. I felt giddy with the thought of holding and nursing this precious baby. There were plenty of children's used items stores, so I would just take my luck at finding a bassinet for the baby to sleep in. I knew that I would be ok on a sofa, if I could only find a bachelor apartment.

"When are you due, dear?" Startled from my thoughts, I looked over to see a slight, elderly lady sitting across the aisle. She smiled warmly, and I couldn't help but smile back.

"In about fourteen weeks," I replied.

"Oh, you're such a lovely dear. Are you going to meet your husband then?" she inquired.

This caught me off guard, because I hadn't actually thought about how I might answer that particular question, if someone asked me. So I said the first thing that came to mind.

"No, Ma'am. I'm a widow."

At this, she became very animated. "Oh! My poor dear, you're so young! Was it an accident, then?"

"Uh…" *What do I say? What do I say?* "…yes. Yes it was. It was a car accident. Some time ago," I lied.

"Well, don't you worry one bit, dear. God will see you through." She said this with a firm nod of the head and promptly turned back to the book she was reading.

Hmmm. I hadn't read a book in such a long time.

I had purchased the newest James Patterson at the drugstore the day before and I fished it out of my bag. It was going to be a long ride. I couldn't spend all of it trapped inside my head, worrying. So I turned to the first page and immediately found entertainment from my favorite author.

Chapter Seven

The next two days went by pretty uneventfully. In the end I decided to stick with the buses, and used the card one more time, before throwing it into a trashcan. My goal now was to backtrack and zigzag a bit, to throw anyone off my trail. I felt confident. It had been five days, and I hadn't heard or seen anything on the news or in the papers. Could it be that David had done nothing? No, that couldn't be the case. He will look for me until the day he dies. It was my mother that I was getting concerned about, but I couldn't call her yet. There was far too much at risk. I had no choice but to continue on.

Four more days of sitting on a bus, reading another book, and making small talk with some of the other passengers. I was exhausted beyond reason. At this stage of my pregnancy, the circulation in my legs was getting poor and my lower back was constantly aching. When we finally pulled into the bus station at Niagara Falls, I was feeling extremely elated that I had finally made it. I had *made* it! Now, it was time to get lost in the shuffle. But first, food and exercise.

Chapter Eight

It was gloriously cool near the mist of the Falls. Tiny droplets of icy water clung to my skin and clothes. It left my hair in drippy, stringy clumps that plastered to my cheeks, and I was truly the happiest I had ever been. If it weren't for my large frontal load, I would have been skipping. Instead, I kept a hand protectively on my belly and relished my first real day of freedom.

There was no way it could be this easy though. I would forever be looking over my shoulder, and I didn't think I would be able to stay in one place for too long over the next few years. That would be OK, though. I had no plans of becoming close friends with anyone in the near future. The last thing I needed was to complicate my life with having to keep a façade up about who I was, and where I came from.

I had spent my whole life so far without friends. I would be fine without any now. I didn't feel the need to be gossipy with other women, nor did I feel the need to have "girl's nights" or heart-to-hearts. That wasn't me. I buried all of that with Emilia. That was enough for girly memories.

Besides, I had a lot to think about. Staying on the run was going to be exhausting, to say nothing of being a new mother. I also had to decide how I was going to support us. I had no skill, save cleaning and cooking. Although I was quite good at sewing, so I could always fall back on that. It was the only thing David ever praised me for.

I mentally chided myself, and had to make a concerted effort to not think about my life with David, and I wondered if I would ever forget about him. Certainly, I suffered with nightmares on a regular basis. Maybe they would stop now that I wouldn't be living under the same roof or in the same city as David. Hell, I wasn't even in the same *province* anymore, and a wicked grin lit up my face at the thought. There would be plenty of time to deal with all those issues, I reminded myself. It was time to find a place to live.

The best place to start would be the classified section of the local newspaper. So, I trotted over to the 7-11 down the street and purchased a paper. I couldn't stand there and read it, so I went into a coffee shop, grabbed a tea, and sat down to read.

I carefully scanned the paper to see if there was any mention about a missing person, but there was nothing. That, in itself, was disturbing. Why hadn't David or my mother called the police? There was absolutely no way that David would be able to guess where I was, and come looking for me. Even if they traced the bank card, they still wouldn't be able to find me. I hadn't spent six or seven days on a bus, zigzagging across Canada from Kaslo, British Columbia, to Niagara Falls, just so I could be caught. No, no. He would not be able to guess where I was, and he certainly wouldn't suspect I had enough intelligence to plan a getaway.

For the next twenty minutes, I scanned the classifieds and found a few rental listings that sounded acceptable. Upon calling them, however, only one was still available, so I made arrangements to see it later on in the evening. I thought about going shopping, but finally decided against it until I had a place to put all of our things. I really shouldn't spend the money or burden myself down with bags. It wouldn't hurt to go looking around though.

I hailed a cab and asked the driver if there were any malls in the area. Apparently, such a big tourist area had a few, so he took me to the one closest to the apartment I was seeing later.

I wandered around for a while and looked at a lot of baby stuff. I didn't know if the baby was a boy or a girl, so I thought I should stick to mostly neutral colors. All babies looked cute in yellows and greens. But I realized that I would have to find out where there was a second-hand baby shop, so I could save as much money as possible.

A few hours had gone by, and it was almost time to go to the apartment. I asked a sales clerk for directions to the address I was looking for and headed over. My duffel bag was small, but it was getting heavy, and I hoped that I didn't have to go to a motel for the night. Once I got to the apartment building, my hopes were raised a bit, because the outside was immaculate. Although there were no flowers yet, I could see that the place would be kept up beautifully into the spring and summer.

The building itself was rather small and very old.

The path up to the apartment was a mosaic pattern of cobblestone blocks, which curved into an S shape. The walkway was lined with decorative patio lights placed every three feet or so. On either side of the walk, the ground was topped with a mixture of red clay chunks and white stone. Each side of the walk also had a large tree, with a huge patch of grass surrounding the trees. I knew it must be even more welcoming in the summer time.

When I spoke to the landlord on the phone, he said the building only had 10 units. Each unit had two bedrooms, a kitchen, dining room, study, one and a half bathrooms, and family room. I also knew that the apartment in question was a six-month sublet, from the woman that lived there. The landlord didn't say why the woman was leaving, but if the tenant didn't mind the fact that there would be a baby in the apartment for at least three of those months, it would work for me.

I rang the landlord's apartment. After a few moments a short, stocky, elderly man opened the door and greeted me with a warm smile. He couldn't have been more than five feet, two inches tall. Only a few inches shorter than me, he stood as straight as he could to look up into my face. He had a very friendly visage, and his smile was contagious.

"Hello there. You must be Kathleen," he noted. He quickly glanced down at my protruding belly, but was graceful enough not to ask any more questions. He already knew that I was expecting, because he asked me on the phone if I had any children, allowing me to explain my situation.

"Yes I am. And you are Mr. Sullivan?" I had told him my name was Kathleen on the phone. Until that moment, I hadn't thought about what I might actually change my name to, so in a haste, I had answered with the first name that had come to mind.

"Come in, my dear. May I get you a tea or a snack?" He led me through the door and closed it behind me. We entered a cozy little sitting room that had a small fireplace and a couple of Lazy Boy chairs.

"No, thank you. I had a bite at the mall." As friendly as this man seemed, there wasn't much time for niceties at the moment.

"All right then, what would you like to know first?"

"Well, I guess, the price." Is that what you would normally ask about first? I had no idea, but Mr. Sullivan just laughed, and quickly gave me all the details of the apartment.

The sixty three year old widow who was leasing the apartment would be spending the next six months in Florida. The apartment was fully furnished, and she apparently had no objections to sub-leasing to a mother-to-be, since she had several grandchildren, and her apartment was child safe. Her only stipulation was a no smoking policy, which was obviously fine by me.

"Mrs. Graham and I are very close friends, my dear, and she trusts my judgment. I don't see why you shouldn't be the person to rent the apartment. Would you like to have a look? You can move in right away. Mrs. Graham left this morning, so the place is empty."

"Really? I can't be the only person to have called about the ad. But, yes. I would love to see the apartment!" I could let my hopes get up just one more time, I thought. After all, I deserved at least that.

"Oh no, dear. You were the tenth. None of the

other callers seemed suitable. You, however, I could tell right away that you will be fine. It's a terrible shame dear that you are also a widow," he said, with a worried look. I had told him over the phone the same story about my husband being killed in an accident that I had told the elderly lady on the bus. "So young," he said, sadly shaking his head. He looked up then and gave that warm, friendly smile and led me back into the hallway.

"Just leave your bag here, dear. If you're interested, I'll come back and get it for you."

"Oh. Uh…that's ok. I'd rather keep it with me. I lost my luggage once, and now I don't leave it anywhere." I returned the friendly smile.

"Well then, at least let me carry it for you. I'm not too old to help a pretty, young lady," Mr. Sullivan teased.

"I can't say 'no' to that, now can I?" With that, I handed him the duffel bag that had a small portion of my life in it. Not to mention all of my money.

We crossed the hall from his apartment and took the elevator up to the fifth floor. There were two apartments on each floor, and the one I might be renting was on the east side of the building. Mr. Sullivan opened the door and led me through.

"This is so lovely," I said. And it was.

We stepped into a little foyer, and on the right, was a sitting room like the one in Mr. Sullivan's apartment, although it had a chaise lounge and a large, stacked bookshelf. On the left was a family room, simply decorated with large doors leading out to a large patio overlooking a park in the rear of the building. We then entered a dining room, which led into a small kitchen and back out into the foyer. On the far side of the sitting room there was a powder room and then a flight of stairs. The study was tucked beneath the stairs.

We went upstairs, and I was very impressed with how cozy and clean the bedrooms were. There was even a crib and twin size bed in the smaller room, along with a dresser and a rocking chair. The main bedroom was decorated with warm colors, adorning large prints on the comforter and drapes, and I felt very comfortable here. The bed looked like it will be like sleeping on a fluffy cloud, compared to the stiff seats in seven or so buses I had traveled on.

"As I said, Mrs. Graham has grandchildren, and sometimes one of her children will visit and spend a few days," Mr. Sullivan pointed out. I couldn't help but notice the fondness that he showed when talking about Mrs. Graham.

"This is perfect!" I said excitedly. "Is it still available, then?"

"Not after you sign the papers and pay the first month's rent." He was smiling at me and thankfully didn't notice my stomach go for a lurch at the mere mention of signing papers.

"Unfortunately, I don't have any identification to show you. My purse was stolen at the airport, from underneath my seat. I didn't even notice, and apparently neither did anyone else." *Please look believable,* I prayed.

"You made a police report, I hope?" Mr. Sullivan asked me sternly, pointing his finger in my direction. I couldn't do anything but smile at him and nod my head.

"Well, I could take the first two weeks payment in cash, if you have it, and then the rest in a couple of weeks.

As for the papers, I can't let that slide, dear. I do need them to be signed. Stay right here and I'll fetch them." And off he went.

"Shit! What's your name going to be?" I hissed under my breath. I couldn't use my real name, of course, nor could I use my mother's name.

Before I could decide, Mr. Sullivan came back with papers in hand and eagerly waited for me to sign them.

"Could I read them, first, Mr. Sullivan? I could bring them back down to you in a little while." With this, I stretched and feigned a yawn, putting my hand to my belly and lower back. "And I can pay you the first month in cash, right now. I have some money on me."

"Good God! Dearie, I hope you're careful with your money. You could be robbed blind!" His tone was not at all admonishing in any way. Rather, it was said in a way that made me feel as if he were being protective.

"I don't have *all* my money with me," I said, with a laugh. "But I have enough. This apartment is a lot less than I was expecting, and it won't leave me short to give it to you now."

"OK then, dear. You come down in a little while, when you're rested, and we'll do the preliminaries then." He reached into his pocket, gave me the key, and turned to leave.

As soon as the door was closed, I locked it, and leaned my head against its cool surface with a sigh. Why had I not thought of a last name? Probably the most important detail, besides my appearance, and I had forgotten. I could think about it while I put my things away and rummaged through the kitchen to see what kind of groceries I needed.

Apparently, Mrs. Graham only purchased what she would be eating one day at a time, because the cabinets were bare, except for the dishes and cooking things. Although, there were plenty of blankets, towels, and other household items stacked neatly in closets. I felt a little awkward going through a stranger's belongings, but then thought Mrs. Graham wouldn't have left her apartment to a total stranger if anything was really valuable. She must be a thoughtful person, because she even left the phone and cable on.

Having spent the last half hour thinking, I finally came up with a name. Kathleen Lockhart. I certainly looked like I had Scottish or Irish descent. I had fair skin, and green eyes, and I've always thought the name "Lockhart" was a cool name. Simple as that. Now, all I had to do was go down to Mr. Sullivan, sign the lease, and pay the first month's rent. Then it was off to the grocery store, followed by a bath and bed. I was so excited, I whooped with laughter.

Chapter Nine

"Kathryn. Kathryn, stop crying. It wouldn't hurt so much if you stretched it out," David was saying. "I could bring you home some kind of pipe or something."

"David! It hurts! Pleeeese stop!" I screamed into the pillow.

David was behind me, forcing himself in. I could feel the stretch and tear of my rectum, and it burned like he was holding a match to the area. With a sudden POP, he finally ripped through and pushed all the way in. I screamed from the shock and bucked to try to get him off me. The pain was more than I could stand, and the only lubrication was the blood from the torn flesh, running down my legs, and smearing down the front of him. It had taken him so long to get in that the Vaseline had mostly rubbed off.

He grabbed the back of my hair and yanked my head off the pillow, bringing his foul, hot breath down to my ear.

"Shut your fucking mouth!" He hissed. "Someone will call the police!"

I could only be so lucky, I thought.

He dropped my head and pounded me from behind so viciously that I thought I would rip in half.

David was laughing, grunting, and pushing, not at all aware that I finally passed out from the pain, slumped over my bunched up pillow beneath my belly.

CHAPTER TEN

I SAT BOLT UPRIGHT, DRENCHED in sweat and crying. It was just a dream. That won't happen again, I reminded myself. He's gone and I had gotten away. But, despite that, I couldn't help but run down the stairs to check the locks on the door one more time. Then I looked out the windows again, in search of a lurking figure. There wasn't one, of course.

I went upstairs to change the soaked sheets and my sodden nightgown, then slipped downstairs to have a tea to relax my nerves. The nightmare was still vivid enough that I could still feel the pain. I knew I would never forget that pain. The sheer suddenness of it, when it happened, left me shocked to the point where my brain had to play catch-up with my senses.

The rape itself probably only lasted a couple of minutes, but it felt like an eternity before my brain finally gave in and let me pass out. I hadn't been out for long enough though, and he came at me twice more that day. Bleeding to death seemed like a possibility at the time, but I hadn't been blessed with that kind of freedom. I did, however, pass out every time. It was months before I could go to the bathroom without excruciating pain or bleeding. By that point, I had gotten extremely thin from subsisting only on liquids and popping laxatives for fear of having a bowel movement.

David raped me like that half a dozen times throughout the years. As time went on, I was able to guard myself against it and turn into myself. I would think about my sister, or my precious Nicolas and Gabrielle. My fury would harden my resolve to someday get out. My fantasies of brutally killing him, or maiming him down there, gave me a deep, primitive satisfaction that carried me through.

And, I had God. Once I found Him again, I found faith again, and the will to see it through. Now especially. This baby moved freely in my womb. The knees or the elbows poked out. With all the love I had to give to this child, I was certain that we would be OK. I knew that the fulfillment of being a mother would allow me to forget about David and the tortures he put me through. I was certain the nightmares would ease, the longer I was free.

This thinking, however, brought my own mother to mind, and not for the first time, I felt a pang in my heart. When would I be able to call her? She needed to know that I was ok, and the baby was ok. I simply could not face her yet. Maybe the police were investigating David and thought he killed me. But why was it not on the news? That was so disturbing to me. When pregnant women go missing, they are splashed all over the television. The only conclusion I could come up with, was that David was looking for me, and I knew my Mom would be bullied into not filing a "Missing Persons" report.

Well, I couldn't find out anything about that situation without putting myself at risk of being caught. I would die before I go back to life with David. Or he will. Too tired to think about it further, I went back upstairs to go back to bed.

Chapter Eleven

I slept well for the rest of the night. Mrs. Graham's bed was very comfortable, and snuggling up in the down comforter was reassuring and warm. The next morning, after a light breakfast of scrambled eggs and toast, I went down to Mr. Sullivan's to get some information about the town. He told me where the library was, the closest government building, the best store to rent movies from, the tastiest restaurant, the finest bowling alley, the top shoe store, and the most important thing, where the walk-in medical center was. I didn't have an Ontario Health Card, as required in Ontario, but I still needed to be checked.

Upon my arrival at the medical center, I picked a number and waited my turn. I was a little apprehensive when the nurse at the front counter finally called my name. I hadn't had any kind of medical care whatsoever, except for the first ultrasound. At the time, the ultrasound was normal, so I never argued with David about going to the doctor again. He made such a big deal out of it, figuring that if I could feel the baby moving, than I was ok. Not the brightest move, I'll admit. But the best I could do under the circumstances.

The nurse led me down the hall, turned into the fourth room on the right, and asked me to sit down. She handed me some paper work to fill out and left me alone for a few minutes.

"I'll be right back, Mrs. Lockhart," she chirped. She was a very attractive red head and was also quite friendly. Had I met her in the company of David, I would have felt very insecure, because David would have gone on and on about how much he'd "want to do her," and "why can't you look like that, Kathryn?" Pretty much making me feel like a worthless cockroach.

There wasn't really much information to give, so it didn't take long to fill out the forms. Mrs. Graham had left instructions with Mr. Sullivan that the tenant could use her phone, so I put that number on the information sheet. Other than that, the address, my name, and a brief history, there wasn't anything else I knew. I did not know my parents' medical history, and my grandparents were all healthy, as far as I knew. So I just waited patiently for the doctor to come.

About ten minutes later, an older woman in a white medical jacket came in the room, smiling warmly. She extended her hand and took a seat across from me.

"Hello, there. May I call you Kathleen?" She waited for my nod. "I'm Dr. Andrea Smart and I'm afraid I have to apologize for the long wait. It can't be helped," she said.

"Hello. It's no problem." I smiled back.

"Just hop up on the exam table, and let's see what we

have." Dr. Smart quickly changed the paper on the table, and I awkwardly hopped up and lay down.

"OK, now I'd like you to lift your shirt and push your pants down in the front a bit, Kathleen, so I can listen to your baby's heartbeat and measure your belly."

Dr. Smart took all my vital signs. I gave her a little bit of information on just one of the miscarriages, and what my sleeping and eating habits were. She wrote all this down and took out a portable Doppler stethoscope, putting it to my belly.

Almost immediately, we could hear strong, regular thumping. Tears sprang to my eyes at the sound, and I couldn't help but giggle.

"Thank you," I quietly said to God.

"Well, Kathleen. You appear a little malnourished, and I believe that your iron is on the low side, so I'm going to give you some supplements to take. Make sure you drink plenty of milk, water, and eat lots of fruits and veggies with meat every day." Dr. Smart took on a serious look now, and my heart began to flutter.

"Kathleen, how far along do you think you are?" she asked.

"About twenty eight weeks, I think. Is there something wrong?"

"The baby's heart sounds well and strong, but I'm a little concerned with the fact that your measurements are on the low side for how far along you think you are. Could you be wrong about the date?" Dr. Smart continued.

"No. No, I don't think so. I've always been pretty regular." I was beginning to feel dizzy with anxiety. Dr.

Smart must have seen it on my face, for she put her hand on me reassuringly and smiled.

"Try not to worry. Your baby definitely has a strong, steady heartbeat. I'm going to have you wait around for a little while, to have an ultrasound and some blood work. Routine stuff. Do you have time for that?"

"Yes! Yes, of course," I said.

"OK then, how full is your bladder?" she asked with a knowing smile.

"Full."

"Then, why don't I get the ultrasound done first?" She turned and left the room, coming back with a portable ultrasound machine.

"This won't give us the top of the line picture, but it is a good machine, so we'll see just fine." Dr. Smart turned off the lights and sat down beside the bed, squirting my belly with cold gel.

She moved the wand around on my bulge, quickly locating the baby's heart and stomach. It was such a wonder to see the baby moving around in my belly. There were little movements that I could see on the screen, but couldn't feel, and then all of a sudden, the baby jolted, and I could feel as well as see it.

Now I knew there were tears in my eyes. As I watched the screen, I could see clearly the perfect outline of the baby's head, and the tiny fingers that were near its mouth. I could see the legs and toes, and the little head with hair on it.

"Oh," I breathed. "That's amazing! Is the baby really sucking its thumb?"

"I think so. Your baby looks very healthy. Perhaps it's just a small baby, and that's fine. Some just take longer to catch up than others do. But let's be safe and have the blood work done. If anything turns up, I'll call you. Just make an appointment to see me in two weeks." Dr. Smart handed me a towel and helped me to sit up.

"Thank you," I simply said.

"No problem. See you in two weeks. We'll discuss your delivery options then." Dr. Smart left the room with a smile.

I made my way to the lab, had my blood work done, and set out to return to my new, temporary home. The day was cool, but I decided to walk because I hadn't had the chance to go outside at my leisure for so long. It was like heaven. The fresh air was so relaxing and it filled me with hope.

On the way home, I stopped at the grocery store and picked up a few items. I hadn't had steak in a long time, and felt that I deserved to treat myself. Just the thought of barbequed steak and a big bowl of salad made my mouth water and my tummy growl. Maybe a little apple pie for desert, as well. Mmmmm.

After a quiet, wonderful dinner and a rest, I decided to go and explore the neighborhood. It was a little chilly, so I pulled out my jacket and pulled on some socks. I wanted to explore the area more closely. When Mrs. Graham came home, I thought perhaps I would stay in the area. It was quiet and clean here. There were large, old trees lining the streets and some of the houses were just as old as the trees, I think. This is what I pictured when I thought of a cozy place to live.

As I walked down the street, it was heartening to see the barest of buds on the trees, and tulips here and there. New life. New life had great potential. Nature had a way of giving the earth what it needed to sustain its existence. Spring was in the air, and I couldn't help but feel blessed and encouraged. These feelings put a bounce in my walk, so I bounced my way around the block twice before my unhappy bladder forced me to go in for a bathroom break.

    I enjoyed a steamy bubble bath and started reading the new book I had purchased at the grocery store. I thought I better get all the reading in that I could. God knows that I wouldn't have time to do it once the baby came. After my bath, I curled up in bed and fell fast asleep.

Chapter Twelve

"OH! OH GOD! STOP IT! David, please stop."

"Shut the fuck up!" He spat in my face, and slapped me hard.

"Please. Please. I'll do it this time!" I was rolling from side to side.

Another slap. Another pinch. I couldn't do anything to stop him. He had tied my wrists together, pulled them up over my head, and tied them to the headboard of the bed. My feet were then spread apart, with my ankles bound on each side of the bed. I couldn't move. I don't think anything could have made me feel more humiliated, and I knew my face was burning with shame. The woman stood by the bed, waiting for David's instructions.

My dream shifted once again to me falling down the endless black hole. But this time, I was alone. Just eternally falling. Clawing at the earth as I sped past, looking up to see the hole gaping open, with David leaning over, laughing.

Chapter Thirteen

I awoke with a start. Yet, again I was drenched in sweat and quaking from the inside out. How long would I have these nightmares? The rest of my life? All I wanted was to forget David ever existed. I couldn't forget if all I did was dream about my life with him. Every time I woke up, the pain of the dream stayed with me. It felt as if it was actually happening again. I shut my eyes tight, and willed myself to calm down. *It was only a dream. He is gone. You are safe*, I thought to myself. And oh, so slowly, I began to relax, and fell back asleep with my hand resting protectively on my belly.

Chapter Fourteen

God, that girl screams a lot, John was thinking. Three nights after she'd moved in next door, he had concluded that she suffered from terrible nightmares. John knew what that was like. It had been over two years now, but the pain was still so fresh.

Tonight was one of those nights that he struggled with whether or not to go on. From his years as a detective, he still owned a gun, yet he knew in the end, he would not use it. Heaving a sigh, he put the gun down then picked up a black and white snapshot of his wife of eight years, Evelyn. And in her arms, his three-week-old son. Little Jonathon. On the table in front of him, lay another photo. This one, however, showed the three of them. They were down in the gorge in Niagara Falls hiking. Jonathon was three. A butterfly landed on his chubby, little hand and a passerby offered to take a picture of the three of them. In the photo, John was sitting on the ground with Evelyn between his knees, leaning back against his chest, and Jonathon was kneeling in front of them, intent on the butterfly that was perched on his hand.

The picture showed perfectly the lines and baby curves of Jonathon's face. His tiny hands were held out almost straight, perfectly still. His rosebud lips curved in a mischievous grin that would melt even a hardened criminal. Evelyn was looking lovingly at Jonathon, her lips curled in the smile that always squeezed John's heart, while her husband gazed down at her, with the love of the world in his eyes.

They had met in high school. *God!* That was forever ago. At least it felt like it. She was a year older, and the first time they kissed, he knew that he would love her for eternity. They had taken a long time to get married and then even longer to have Jonathon. John wanted to make sure they had a house and savings before having a child. After university, and then the police academy, John and Evelyn finally got married. Two years later, they bought a house and three years after that had Jonathon.

Around the same time that Jonathon was born, John had been promoted to detective, earlier than most, but he was an exceptional police officer. His record was impeccable. He was the one that other cops either looked up to or envied. Not only for his talent at getting the bad guy, but for his home life as well. Whenever there was a police fundraiser, a Christmas party, dance, or BBQ, John knew that every other man there wished for the chance to have one night with his wife. He saw the covert looks of appreciation. He was aware of the subtle brushes against her, when this guy or that guy walked by. He had to admit that he was proud to have a wife that other men admired. Evelyn wouldn't say anything, but he knew it bothered her sometimes, especially when some of the women openly glared at her.

Saying Evelyn was beautiful was such a weak statement, that it seemed almost an insult. She was tall, and had long, blond hair that hung straight and luxuriously down her back. She was very athletic and lifted weights regularly. She had rock hard abs and *killer* legs. Every time John looked at her, his heart stopped. Her mouth was just the right fullness. Almost too full. Her eyes were brown, the color of whisky. He swam in those eyes and got lost looking into them while they made love.

Evelyn was a kindergarten teacher, but after she gave birth to Jonathon, she decided to stay home with him. She would go back to work when they had one or two more children after the children grew up a bit. She loved her job, but she loved her baby more. And with John's unpredictable hours, he agreed that it was a good idea for Evelyn to stay home. He didn't want anybody but his wife taking care of their child.

That was six years ago. They had been gone for almost three. Today would have been Jonathon's seventh birthday. Would have been. Except that he was buried with Evelyn only weeks after his fourth. That was the day John's life ended. Every second of every day since then, he blamed himself for their deaths. He quit his job as a Detective. He could never go back to it. It was his job that killed his family. It was because of his job that he lay awake in a sweat, aroused and anguished because he had just dreamt about making love to his wife. He could smell her when he woke. He could feel the way her hair tickled his skin when she snuggled into his shoulder. Could still feel her soft, warm skin brush up against his, or the way she held him tight, arching her hips up to his, crying for him to keep going, and then when he was spent, he would simply lower his body to hers, kissing her deeply. God, he missed kissing her.

He had experienced one of those dreams tonight and had refused to go back to sleep. If he slept, he knew he would dream again, and he would cry and see his little boy. He would be playing catch or showing Jonathon how to ride his tricycle. The dreams came like that. *Always,* came like that. He would dream of Evelyn, and then would dream of Jonathon. Then he would dream of the fire and the damned police.

John knew that it was his fault that his family was gone. It was the job. He had put away this pimp, who used to take young boys off the street, and sell their bodies to all the sick bastards in the world that had secret fetishes for boys. John had been after this guy for nine months, posing as an interested client. He managed to get not only the pimp, but 85% of the men, as well. But these weren't just any men. These were schoolteachers, lawyers, preachers, and priests. These were his next door neighbors. The guy down the street he would see on Saturday mornings, outside mowing the lawn and playing ball with his kids. The guy that John would least expect to be a child rapist, because that bastard had spent the last five years coaching t-ball and soccer.

John arrested 149 of these sick perverts. (Not nearly enough.) That fateful day, several years ago, had been a good one. He had spent hundreds of hours coordinating the arrests and all the departments that were involved. Of course, the defense had wanted to keep these men's names private, to protect their innocent families. John had agreed, but had felt strongly that it was even more important for the communities where these men lived to know that they had sexual predators living amongst them. He would live to regret that decision. While he was basking in the glory of the biggest arrest of his career, he was oblivious to the woman that was befriending his wife at the park where Evelyn brought Jonathon to play.

Her name was Lucinda. She was an average woman. Three kids at home. Two in school, and one three-year-old little girl named Emma. Jonathon loved playing with little Emma. He couldn't wait to get to the park everyday, and the two women became fast friends. Evelyn had invited Lucinda over for coffee one afternoon, and John had thought nothing of it. She seemed to have her shit together, especially considering she was as single mother. But that was his mistake. He should have known. After all, who would think that one of the predator's wives would have been pissed to have her husband arrested for the unspeakable crimes against children he was committing?

John never knew at the time that Lucinda's husband was one of the arrested men. He should have been on guard, but he wasn't. He should have studied the families of the men more closely. Even thought he had, but somehow Lucinda slipped through his fingers. She got to him in the worst possible way. She took his family, and it was his fault.

In the months following the arrests, only a handful of the men went back to their lives. Apparently, society and their families decided to forgive (or ignore) the fact that these men paid to rape young boys. The Catholic priest was relocated, because even though the Catholic Church frowns upon a couple in love who have sex before marriage, refusing even, to marry such a couple, will relocate "men of the cloth" who are molesting children. The two cops who were caught in the sting were suspended *with pay*, and then got off somehow. Several teachers were also given just a slap on the wrist, somehow still managing to keep their jobs. John would never understand how a person could go to jail for life for committing fraud, yet when it came to our innocent children, a man or woman could get off without spending any time in the slammer. It's what drove him as a cop.

Lucinda's husband, however, was the ring leader. His name was Trevor and he was a pediatrician. Not only was he paying for sex with young children, he was molesting his young patients as well. One of the children was a two-year-old baby boy. That one especially got to John. Trevor admitted to performing fellatio on the baby. He always insisted that the parents remain in the waiting room while he "performed his services." One of the nurses suspected something was going on and hid a video in the exam room. It was her job to clean the rooms in between patients, so she was confident that he wouldn't find it.

Lucinda's real name was Trina. By the time she had befriended Evelyn, her hair had been cut and died to alter her appearance. She even went as far as getting colored contact lenses. She was irate that her husband's career and good name as a physician had been so badly dragged through the mud. Not to mention that his license as a physician had been revoked and he would be spending a few years in prison. Her life had been so bad after the arrest that she had to move and change her and the children's names. Lucinda/Trina had no skills, having been one of Trevor's patients and then marrying him when she turned eighteen. After the marriage, they had moved from Edmonton to Vancouver so he could start a new practice and get away from the scrutiny of the parents of his previous patients.

Trevor was very good at convincing people he was a good man and a good physician. His new practice began to thrive. The unsuspecting parents blindly took their innocent children to this great new doctor. It didn't take long for him to find out about the pimp and the young boys either. Trevor's practice was at the very heart of the city. He often worked late into the night, and it was convenient to have the boys come to the office once the staff left.

When Trevor was arrested, thirty different parents stepped forward, suspecting the worst. The parents of the two-year-old baby became concerned when the child began obsessively touching himself after they had been to see the doctor. They were finally convinced something was wrong, however, when the baby ran around the house chanting, "Kiss my pee-pee." The doc confessed.

His wife Trina went into hiding with their children while the trial was in progress. John thought that she must have been on the brink of snapping during that time, but quickly forgot about her in the glory of his career-making arrests. He should never have done that. He should have recognized *why* Trina seemed so familiar to him; should have gone back and studied the pictures from the case. John could have seen it coming, what happened after the trial, but he was ignorant, and blind, and too vain in his success.

The trial itself was a complete bloodbath. Two of the

fathers barged into the courtroom, ready for a fight. One was the father of a runaway turned prostitute; the other was the father of the two year old. They agreed to cause a disturbance and a riot ensued. The fathers only wanted to beat the doctor, maim him somehow, but one of the victim's mothers grabbed a guard's gun in the chaos and managed to shoot the good doctor in the head *and* the groin before someone stopped her. He bled out right there on the courtroom floor before the ambulance even arrived. As the shock of the situation sank in, the entire courtroom went deathly quiet.

John's thoughts on the day? Well, let's just say that his job had already been done. What happened in the courtroom was not his fault. What happened after was.

About a year after the whole courtroom incident, Evelyn sat down with John for dinner and happily told him about a new friend she had met while taking Jonathon to the park. Of course, Jonathon didn't want to be left out and piped up about *his* "new fend daddy," referring to Lucinda's youngest child. John still choked up every time he remembered the way Jonathon talked about his trips to the park. He recalled very clearly the sound of Evelyn and Jonathon's voices, especially after he woke from dreaming about them.

About a month later, Evelyn had invited her new friend Lucinda and her three children over for dinner. She had visited a couple of times in the afternoon with Emma while her two older children were at school, but this was the first time that Evelyn and John would be meeting the other children.

They seemed like happy kids. Max was a bright ten-year-old boy, who although seemed distant, was polite and normal enough. T.J. was the oldest. She was thirteen, but dressed like she was eighteen, and had the attitude that a thirteen-wannabe-eighteen year old girl has--either giddy and stupid, or rude and calculating. She was all of the above.

It was a Thursday night, and John had to go into the station for an overtime shift. He left right after dinner, bid the ladies good night, and kissed his boy on the top of his head before ruffling his hair on the way out. Two hours later, a uniformed officer pulled up to the location where John was working a double homicide. The officer told him he needed to get home. The uniform refused to give him any more info. He just nervously gave John the captain's orders.

It took John fifteen agonizing minutes to get to his neighborhood. The second he smelled the smoke, he *knew.* He knew it was coming from his house. He remembered clearly the way his stomach clenched. He remembered clearly how annoyed he was that the uniform didn't tell him that his house was on fire. Evelyn was obsessive about the smoke detectors working, and made sure she knew the fastest fire escape route. He was sure they would be safe. It wasn't even dark out yet, so he fully expected to find them waiting on the front lawn.

John turned onto his street. He had to stop a few houses down because of the fire trucks and ambulances. Why the hell did they need three ambulances? Panic set in fiercely, and he could feel his gorge rise, mixing with the burning in his nose and throat. He ran. It seemed like minutes, but was only seconds. He got to the police tape and was stopped by a uniform that didn't know who he was. The captain was there, however, and quickly came over to see John. Why the *hell* was the captain there? Where did all the police cars come from?

The captain stopped him, but John pushed through. That's when he saw them. Six body bags. *Six!* The next few minutes were a blur. He only remembered being at the bags and opening them. One by one. The fourth one was Evelyn. Oh God. His wife. His lover. He became a madman then. Attacking anyone that came near him. His hands were covered in blood. Whose blood, he didn't know. He only knew that his life was gone. Lying right at Evelyn's feet was the tiny body bag. This time, a couple of cops tried to subdue him. John pulled his gun and threatened to kill anyone who came near him.

They were smart and backed off. He threw himself at that miniscule body bag and ripped it open. He vomited and retched. He sobbed until there was nothing left. He picked up the body of his only son. It was still warm. Just a little. He swathed his child in his jacket and lay down beside his dead wife, holding their son with one hand and wrapping the other around her cold, slightly charred body. He was sticky with their blood and smelled of bile, fear and smoke. Eventually, someone sedated him, and he vaguely noticed that his house was burning. Knew that his wife, his child--

He was jolted out of his self-loathing by the sound of muffled crying. He strained to hear. Yes. There it was. She was crying again. The girl next door was weeping and screaming *again.*

He couldn't take it anymore. That's it. John made the decision and went to the desk where he kept the gun, put it away, and headed for the door. He was thoroughly annoyed with the fact that her nightmares, if that's in fact why she was crying, were interrupting his self-loathing. Almost every night, she woke him up with her nonsense. It was time to meet the girl and give her a few suggestions for some good sleeping pills, so he could get a night's rest.

CHAPTER FIFTEEN

BANG! BANG! BANG!

I bolted up, and nearly fell off the bed. **Oh my God! David found me!** Oh god. What was I going to do?

Bang! Bang! Bang!

OK. OK, I can look through the peephole. I didn't have to open the door. So with my heart in the back of my throat, I tiptoed down the stairs and into the kitchen to grab a knife. Not just any knife, but *the* knife. Mrs. Graham had an assortment of knives that would cut through steel. I found the biggest one.

Now that I was armed, I crept to the door and looked out the peephole. *Who the hell was that?* I wondered. Why would there be a strange man banging on my door in the middle of the night? I peeked again. He looked pretty agitated. Was he a private investigator that David had hired? Was David hiding around the corner, waiting to leap out and lunge at me?

Bang, Bang, Bang.

"OK. OK, I'm coming," I called.

Tentatively, I opened the door. I kept my left hand

behind me, with a secure grip on the knife. The man stood there with a look of pure horror on his face. He looked down at my belly and then slowly back up to my face. How rude.

"Can I help you?" I asked. A little testily, I'll admit. He stood there gawking at me.

"Hello. Um...I don't know if you realize this," I began, "but it is the middle of the night."

This seemed to snap him out of whatever trance he was in, because he jumped and looked at me as if I had just appeared before him. He stammered incoherently and then just turned and walked away. Well, how strange was that? I watched him go into the apartment next door and slam the door.

Now that I knew it wasn't David, I breathed a sigh of relief, closed the door, and willed myself to stop shaking. It was three o'clock in the morning, and even though I was a bundle of nerves, I was now wide-awake and ravenously hungry. Toast and tea would calm me. OK, maybe, toast, tea, and a slice of the apple pie that I picked up at the bakery earlier today. I was definitely entitled to some comfort food. My life had been hell, and I was going to pamper myself while I could.

Slammed with another pang of guilt, because I knew my mother was at home worrying about where I was, and whether or not I was alive, I sat down with my food, and pondered the strange man next door.

I had only glimpsed him once since I had been here. I knew that our bedrooms must be against the same wall, because sometimes I could hear his television or his alarm clock. Looking at him up close, however, I got a better picture. He was older than I thought and in much better shape. He wasn't wearing a shirt, which I hadn't noticed through the peephole. The image of a well-muscled body was at the front of my mind.

I pushed *that* image out of my head, and decided instead to abandon my idea of a snack, turn on some soft music, and read a book. Tomorrow I would go next door, and introduce myself. Perhaps I could invite him over for coffee and pie. He did seem kind of rude, but maybe he was just expecting Mrs. Graham, although I was sure Mr. Sullivan let my neighbors know that I was sub-leasing the apartment. I really didn't want to make friends with anyone, but it wouldn't kill me to be neighborly. I only hoped that he was nice, because it was really creepy, the way he was standing there just staring at me. It wasn't that he was staring at me; it was *how* he was staring at me.

There had been utter disdain in his eyes. Maybe I wouldn't go to introduce myself. After all, he didn't even have enough decency to tell me why he was waking me up at three o'clock in the morning. No. I wouldn't introduce myself. I had spent my life going to men and biding by their demands. I needed to break that cycle. If my neighbor wanted to make nice, he was going to have to come to me.

Having made my decision, I was suddenly very tired again, and ambled my way up the stairs, which was getting more and more difficult with the added weight, and plopped myself onto the bed, falling asleep almost as soon as my head hit the pillow.

When I woke late the next morning, I was once again famished. It was around eleven in the morning, so it was no surprise that I was so hungry. I decided on a bagel with cream cheese and a large cup of steaming coffee. It was a wonderful way to wake up, despite the fact that the coffee was decaf. One more reason to hurry up and have this baby. Real coffee. Mmmmm.

I really didn't have much more to do to get ready for the baby, so the time I had was all mine. Even though I had always been alone in the apartment while David was at work, this was totally different. I was so grateful for this time to put my thoughts and feelings together. No matter what, I would never go back to David. I was getting increasingly aware, however, that I needed to figure out a way to keep hidden. We would be fugitives for the rest of our lives. Unless, by some small miracle, David choked to death on his beer.

David would have me arrested for kidnapping, despite the fact that he wanted nothing to do with a baby. Of course, he would have to find me first, and I hoped that I had sufficiently covered all my tracks.

After finishing my breakfast, I did some light housework and then decided to go for a walk. It was still pretty cool outside, but refreshing, so I couldn't pass up the chance to go out and enjoy it. So I pulled my hair back into a ponytail, yanked on a baseball cap, and threw on my sneakers and a windbreaker. The windbreaker barely fit over my basketball sized belly, but I wouldn't need it for much longer if the weather kept up.

About three blocks down from the apartment, there was a park and a creek. The banks didn't seem to be too steep, so I made my way carefully down to the water to walk along and skip pebbles across the surface. It was beautiful down there, and before long, I had gone a fair distance, all the while turning my face up to the sun as

FREE

I walked. To be able to breathe in the smells of spring, with a faint scent here and there of animal, was heaven. Even the odor of old decayed land, buried under snow for months on end, was refreshing. It reminded me that, like nature, the old, decayed part of me was slowly, with each passing day, disintegrating. The new me was growing with the spring season, and I was starting to feel clean, revitalized, and new.

My bladder was filling up, so I found a bush to squat behind, did my business, and came staggering out, smack into a solid mass of…man. I jumped back, startled, and put my hands out in front of me to ward off being hurt. He grabbed my wrists and I instinctively flailed and shrieked. After a moment, I realized that he wasn't struggling or doing anything other than holding me by the wrists, so I stopped fighting and opened my eyes. To my horror, or relief, it wasn't David, but my neighbor from the night before.

"Let go of me," I growled as I wrenched my hands free.

He let go, took a step back and fixed me with a glare.

"What are you doing down here in your condition, on your own?" he demanded.

"Excuse me?" I puffed my chest out, without any intimidation, mind you, and glared back up to his face. "What makes you think I'm alone?" I shot back. I really hoped that he couldn't see how terrified I was.

Instead of answering me, he just deepened his glare and tilted his head slightly, as if to say, "Do I *look* stupid?" He turned and started walking away, back toward the creek.

I stood there feeling foolish and a little angry that he had been standing right in the vicinity of where I had been urinating. He could have seen me! I was terrible with confrontation, so instead of saying anything to ensure my dignity, I stumbled out onto the path and made my way down to the creek as well. My neighbor didn't turn to look back at me, but I was certain that he knew I was following in his steps. I was more than curious about this older man who had just about banged my door down last night and then left me standing there like a dummy.

"My name is Kathleen." I said to his back. He was either more boorish than I thought or he had a hearing problem.

"I *said* my name is Kathleen." If he couldn't hear me this time, every other creature down here could.

"I heard you," he said simply, and after a few moments I realized that he wasn't going to introduce himself to me. Yep. He was just plain rude.

"You know, you scared me to death last night when you almost broke my door down. You terrified me down here, and now you don't have enough decency to give me your name?"

"If I had *wanted* to break your door down, I *would* have broken it down. We aren't going to become friends, so I don't need to give you my name. What are you doing down here anyway? Following me?" This time he had turned to face me with his arms crossed over his large chest.

"Me? Why would I follow you? Are you following me? I was down here first, you know." Now he was really pissing me off, and I wasn't quite so afraid anymore.

"Lady…"

"Kathleen."

"*Lady,*" he said through clenched teeth, "I am down here at this time on most days."

"Doing what? Waiting for women who are alone, so you can follow them?" I knew I sounded like a little kid, but I couldn't help myself.

"Lady, you are so far from the truth. You shouldn't be down here by yourself in your condition. If you fell, you could be seriously hurt. Do you have a cell phone?" he asked in an accusing tone.

"Well, no..." OK, I could see his point. Not that I would admit it.

"No. Well, I happened to see you walking along the creek, and then you disappeared for a while, so I thought you might have fallen. When I realized what you were doing, I went to turn back, but you came barreling out of the bush before I could." He had stepped closer to me, and I really felt like a little kid. I had to look *way* up.

"You were spying on me?" I demanded.

He looked at me as if I had spoken a foreign language and turned around to stalk off.

"You still haven't told me your name." I called after him. But he ignored me and kept walking. Fine. I would just ask Mr. Sullivan who this rude man was.

It figured. I finally get away from an abusive husband and now I have to deal with a disrespectful neighbor who wakes people up in the middle of the night without even giving an explanation. Not to mention that he seemed to be a big bully.

I took my time getting back to the hill that I needed to climb in order to get out of the lush green grass and budding trees from down in the creek. Coming down the slope was challenging, but I quickly realized that I probably couldn't get back up. After about ten minutes of trying different angles, I heard a loud, impatient sigh behind me. I knew who it was before I turned to look. My neighbor was standing there with a smirk that said, "I told you so." I thought that I would very much like to wipe that smirk off his face with a handful of muck, but decided better of it.

"You only said that I might fall," I replied, "not that I might not be able to get up." I stood up straight to try to gain some dignity back.

"You should have known it yourself." He easily walked up and passed me. When he got in front of me, he turned and reached his hand out. As if.

"No thank you. I can manage." I wasn't giving this stranger the satisfaction of being right.

"Fine." He turned and went up the rise. I watched in disbelief. He wasn't going to stay and help me? I really didn't think I had ever met someone so bad-mannered. He hadn't even stayed to make sure I got up the hill alright.

It took another twenty minutes or so, but I finally reached the top. I had made most of the journey on my knees, so I looked like a wreck when I emerged from the brush. I had a great deal of mud and decayed leaves under my fingernails, and my jeans were stained from the knees down. I was in a fine mood, I can tell you. Hopefully, I wouldn't run into my neighbor again anytime soon, I thought miserably.

When I got back to the apartment, I ran into Mr. Sullivan just outside the front door.

"Hello, sweetheart. How are you today?" he asked me with a smile in his eyes.

"I'm fine. Thank you. How are you, Mr. Sullivan?" I returned the warm greeting, pushing the thought of my bitter neighbor out of my head.

"Just fine, deary. My goodness. You're a mess," he exclaimed while taking in my appearance. "John said you were down in the creek, and being stubborn, I might add."

"John? Oh, John. Is that the man next door to me? *He's* the stubborn one. He wouldn't even give me his name." I complained.

"Oh. That's just him, deary. He's a loner, but he's harmless."

"Well, I think it's rude. Anyway, Mr. Sullivan, would you like to join me for dinner this evening? I could use some company, and I thought maybe we could play a game of cards."

"Oh, I would love that deary. What time would you like me up there?" Mr. Sullivan asked.

"Six."

"OK. I'll see you then." He turned and went inside, and I headed to my apartment. I showered, changed, and threw my clothes in the washer. Thankfully, Mrs. Graham had an apartment-sized washer and dryer, so I didn't have to trudge to a community laundry room. Good. One less place there was a chance to run into *John*. After I was dressed and refreshed, I set about making spaghetti for Mr. Sullivan and myself.

He arrived promptly at six with a little bouquet of flowers in his hand. He had cleaned up as well and was dressed in "going out" clothes. I couldn't help but smile to myself, and appreciated the gesture. This man could be a father figure to me. Or rather, a grandfather figure. I didn't remember my grandpa very much, because he died when I was only five. What I do remember, though, is his military brush cut and the fact that he was round and cheerful. Mr. Sullivan was like that. So, for me, he could be grandpa, and that warmed my heart. I would have to visit him once Mrs. Graham came home and hoped that I might be able to find another apartment close by.

We sat down to eat and then retired to the sitting room to have some coffee after the dishes were washed, dried, and put away. I brought out some biscuits and cupcakes for dessert. We were sitting quietly for a time and then decided to play some cribbage. Mr. Sullivan had to remind me of the rules, because I hadn't played since Emilia was alive. I remembered why I didn't like playing that particular game, because I could never win.

"How much more time do you have, Kathleen?" Mr. Sullivan asked. It took me a moment to realize that he was talking to me, because I had forgotten that I told him my name was "Kathleen". Whom else could he be talking to, right? Duh!

"About fourteen weeks," I replied with a smile.

"Do you know what you're having?"

"No. But I think I can wager to say that it's a 50-50 chance that it's a boy or a girl," I said with a giggle. Being with Mr. Sullivan made me suddenly realize how much I craved human kindness and a friend.

"You got that right" he said with a low, grandfatherly chuckle. "Do you have any names picked out?"

"No. I haven't really given it much thought, yet."

"Well, you better pick one soon, young lady, or we'll be calling it….'It'." He laughed at his own joke.

"What's your first name, Mr. Sullivan?"

"My name? Oh, it's Charles."

"Well then, if I have a boy, I will name him Charles," I said.

"If it's a girl, you can name her Charlene," he offered.

"Done."

We played for little longer, and then I asked what had been on my mind all day. "Who is John? I mean, I know he's my neighbor, but who is he really?"

"All the ladies ask about John," Mr. Sullivan said with a laugh. "I guess if I was a lady, I would ask about him too. He's a fine man."

I know I was blushing, because my face felt itchy with heat. "Well, yes. He is attractive…"

Mr. Sullivan smirked and winked at me.

I stood there gaping at him, hoping that my face wasn't as red as it felt. "OK. But that's not why I'm asking. He seems quite brooding to me. He actually banged on the door in the middle of the night, and when I opened it, he just stood there staring at me as if I was from outer space. Then he just turned and walked away. And this morning, he didn't even offer an apology!"

"Oh, that? He says you cry out in your sleep a lot, and he wanted to see that you were OK," he said offhanded. "As to why he just stood there, I don't know. I could ask him if you like."

"No!" I said, nearly falling off my chair. "I mean, that's all right. I'm sure I probably won't see him again. I cry out? Maybe I'll leave him a note telling him I'm sorry if I woke him," I offered.

"I'm sure you don't need to bother, dear. John is a character. He doesn't bother with people, so I wouldn't put yourself out. If there's an issue, he'll be back. But don't be afraid of him. He wouldn't hurt a fly. His bark is big, but his heart is bigger."

Ha! You could have fooled me, I thought. But, I had to admit, that I was intrigued. I felt drawn to this strange, brooding man. Aside from his physical appearance, I mean. There was no denying how attractive he was. He had to be around six foot two, with sandy brown hair and brown eyes that could stop any woman's heart.

Mr. Sullivan bid me good night and left me alone to wonder about John. His face had been shadowed in the dark hallway the night before, but down by the creek, I had seen his features more clearly. I noticed that he was even older than I initially thought. Maybe close to forty. He had deep lines etched at the corners of his eyes, and his mouth was beautifully set, with the corners curving up slightly. God, that was sexy! His jaw line was square and chiseled, and he had a nose that had been broken sometime in his life--somewhat long and a little crooked. And his well-muscled arms, chest, and abs...

Ugh! Shake your head girl! Go to bed. So I did and dreamt about John. Yes. *That* kind of a dream. No. I *didn't* get up and pound on his door. Yes. I really, *really* wanted to. It must be the pregnancy. I did not normally think about men like this. I was too afraid to even look at men. Now, I was overcome by hormones.

I couldn't go back to sleep, so I went out to the patio to look over the park and see the stars. It was a chilly

April night, but the sky was crystal clear, and I could see a billion stars. The air was swirling around the corners of the patio, and my eyes watered from the mixture of wind and cold. My nose began to run as well, and I knew it was glowing red and shiny. I felt perfect.

I had been kept a prisoner for so long. Day after day, I had wished to be able to just go for a walk and feel the air on my face. The only time I got out was to go grocery shopping or to my mother's. And that didn't count, because I wasn't free to sit on a park bench and just...*be.* I couldn't wait to be able to walk outside with the baby. Or, in the fall, sit the baby in leaves and watch while he or she plays in them. I couldn't wait to frolic in the snow, walk this child to school, play ball, or go swimming. I was going to do everything that nobody did with me after Emilia's death.

There would be dance lessons, or baseball, or soccer, or gymnastics. There would be play days with friends and maybe even carpooling with other parents. I wanted this child and me to have a normal life. As normal as fugitives could have, that is. I was absolutely petrified about the prospects that I was facing.

What if I couldn't get a job? What if I couldn't find a suitable apartment or we were found? What would I do then? I truly believed I could kill David if I needed to, but what if I was charged with manslaughter, instead of being let off for defending myself? I had no clue how the judicial system worked. Maybe I would go to jail for taking the baby, even though it isn't born yet, and the police wouldn't believe me when I told them that David beat me and locked me up. He was very convincing. Hell, he convinced my mother for, how many years?

That all the bruises and fat lips I always had were from my own clumsiness. How gullible for mom, though.

I needed to calm down. Now, I was being ridiculous. He was not going to find me. After the baby comes, maybe it wouldn't be a bad idea to relocate. Maybe I should think about relocating a few times over the next few years, just to make sure. I could find *somebody* to make me a fake I.D., or some landlord that would take only cash with no paper trail. Other people have done it. So could I. I stretched and headed back to bed.

Chapter Sixteen

John sat on his sofa and flicked on the television. He really didn't want to watch anything, but everything else he had tried wasn't working. He knew the girl next door was pregnant, because Charles told him. But when he *saw* her, it had been like a bolt of lightning had pierced him through the heart. Yes, he had seen pregnant women since Evelyn and Jonathon's demise, but when he saw *her*...it was like going back in time.

She said her name was Kathleen, but to him, it was Evelyn back in university. She was shorter by a few inches, a little smaller in frame, and she had green eyes instead of brown. But, God, she could be Evelyn, or at the very least, Evelyn's sister. John had not expected that and it was taking a toll on him. Then to see her down by the creek, made him want to turn and run. But, at the same time, he was compelled to watch her. Of course, he *knew* she wasn't Evelyn, but that didn't stop him from *wanting* to simply gaze at her, if for nothing else than the familiarity of the resemblance.

He also noticed that this woman had the indignant

attitude reminiscent of his wife. Kathleen was a scrapper, he mused. He needed to make sure he didn't run into her, too often. Seeing her made him feel again, and he didn't want that. It was difficult enough to get through each day with the grief still so strong in his heart. He didn't need to have a visual reminder of what was missing in his life. He would have to keep his distance, and if he did see her, his strategy would be to treat her like she had the plague. Besides, she was only going to be here until Mrs. Graham got home. He only hoped that his will was strong enough to get him through.

John managed to get through the next three days without seeing Kathleen, but on the fourth day he ran smack into her coming around the corner of the hall heading toward the stairs. A wave of nausea hit him at the sight of her stumbling back toward the stairs. He lunged forward and grabbed her arm to steady her on her feet.

"Watch where you're going!" she snapped.

"You're welcome, Princess," he growled, and strode down the hall, entering his apartment. He slammed the door so hard that the walls shook, and one of his paintings fell to the floor.

A few seconds later, there came a banging on the door, and he had to smile to himself, because he guessed she was hitting it as hard as she could, although it only came through as slightly stronger than a regular knock. He pulled open the door so fast that she nearly fell through.

"You're an ogre! You practically pushed me down the stairs, and you don't even have the decency to ask me if I'm alright. In case you haven't noticed, I'm having a baby." He was amused to see her standing a foot in front of him, looking up with her hands on her hips. Her face was flushed with anger, and it made her look like a teenager having a hissy fit. She was a full head shorter than he was, and despite himself, he wanted to tease her.

"I didn't bump you in the front, it was the side. And I grabbed you before you fell down the stairs. *You* were not watching where *you* were going," he said evenly.

"It's still rude. First, you wake me up in the middle of the night, then you leave me down by the creek, and then, you don't even have the courtesy of giving me your name." Kathryn was still fuming, and the more she fumed, the more he found himself amused.

"My name is John. Happy?" He was inching forward, and when she was backed up enough, he smiled and shut the door. Behind it, he could hear her grumbling, but after a few moments the sound faded and he heard her close her door.

That should do it, he thought. He was pretty effective at keeping people away. Hopefully she would get the hint and leave him alone. Maybe he should get away. John hadn't been fishing in a while. He had no jobs booked for the next few weeks, so he decided to plan a week long fishing trip. He then reserved a Cottage up North in Muskoka, for the following week. There. That gave him one less week to worry about.

The following day, John was getting ready to leave for his daily hike, when there was a knock on the door. Much to his annoyance, it was Kathleen. He was just going to close the door in her face, but she was expecting it and stepped in before he could.

"Can I help you?" he asked with as much exasperation that he could conjure up.

"Actually, you can. My...Mrs. Graham's toilet is leaking, and I can't find Mr. Sullivan." It was killing her to ask, he noticed, but she didn't have a choice and he reveled in it.

John sighed very loudly, grabbed his tool pouch from the front closet, and followed her out into the hallway. Once inside Mrs. Graham's apartment, he went to the bathroom to see what the problem was. The toilet was indeed leaking. Actually, it was spewing, and he rushed to shut off the valve. He then quickly checked all the other water sources in the apartment and ran downstairs to the basement to shut off the water entirely, just to be on the safe side.

"When did it start leaking?" he demanded when he came back up.

"Not long ago. I went to get Mr. Sullivan right away, but he wasn't here. I tried to get back upstairs as quickly as I could." Kathleen was also annoyed. "I'm not *stupid*."

"Well, I need to get some more tools before I can do anything," he muttered. She didn't know that he was feeling complete dread at the thought of being in the same vicinity as her for any length of time. Every time John looked at Kathleen, the wall he built around himself, cracked a little bit more. Despite his efforts, life was seeping through each crack. He was intrigued by Kathleen, and seemed not able to stop goading her on.

Chapter Seventeen

John was coming back into the apartment just as I was finishing the sandwiches. If he wanted to be a jerk, that was his choice, but I wasn't going to stoop to his level. The least I could do was offer him lunch for coming over to fix the toilet.

"Would you like a sandwich?" I asked with as much courtesy that I thought he deserved.

"No. I mean, no thank you, Princess."

"My name is Kathleen."

"I know. You told me." He just carried on, not even bothering to look at me. It was infuriating.

"I would appreciate it if you would call me by my name. It's insulting when you call me 'Princess'." It was getting very hard to stay polite, but I didn't have to worry about it, because John was already most of the way up the stairs to the bathroom.

I don't know why this man didn't scare me. At first, I felt intimidated, but not now. I think this was the first time in my life that I wasn't fearful of a man. Besides Mr. Sullivan, of course. When I was little, even the men my father brought home were somewhat nasty. Some of *them* would even pinch or slap my mother on the rear end when she walked by, while serving them beer or snacks. She would just stiffen up before walking away. Given my experiences with them, I should be wary of all men. But, for whatever reason, I knew that John was putting on an act. He was pushing me away, which was strange considering that I was a total stranger. I was only vaguely interested in getting to know him before. Now, all I could do was think about him and what bubbled beneath the surface of such a man. What could have happened to make him want to be alone in a conscious effort to repel people away.

Mind you, that was what I was doing. Aside from Charles Sullivan, I wanted to keep people away as well. I didn't trust people. Especially men. The thought of it hit so suddenly, that I had a momentary surge of dizziness. And then I started to cry. I didn't want to meet another man now, but what if I did some years down the road? Would I ever be able to move past my deeply ingrained distrust for men? Sure, I didn't feel afraid of John, but that didn't mean that I trusted him either. Not that I needed to. When it was time to leave here, I could always avoid him when I came to visit Mr. Sullivan.

I was still feeling sorry for myself and crying when I began to put the sandwiches away. I wasn't hungry anymore. When I turned around, John was standing there at the end of the counter, staring at me with the same expression of horror he had worn on his face when he banged on the door that first night.

I immediately felt embarrassed and then angry.

"Do you like to watch pathetic women cry?" I snapped.

"No," he began slowly. "Look, I'm sorry. I tend to be rude. Thank you for the offer of lunch," he managed.

"Oh, you think I'm crying because of you?" I sputtered a laugh. "Don't flatter yourself."

That hit a nerve, because he just said, "Fine," and went out the door, which really pissed me off, because he didn't say if he fixed the problem, and I had to use the bathroom.

I tried to turn on the kitchen tap to see if the water was running. It wasn't. *I'll just have to go use John's bathroom,* I thought defiantly. So I went to the door, and just as I reached it, he came barging back through, hitting me on the face with the edge of the door. I cried out. It happened so fast, that the shock of physical pain sent me reeling back to my life with David. I threw my hands up and jumped back to avoid being hit again.

"Oh, God. Princess, are you OK?" It took a second to realize that it was John speaking to me, and not David. If I thought he had an expression of horror before, he certainly had it now.

I gingerly touched my lip and tasted blood. It stung like hell, and already felt puffy. "It's OK," I said. "Why were you barreling through like that? You keep popping up in front of me without warning." If I sounded whiny, it was because I was trying really hard not to cry.

"I'm sorry, Prin-Kathleen."

I could tell he really meant it, and he looked at me softer now.

"That's alright. It was an accident. I'll just put some ice on it. Can I please go use your bathroom? That's what

I was coming out to do." My speech was a little slurred, and I'm sure I sounded very much like I had been to the dentist and had Novocain to freeze my mouth.

"Yes. The apartment layout is the same. You'll find some clean wash cloths in the closet at the top of the stairs for your lip."

"Thanks." I went to his door and stepped inside.

It was like walking into a cozy cottage. All the furniture was dark, rough wood, including the dining room table. There were a few pictures of wildlife in the sitting room, but the apartment was otherwise bare of decoration. The floor was hard wood, stained a few shades lighter than the deep, rich brown of the furniture. John had a few throw rugs on the floor of the dining room, sitting room, and the foyer. It almost had a Native American theme. It was absolutely breathtaking.

I made my way up the stairs and found that the décor was pretty much the same throughout. I could live here, I thought. It was comforting, inviting, and warm. Not what I would have expected from his demeanor. He clearly appreciated the simple things in life. No extravagance here. My kind of taste.

Once I had used the bathroom and found a wash cloth, I made my way down to the kitchen to get some ice. I could've gone back to my place to get ice, but I wanted to stay in John's apartment. I felt oddly safe here. Though, after a few minutes, I couldn't stay any longer before he got suspicious, so I reluctantly went back to my apartment. John was still in the bathroom, so I went up to see how things were going. By this time, we were both calm, and I knew that we had turned a corner.

"Do you know what the problem is yet?" I asked,

leaning as far as my belly would allow me, to see into the toilet.

"Well, I know the problem isn't *in* the toilet," John said.

"Oh. I guess not." I stepped back as he stood up. "Do you think you can fix it?"

"I don't know until I figure out what the problem is. I need to go into the wall under the sink. I can't do that until Charles gets back, though. He may want to call in a plumber."

"You're not a plumber? I thought you were, because of the tools, and you seem to know what you're doing," I observed.

"I do know what I am doing, but I'm not a plumber. I just do contracting."

"Oh. Would you like a sandwich now? Since you have to wait, you might as well eat."

He hesitated for a few minutes, then finally said yes, so we went downstairs to the kitchen. I gave us each a glass of milk and an apple to go with our sandwiches. I had to cut my fruit up into small pieces, because it hurt like hell to stretch my lip. It was quite puffy by now. We ate quietly, which was kind of uncomfortable, but not squeamishly so. When we were done, John thanked me and helped me clean up. He said he would be back later on when Mr. Sullivan got home, but in the meantime, he welcomed me to come back to use his bathroom, should the need arise.

This man was wounded, somehow. That much was for certain, but I didn't know the extent or cause of the damage. Underneath the granite wall of self-protection, was a man who was capable of gentleness. Maybe we could be good friends. Nothing more. Yet, I was curious as to what else could happen, but then stopped *that* thought in its tracks. I didn't risk my life to escape from the prison my husband created, to go right into the arms of a stranger. I needed to be alone. Though I couldn't help but wonder about the protection that John would be able to provide if David found me. Unfair as that was, I had to know that if I was found, I would have a friend to turn to. As each day passed, I was finding the thought of a friend more and more inviting.

I had an appointment with Dr. Smart, so I got ready and walked down to the clinic. As long as I could walk, I would. When I got there about fifteen minutes later, I signed in and waited my turn for the doctor. It was a good thing I brought a book with me, because I ended up waiting for over an hour and two more trips to the bathroom. Your bladder doesn't hold much when there's a miniature person bouncing on it, let me tell you.

Finally, Dr. Smart greeted me and ushered me into her office.

"Well, how are you doing Kathleen?" she inquired. When she looked closer, she noticed my broken, swollen lip. "How did that happen?"

"I had a collision with one of my neighbors in the hall this morning. But it doesn't hurt too much. I'm actually feeling really good," I replied with a smile, then winced, tenderly touching my broken lip.

"Are you extra tired, or do you have the sniffles at all?"

"No," I said slowly.

"OK then. I was curious because your blood work

came back with a slightly elevated white cell count," she said.

"Does that mean that there is something wrong?" I asked, a little nervously.

"No. You're probably just fighting off a little virus. But, if you do start to feel ill, or especially tired, please come see me right away," she advised. "Now, let's get you up on the table so I can measure your belly and listen to the baby's heartbeat."

I hobbled up, pushed my jeans down in the front, and lifted my shirt up to my bra. Dr. Smart took the measuring tape and measured across and down the length of my rounded belly. She frowned a little bit, but didn't say anything. She took out her stethoscope and put the cold metal to my belly in a few different areas, spending a few seconds in each spot. She then took the stethoscope out of her ears and handed it to me, while still holding the metal part to my belly.

"Here, Kathleen. You can hear the baby's heartbeat clearly. You're a little small still, but that baby has a good, strong heartbeat. Keep up the good work." She smiled down at me while I put the earpieces in my ears. I smiled up at her when I heard the sounds of my tiny baby.

Sure, I felt him or her moving around all the time. Of course, when one is getting near the end of the pregnancy, moving around is an understatement. I sometimes felt as if the baby was trying to tear out of the cramped space it was in. It's probably a good thing that we don't remember being confined and born ourselves. It must be pretty scary coming out of your own little world where everything is warm and fluid. "It's OK, baby," I said to my belly. "You can stay in there as long as you want. Well, not *too* long, but awhile longer, for sure."

"Kathleen," Dr. Smart stepped back so I could get off the table. "Unless something comes up, I will see you in three weeks, and we'll discuss your delivery options."

Everyday that I was free gave me more hope, and with more hope, came more relaxation. When I thought about it, I realized that I *was* relaxed, and I couldn't remember really ever feeling this way. When I was little, especially after Emilia died, the only time my mother and I felt somewhat calm, was when daddy was gone for a few days at a time. Daddy went on business trips a couple of times every month. As foreman in a steel factory, he had to go to other company locations, for various reasons; business meetings, union functions, and whatever else he had to do.

When I got back to the apartment, there was a note on the door from John. It simply said that I needed to go to his apartment when I got back. I crumpled the note and stuffed it into my windbreaker pocket. When I got to his door, I rapped lightly. He opened the door right away, with the usual scowl on his face.

"Hi," he said, and stepped back for me to come in.

"Hi. I didn't tell you earlier, but your place is magnificent." I looked around again as I stepped into the room.

"Thanks. Look, Charles will be up here in a few minutes and he wants to talk to the both of us. Something about the plumbing, he said. While you were out, a plumber came by."

"I know. He was still outside when I got back."

"Have a seat and I'll get you a drink while we wait.

Although, I don't know why Charles needs to talk to me. I'm not the one with the problem." He was starting to look and sound annoyed again, but I just brushed it off as him being his normal, rude self. The more I looked at him, the more I noticed that he was carrying a deep exhaustion. I, on the other hand, felt alive and free. I was actually surprised at the level of energy that I had, considering how many years I'd been living without any.

Fighting for your life on a daily basis takes its toll on you. I guess being out in the fresh air and having sun shine on my skin was making a difference. I was even starting to develop that pregnancy glow that you hear people talking about.

John basically ignored me until Mr. Sullivan came up to his apartment.

"Hello, my dear," he said in greeting.

"Hello."

"Well, John, you're not going to be happy about this," he began.

"What am I not going to be happy about, Charles?" John asked evenly.

"The water to Mrs. Graham's apartment will be out for the rest of the week," he simply said.

"What does it have to do with me?" Even as John said it, I could see it dawn on him, and he said very quickly, "No. No."

"No what?" I asked. (Again, I'm not quick on the uptake.) The two men just glared at each other, though. "What's going on?"

"Deary, you are going to have to stay here, in John's apartment for a few days," Charles explained to me

"No. She can't, Charles. You know she can't," said John.

"She can, and you'll be gracious enough to let her," Charles said, not backing down or being intimidated in any way. I was very impressed.

"Why can't she stay with you? You have another room," John replied, seething.

"The grandkids are going to be here for the week."

"Then why can't she stay with someone else?"

"Um...*she* is in the room," I said, a little annoyed myself.

Charles looked at me as if I had just appeared. "I'm sorry, my dear. I know you expect that kind of discourtesy with John, but please forgive me for following in his footsteps."

John just stood there, glowering at Charles. Then he spun on his heel and stomped off to the sitting room. "*Fine!*" Stomp, stomp. Then to me he said, "Make yourself at home, Princess."

"He's a bit childish, isn't he?" I asked Charles as we watched John stomp off. "Could you please tell me what's going on?"

"Yes," laughed Charles. "He is very childish. Always has been."

"I heard that, old man!" John called from the sitting room.

"Let's just ignore him, dear. He'll simmer down. But you do need to stay here in John's apartment for a few days."

"Oh-h no!" I said, holding my hands out in front of me as if to ward him off. "I'm not staying with him. He scares me. He's mean and he hit me in the mouth, barging into my apartment earlier." I leaned forward to point at my puffy, pouting lip.

"You were *standing* behind the door!" bellowed John.

I got closer to Charles and whispered, "I wasn't standing behind the door, I was moving toward it, to go out."

"I know he's a bit mean, dear. But it's an act. He wouldn't hurt a fly. Unless you want to stay in a hotel for the next few days, you'll have to stay here. There will be no water running in Mrs. Graham's apartment."

I couldn't afford to stay in a hotel. I had to conserve my money for as long as I could.

"OK. If it's only for a few days, I'll stay here."

John strode moodily through the door, "Don't I get a say in this?" he asked.

"No," Charles and I said in unison.

John just stood there, gaping at us in disbelief.

"Close your mouth, John. It's unbecoming," Charles said flippantly. That really seemed to hit a nerve, because John looked as if he had murder on his mind.

Chapter Eighteen

I brought some things over to John's place and put them away in the spare bedroom. The room was just as cozy as the rest of the apartment, with an oversized bed and huge pillows. John was pretty pissed, so I decided to stay in there for a while, out of his way. I knew he desperately didn't want me here, but my will was getting stronger, so I knew I could put up with his moodiness for a few days.

I must have fallen asleep, because I woke a while later to the smell of food. My mouth watered and my stomach clenched in protest at being so empty. I quickly ran my fingers through my hair and patted down my clothes in an attempt to look a little less rumpled. As I came down the stairs, John was cooking something that smelled wonderful.

He heard me coming down, looked at me, then turned away to continue his preparations. When I got close enough, I could see that he was tossing a salad and had pulled some baked potatoes from the oven. He had also torn some wedges from a loaf of pumpernickel bread that was resting on the counter.

"I hope you're not a vegetarian. I grilled some chicken for dinner," he said without turning to look at me.

"It smells wonderful." And it did. "Can I set the table?"

He seemed to stiffen when I spoke, but regained his composure so quickly that had I not been looking at him, I wouldn't have caught it. Again, I wondered what could wound this big, strong man so. Could he tell how wounded I was? *Maybe, he just doesn't like you, Kathryn, and you're flattering yourself.* Maybe. I sighed loudly, and he turned with a questioning look on his face.

"Is there something wrong, Princess?" John was still very much annoyed, but appeared to be making an effort not to bark at me.

"No. It's just been a long time since I've eaten a meal like this." I was trying not to let my own irritation creep through. He made it perfectly clear that he didn't want me there.

I set the table for us. He poured himself some white wine and me a glass of milk. We first ate the delicious chicken and potatoes, and finished off with the bread and salad. John had mixed an olive oil dressing with balsamic vinegar, a little salt and pepper, and a sprinkle of parmesan cheese. It was scrumptious.

"John, this is very good. Thank you, so much." I really meant it. I was very grateful. "Look. I know that you don't want me here, and I promise I won't get in your way. I just really can't afford to stay in a hotel on my budget."

"It's OK. It can't be helped, I guess. So just make

yourself at home. I'm going fishing in a couple of days anyway, and if your apartment isn't ready by then, it won't matter." He was actually looking right at me. I think it was the first time he really looked at me. Even when he hit me in the mouth with the door, he was careful not to give me strong eye contact. Maybe we were making progress. I had to hide a smile.

"Oh. Where are you going fishing?" I asked.

"Muskoka. Have you ever been?"

"No, I haven't. I went to a cottage once with my grandparents when I was little, but other than that, I haven't been anywhere. Not even a honeymoon." Oh shit! Why didn't I just blurt out that I had a crappy life and husband waiting for me somewhere? It caught his attention, because he leaned forward and looked at me quizzically.

"Are you married, then?"

"Widowed." Please, please don't let him see through me. "My husband was killed in a car accident." *Look down, look glad... I mean, sad.*

"Where are you from?" he asked.

"Where are you from?" I countered.

"Here. I was born here, moved away for a number of years, then moved back after…uh, after I changed jobs," he stumbled.

Ha! He was hiding something. What if he's an axe murderer? No. He was kind. It was in his eyes, even if it wasn't in the rest of his demeanor. I just had to be careful not to give myself away. Thank God he didn't ask me more about my husband. I needed to give that subject a hell of a lot more thought, so people who were curious wouldn't catch me off guard.

"When are you due, Princess?" John had returned to his more courteous side.

"In about twelve to fourteen weeks. You know, I would really appreciate it if you wouldn't call me, 'Princess.' I did ask you that already."

"How far along were you when your husband died?" He was pushing now.

"I hadn't known yet. I'd rather not talk about it. I came here to get away from all that." I was starting to get a little frazzled, and I knew I had said too much as soon as the words came out of my mouth.

"Where are you from?"

"Uh…I'm from Kaslo, British Columbia. Near Kootenay Lake," I blurted out. It was the first thing that came to my mind. Unfortunately, it was the truth. *Double Duh!*

"Really? I used to live in Victoria. Never been to Kaslo. Is it nice, then?"

"You know, I don't want to talk about me. Why don't you tell me about yourself?"

"There's nothing to tell. I moved back here a couple of years ago, and I'm a contractor. Boring, simple, and exactly the way I want it," he said, with a smile. That small grin transformed his face into an amazing mixture of good looks and strong character, which quite simply took my breath away.

"I think I'm going to go for a walk. Would you like to join me?" I hoped that he didn't, because I needed to be alone for a while to contemplate things.

"No thanks. I'm going to stay here. I have some quotes to work on before my fishing trip."

"OK. I'll see you later." I quickly cleaned off my

plate, put some of the food away, then grabbed my jacket from the hall closet and slipped my feet into my sneakers. Off I went, eventually venturing into a small little book store. It was lovely and had a good selection of both used, old books and new. Before I knew it, a couple of hours had gone by, while I lovingly ran my fingers over some of the old, dusty leather bound works of art. I loved to pick up this one, or that one. Reading the backs, or the first few pages. The whole store smelled of dust and old leather with a musty undertone.

Chapter Nineteen

John cleaned up the rest of the dishes and tidied up a bit. He then ran up to the bathroom to make sure it was clean enough for a guest to use. A guest. Yeah, right. She was a nightmare and a woman, and looked so much like Evelyn that his heart nearly stopped every time he looked at her. Kathleen's voice was soft and she was a spitfire at the same time. He could look into those eyes and get lost in them. Yet, he could die in them, too.
True. He hadn't been with a woman since Evelyn. Not even for coffee. He still felt like he would be cheating on her if he went out with someone. Gently, he took her picture out of the desk drawer and looked down into her face. He still felt so much grief. Remembering clearly what she smelled like. He remembered the taste of her, and how she felt in his arms, and in his bed.

Being around Kathleen was getting to be increasingly difficult. He couldn't help but to inhale her scent, as he so often did with his own wife. John was experiencing stirrings that had been lying dormant for the last two, almost three, years. He was confused and angered by it. He was also a little sad, feeling somehow that Evelyn wouldn't forgive him if he carried on with his life. *He* couldn't forgive himself if he got on with his life. It seemed too much of a betrayal.

At least Kathleen wouldn't be here for long. Mrs. Graham would be coming home soon. John would just have to stay away from Kathleen as much as possible, especially when that baby came. The last thing he needed was to become attached to a baby, then lose it because it wasn't his and he had no claim to it. That's why he had detached himself from his nieces and nephews, unfair as that was to them. He knew he could not be a friend with Kathleen. That would be complete torture.

He put the picture of his wife away. John kept it in a drawer because it was just too painful to see on a daily basis. It had taken him almost a year to put Evelyn and Jonathon's stuff away in the first place. It crushed him every time he put their pictures away, but, it cost him much, much more to keep them out.

John made a stiff drink and sat down to read for a while, but his thoughts kept coming back to this strange young woman who had suddenly been thrown into his life. She was lying about who she was, or where she was from. He had been a cop for enough years to know when someone was lying. And she was not a good liar. He still had some pull in the police world. Maybe he would do a little digging to find out who she really was.

She said her name was Kathleen. John would find out from Charles tomorrow what her last name was and go from there. He also hoped that Charles would give him her social insurance number, if he asked nicely enough.

He couldn't help but wonder about the nagging

twinge of unease that was forming in the pit of his stomach, though. John didn't know why, but he *knew* something was off about Kathleen's whole story. When he asked about her husband, he sensed that her reaction was phony. The grief simply wasn't there. John had had over two years to practice pretending that he was getting on with his life. Of course, losing a child was a whole different ball game. That grief could not, and would not, be hidden, no matter what you tried.

His thoughts were interrupted with a knock at the door. He opened it to find Kathleen standing there timidly.

"Sorry," she said, looking up at him. "I didn't have a key, and I didn't want to assume I could just walk in."

"If you're staying here, Princess, you can just walk in." Unconsciously, he stepped forward and almost brushed up to her belly. He was so taken aback by his response to her standing there, he didn't know what else to do but to turn and walk away. He walked straight into his study and closed the door. This woman was turning his life upside down. She was breaking his resolve in so many ways. Quickly too.

Chapter Twenty

I needed to think about a lot of things. How could I keep John from asking me so many personal questions? Obviously, I hadn't put enough thought into keeping my secrets. If John, or should I say, if I let John get too close, it could be very dangerous. I needed to come up with a plausible story about David. I also needed to be able to show a little bit of grief when I was asked about my dead husband. The only way I could do that was to think about Nicolas and Gabrielle.

John was a mystery for sure. I could not get him out of my head. Maybe I was just obsessed with somebody else's problems and intrigued by the thought of helping some other poor soul.

I remember the first time David and I had slept together. It was basically, wham, bam, thank you Ma'am, and then he rolled off. It stung and I bled a little. I hadn't known that a woman bled the first time she had sex.

He said over and over, "I won't do that to you again." I think he felt guilty because he had bugged me for three days to have sex with him. It was either that or give him a blowjob, and there was no way in hell I was going to put that *thing* in my mouth. David didn't touch me sexually again for two months after that first time.

Once he got over his guilt, however, he came at me all the time. Eventually, David finally got to me, and I had to perform…ah-other duties. It had just been so vile.

David did not have the best hygiene habits and the smell of old sweat and…and *male*, was so overpowering…well lets just say I ended up vomiting. That was the first time he ever hit me. At the time, I thought I deserved it.

Of course, David apologized for hitting me. I remember lying on the floor crying because I was so repulsed, yet at the same time, I felt really bad for not being able to please him. It had been so very confusing. I was so scared that I had damaged his ego somehow. After all, it was my job as his girlfriend to please him, and anyone would be upset at being thrown up on, right? David never let me forget that.

"Kathryn, if you learned how to please me, I wouldn't feel the need for another woman." Somehow, he managed to get me to believe that, too. So, I tried very, very hard to learn how to please him. Eventually, I mastered the art of getting past the smell of him, and the taste, and began to perform my duties. I knew that he still cheated on me, though. In my brainwashed mind, I reasoned that I simply was not good enough for him, and that's why he cheated. Obviously, I would never know how to please a man.

David was sometimes encouraging, but most of the time, he would belittle me. I could never do anything right. He was often frustrated with me and held my head, ramming himself deep into my throat, like the night of our wedding. A few times over the years, I would gag, (I couldn't help it) and he would grip my hair like he was going to rip a piece of my skull off.

I started retreating into myself. Every second of every day was filled with a gut wrenching fear. I was consumed with dread at the thought of what David might do if I said the wrong word, cleaned the glasses before the silverware, or made the floorboards creak when I walked into a room. Even when David wasn't home, I lived in fear like that, in case he found out that I had eaten breakfast before cleaning, or some other minor offense.

Soon, he started with the prostitutes. He brought a new one home with him a couple of times a week. At first, he would order me into the living room, while he had his way with her in our bedroom. I was so confused. Humiliated. All the time, David reminded me of how much of a failure I was. So, why shouldn't he bring home somebody else? After all, my inadequacies were forcing him to have to pay for sex. Once again, according to him.

After the second week, David started calling me into the bedroom with them. My skin crawled when I saw another woman in my bed laying naked and waiting for my husband to join her. My brain screamed in protest, yet I could never say a thing, or I would get a punch in the mouth. Part of me was happy to not be on the receiving end of David's advances and part of me felt truly betrayed.

Supposedly, if I watched, I might learn a thing or two. When David got bored with that, he wanted me to join in the fun. There was no way in hell I was going to participate, until, of course, David smashed his fist into the side of my face and knocked one of my teeth loose. I wiped the blood off my mouth with the back of my hand and *apologized* for upsetting *him*, before I asked him what he wanted me to do.

"Simple, Baby. I want you to go down on her" David had said, with pure malevolence on his face.

I felt all the blood drain from my head, and I started to shake. *Play dumb*, I remember thinking. "I don't know what you mean." I whispered. My head hanging low.

Smack. "Yes you do, you dumb bitch!" he screamed.

"Hey. Don't do that!" The whore got up on her elbows to protest. She immediately cowered back down, though, when David turned his lethal glare on her.

"Kathryn," he snarled through clenched teeth, "you damn well know what I mean."

I started to cry. I couldn't help it and hated myself for being so weak. "No, David. Please," I whispered.

He landed another smash from his fist into the side of my head. "*Now!*"

I jumped and ever so slowly, I climbed up on the bed. The whore looked at me apologetically, and I could tell that she wanted to get it over with and leave. She softened her attitude a bit and reached her hand out to me. "Come on honey. It's not that bad. I'll help you," she said in a quiet, soothing voice. So, in the end, this whore and I became allies of a sort. She guided me as to what to do. I gagged a few times, but thankfully didn't lose my dinner until the whole ordeal was over and done. Finally, David let her go, so I could finish him. She looked back at me with sincere concern on her face. David never brought that one home again, but I would be forever grateful for her attempt to make a vile, humiliating act of sex as easy on me as possible.

David was not as concerned. Actually, he was irate that I would disobey him in front of another woman. Boy, did he make me pay for that. He gave me a severe beating that left me lying on the floor with blood and saliva drooling down the side of my face. It was a full three weeks before I could go out in public. I hurt for even longer. An eternity, really. My bedroom had become 'the torture chamber.'

How could I fake grief for a man that brought about my own yearning for sweet death? I wished day and night to be up in heaven with Emilia, Nicolas and Gabrielle. No matter how I tried, I could not fake grief for David.

Chapter Twenty One

I had walked for about as long as I could without needing the bathroom. When I got back to John's apartment, I planned to go up to my room and avoid him as much as possible.

John was busy in his study when I got back, so I hadn't needed to come up with an excuse for not staying up. Thank God for small miracles. Once in the spare bedroom, I took out a journal that I had purchased the day before and started writing. I desperately needed to write things down, or I would never be able to control my emotions. It was so frustrating! First, I controlled my emotions to avoid being abused, and now I had to manage my emotions to avoid falling in love. Life was so not fair. Would I ever be happy?

Chapter Twenty Two

The next day, John was gone when I got up. He had left a note on the table that read, "Kathleen, please make yourself at home. I will be home for dinner. I don't expect you to cook, so I will bring home some take-out. Have a good day. J."

So he was considerate after all. I made myself a light breakfast of toast and coffee and went out on the patio to continue my writing. After a couple of hours, my hand began to cramp, so I put my sneakers on and made my way to the supermarket. I picked up some steaks and marinade to grill for John tomorrow night. Then I headed to the Farmer's Market to gram some veggies for the grill as well. The Farmer's Market had fresh produce and my mouth watered for some cherry tomatoes that I was planning of having in a spinach salad for lunch. Even if Mrs. Graham's apartment was ready by then, I wanted to thank John and make him a wonderful meal. I also picked up a simple thank you card for the hospitality.

It was an overcast day and smelled like rain. The breeze was cool, as it still is at the end of April, but was inviting and comforting. I could stay outside all day long. I stopped to sit on the bench in front of the apartment building and lifted my face up toward the sky. *Angel's, protect me, please. God, give me strength. Thank you.*

"What are you doing?" I was startled by John standing in front of me.

I smiled a little at him. "I'm just enjoying the fresh air. I normally don't get out much."

"I see. Are you ready for dinner?" John didn't smile, but he also didn't seem annoyed, so I took it as a sign, and silently thanked the angels again.

"Yes. Actually, I'm starved. I could eat a side of beef right about now. Pregnancy is so strange." I patted my belly, just as the baby stretched.

John followed my hand and saw the movement. "Looks like the baby is hungry too." This time, he did smile.

"Would you like to feel it?" I asked, and immediately regretted it when I saw the sheer terror in his eyes. This time, he wasn't quick enough to hide his reaction.

"I'm sorry," I said quickly. "I forget that not everyone wants to know what goes on in a woman's belly during pregnancy."

John recovered nicely. He reached out his hand for me to take, and said, "It's OK. I'm sorry I reacted that way. Here, let's get you up and fed before you shrivel up from starvation."

I stared at his hand for a moment, and then took it in mine.

CHAPTER TWENTY THREE

JOHN CURLED HIS LARGE, STRONG fingers around her tiny ones and felt a rush of adrenaline. He dropped her hand suddenly, as if it had burned him, and flinched when he saw her cringe at his actions. To make up for it, he put his hand on the small of her back and gave her a gentle push forward. That was much better. He wasn't touching her skin that way.

Kathleen opened the door to the apartment and they stepped inside. She got her shoes off first and took the bags from his hands. He had picked up some Chinese food, much to her delight. John took out the rice and honey garlic ribs, while Kathleen took out the chicken balls, sweet and sour sauce, and chow mien. She then took out some plates and glasses while he took out the silverware.

They ate in silence for most of the meal, and then John asked her if she would like to go see a movie.

She almost choked on her food. "I've never been to

see a movie. Well, when I was little, my mother took my sister and me. I think we saw Cinderella, but I really don't remember."

"You've never seen a movie as an adult?" he asked with obvious disbelief.

"No," Kathryn said defensively. "Not everyone has, you know."

He had to laugh at her. He couldn't help it. She was so child-like. He was reminded of little kids when they said stuff like, "my dad is bigger than your dad."

"Don't laugh at me, John. That's not nice." She was actually pouting and was totally unaware of it. Her innocence was so totally unexpected, and sexy. It drove him mad, and he had a fleeting thought of carrying her up to bed right there and then.

"I'm sorry, Princess. Would you like to go to a movie, or not?"

"Yes. I would like to. Nothing with a lot of violence, though."

"Now you've ruined my night," he teased.

They ended up going to see a comedy. Kathryn had laughed so hard, it made her belly ache. John was very relaxed, but still had his guard up. He was very aware of how much they were both trying hard not to brush hands together in the popcorn.

When they left the theatre, Kathleen suggested that they go for a walk, so she could get the circulation back in her legs. They drove back to the apartment, parked the car, and started out down the street. It was pretty cold outside, so they didn't stay out for long. John also noticed that their silence with each other was slightly less uncomfortable now that they had relaxed at the movies and laughed out the tension.

When they returned, John reached the door to his apartment first. There was a note on it from Charles, asking him to call when he came home. They got their shoes and jackets off, and John picked up the phone. A few minutes later, Charles came in looking very grim. *Uh-oh. What now?*

"Hello, dear," Charles said to Kathryn.

"Hi, Charles. How are you today?" she politely asked.

"I'm doing OK, but John won't be for long."

"Why not?" John put his shield back up in the blink of an eye.

Charles only hesitated for a minute, looked John over carefully, then sighed in resignation. "John, there's a much bigger problem with the plumbing than we thought. We are going to have to shut your water off and punch a hole in the spare bedroom and bathroom, so the plumber can change the pipes." Charles put his hands up to stop John from interrupting. "Don't say anything just yet. The building is old, and the original plumbing isn't going to hold out for long. I know you have a fishing trip planned for the week, so I'm suggesting that you take Kathleen along with you." He then turned to look at Kathryn, and added, "You don't have anywhere to be for the next week, do you sweetheart?"

She was so dumbfounded by the thought of going away to a remote cottage with John that she could only stand there and shake her head. Her mouth was hanging open as well. As was John's. John snapped his shut into a thin line and gestured for Charles to follow him to the study, where he slammed the door after taking one last glimpse at Kathleen, who was still standing there with her mouth agape.

"Charles, you *know* I can't do that," John hissed. "It's bad enough that she's here with me, now."

"John, you're being unreasonable. You don't seem to be suffering too much," Charles observed.

"I'm not ready for it. In case you haven't noticed, she looks like she could be Evelyn's sister. *And*, she's pregnant," John shouted. "Thanks a lot for the warning, by the way. You could have told me."

"What would I tell you, John? There's a woman next door who looks like your dead wife?" Charles raised his voice to match John's.

Kathryn was standing in the kitchen and she could hear every word. So that's what he was hiding. His wife was dead and Kathryn reminded him of her. No wonder that first night, he just stood in her door gaping at her. He was horrified. She was horrified. How stupid could she have been to think a man like John could actually feel something for her? He just wanted to stop thinking about his dead wife. What was her name? Evelyn. Without thinking, Kathryn turned and ran out the door.

John heard her go and stopped talking in mid sentence. He went out of the study into the kitchen.

"Great. Are you happy Charles?" He spun around.

"It's been over two years, John. Almost three. You need to get on with your life," Charles pleaded.

"I'm not ready." John didn't shout this time. He just sat down and buried his face in his hands. "Charles, you can't force me to forget."

"I'm not trying to make you forget. But, you are

allowed to be happy. I'm only asking you to take the girl to the cottage with you for the week. I'm not asking you to get involved with her. So what if she looks like Evelyn? She's not Evelyn, and might I remind you that she is also a widow."

"You're right. She's not Evelyn, and she's widowed. But I'm sure she didn't cause the death of her husband. How am I supposed to forget what I did and move on? Is Evelyn moving on? Is Jonathon moving on?" John was almost desperate. Charles felt for him, but he needed to be tough right now.

"John," Charles began in a low voice. "What happened to them was not your fault. It was out of your control. Nobody saw it coming."

"I know. I know, and I'm sorry. I know you mean well, but I know I will never forgive myself. I need to go out in the fresh air and think." John got up and put his shoes on. "Could you please look for Kathleen while I'm gone? Make sure she's OK. I've gone and fucked everything up, again." Before Charles could reply, John was gone.

Chapter Twenty Four

I didn't really go anywhere. I just sat on the stone bench in the garden behind the building. I was still reeling from the revelation that John's reaction to me from that first moment was due to my resemblance to his dead wife. I couldn't be angry with him. Obviously, he loved his wife. I did not love or miss my husband. I missed what I thought my life with David should have been. But, I knew it wasn't at all the same as what John was going through.

"There you are. Are you cold, dear?" Charles walked up to the bench and sat down. He reached out and put his hand on top of mine, which was resting beside me on the bench.

"No. I think I'm going to just leave. I can go to a hotel until I find something else. John obviously doesn't want me around, and I don't blame him."

"You will do no such thing, young lady. I've grown very fond of you, and believe it or not, so has John. I know you can't tell, because he's sometimes a brute, but he likes you. I know." Charles was getting animated as he spoke.

"I remind him of his wife and if I'm not mistaken, I heard you say that his wife has passed on," I said, feeling very alone and confused at the moment.

"There are some things about John that you don't know dear, but I'll leave that up to John to tell. I'm in hot water with him already." Charles smirked.

I sat quietly, not knowing what to say. I wanted to know more, but I could sense there were details that he wasn't ready to share.

"Have you known John for very long? You seem to know a lot of personal stuff."

"Yes, indeed. I raised him." Charles leaned back a little, thinking for a moment before continuing to speak.

"John's mother and I were married when John was about three years old. Two year's after that, his mother, Nancy, died of ovarian cancer. It was sudden and painful. John's father dropped off the planet the second Nancy told him she was expecting, so when Nancy passed, I wanted to keep John with me. I had developed a strong bond with him. He was my boy." Charles was clearly very proud of John.

"I know your grandchildren are staying with you, so does that mean that John has siblings?" I asked. I wanted to know as much as I could.

"No, dear. I remarried about eight years ago, and the kids are my wife's. *Were* my wife's. She passed on last year of a stroke," he said, wistfully.

"Oh, Charles. How awful!" I said, and reached up to touch his arm. He patted me on the hand, and we just sat there for a while, listening to the rustle of the dead winter leaves that the melted snow had uncovered.

"Kathleen, how long ago was it that your husband passed on?"

My breath caught. I still didn't know how to answer questions about David. I was desperately afraid to trust anyone for fear that they might turn me in. Now that I knew John used to be a police officer, I knew he must be able to see right through me. I would just have to wing it.

"My husband has been gone for six months. I didn't know I was pregnant when he passed. But it's not the same for me as it is for you and John. My marriage wasn't a good one. I was fourteen when I met my husband. He worked with my father, and when I was seventeen, I became pregnant, and we got married. My father died of a heart attack on our wedding day, before the ceremony took place. My mother didn't want to waste my father's money, so we went through with it. It was very creepy. Our family was what you would call dysfunctional." I knew I was saying too much, but I had the feeling that Charles would keep my secret.

"My husband wasn't good to me, and my mother wasn't able to help me in any way." I looked at Charles, who had been listening thoughtfully to every word.

"What happened to the child, dear?" he asked.

"Oh. Um, the baby died on my wedding night. The doctors said it was the stress and the events of the day." I didn't need to tell him that the day was worsened by the fact that my new husband raped me.

"You poor dear. I knew that you harbored a terrible secret. I can see it in your eyes, the same way I can see it in John's eyes. Life is short, as you know. It seems to me that you could also use a week at the cottage."

"Could you please," I faltered, and bit my lower lip before slowly continuing. "Could you please not say anything to John? You see, my mother doesn't know where I am. I'm not ready to face her at the moment."

"Your secret is safe with me, on one condition," Charles said.

"What's that?"

"That you get in touch with your mother soon. It's none of my business why you left wherever it is that you come from, but a mother needs to know that her child is safe."

"I'll talk to her soon," I promised. "Thank you, Charles. I guess I'll go pack for the cottage. As scary as that seems."

"You're welcome dear. About John, just give him a chance to warm up to you. He's my son, and I know him better than he knows himself." Charles got up from the cold bench and held out his hand to help me up.

I stood on my toes to give Charles a peck on the cheek before going in. I was nervous about facing John, but I wanted him to know that he was OK with me. I would stay in a completely different room for the whole week, if he wanted me to. But I didn't want to give up this chance to get away from it all, to be in nature. I needed that for my healing process, and John was just going to have to give in.

I found him sitting on his sofa, staring blankly ahead. He slowly turned to look at me, than patted the sofa beside him. I sighed deeply and moved toward the sofa.

When I sat down, I sat far on the other side of John. He only gave me a small, tired smile.

"I'm that bad, am I?" he said. "I don't blame you. I can be an ogre."

"I am grieving the loss of my son, John, so if you need to talk—"

John was genuinely shocked. "I didn't know. Of course I didn't know, he paused for a moment. "My son's name was Jonathon. My wife was Evelyn. It's been two years and eight months since that day."

"My Nicolas was premature. I only got to hold him for a little while before he died. He was so tiny, I was afraid to touch him." We sat quietly for a few moments before John spoke and startled me out of my thoughts.

"Look, if you want to come with me, that's fine. It's just that, well, you look very much like my wife did when we were in university, and the shock of meeting you is still kind of throwing me. I'm sorry that I've been an ass. Really, I am."

"That's OK, John. I totally understand. Could I see a picture of your family?" I was extremely curious as to how much I looked like his wife.

"Sure, let me get one." He went to the desk in his study and produced a family picture of the three of them. "We were down the Niagara Gorge, on that day. I'm assuming Charles told you he's my step-dad?" He waited for me to nod, before continuing. "We were here visiting Charles and had decided to take Jonathon for a hike down the Gorge.

"It was one of those days that isn't extraordinary for any particular reason, but that stays with you. The kind of day one might take for granted." It broke my heart to see such sadness in his face.

I looked at the picture. "I'm actually quite shocked at how much I look like her. I could be her sister. And your little boy looked just like you."

"Yeah. Thank you. He was my pride and joy." John looked away for a moment and I knew that he was trying to get control of his emotions. I, on the other hand, could not control mine, and I began to cry. I wondered if our children were friends up there in Heaven, as well as what exactly happened to this man's family.

"Are you OK?" John slid closer to me and handed me a tissue.

"Yes, I'm OK. Are you?" I choked back a sob.

John just chuckled. "Yes, and I'm fine. Now, let's put this hokey stuff behind us before Charles comes in and gives us both shit."

I sniffled again, wiped my nose and turned to John with a smile.

"So, tell me," he said, lightening the mood. "Do you like to fish?"

"I don't know. I've never done it before."

"First, you've never been to a movie. Now, you've never been fishing?" His brows rose up in question.

"No, I haven't. But, I hear it's relaxing, and I could use some of that," I said with a pat on my belly and a smile. "I better get as much R&R as I can before this baby comes."

"That's for sure. I have an extra rod, and everything we'll need. All you have to bring is your clothes. "Muskoka is beautiful this time of year. It's a long drive, though. Are you up for it?"

"I think so. But you'll have to stop a lot for me to stretch my legs."

Was I dreaming? Was I actually going away with a man I just met, to a secluded cottage? John must have been able to read the look on my face.

"Are you nervous to go away with me?" he asked.

"Just a little. I've never been on my own before. Decisions were always made for me."

"It's OK. Charles can vouch for me. I used to be a cop."

I could only nod and laugh. "How could I refuse, then?" I asked.

"You can't. Now, let's go pack and we'll leave at dawn. I really want to get there by mid-afternoon. That way, we'll be able to hike a bit to get the circulation back in our legs."

"That sounds perfect. I'll go get my stuff together. I suppose we will just grocery shop while we're there?"

John nodded, said goodnight, and we both went to our rooms to pack. I was pretty excited, but the nervousness I had been carrying around with me since I met John was still in the pit of my stomach. My life had changed so drastically, in such a short time, that I was left reeling from the roller coaster of constant changes.

Only a month ago, I left a life that threatened to swallow me whole, yet it seemed like a lifetime ago. At least, some parts of it seemed that way. When I dreamt of David at night, it always seemed like it had just happened. Yet, at the same time, it was as if I was dreaming about someone else's life. Maybe it was someone else's. I was changing just as much as my life was.

I was definitely emerging from my cocooned self. I

felt different. I reacted differently, and I was thinking differently. Could it just be because there wasn't the constant threat of death hovering above me? The constant threat of being found was almost as bad, but not quite the same. I knew that David wasn't going to come home and lock me into the apartment or beat me if I did something wrong. A threat is still a threat though, and I would forever be looking over my shoulder.

Just the other day, I had been certain that I was being followed. Terrified that it was David, I had kept to area's where there were a lot of people. Eventually I realized that I had not been followed by anyone, yet that didn't quell the fear that engulfed me every single time I left the apartment building.

In my mind, I pictured the baby and me being free and happy. That would become a reality to an extent, but we would never be completely *normal*. I had to be grateful for any amount of freedom, and I was. Anything was better than the baby and I living with, or anywhere near, David. Eventually, I might be able to convince my mother to sell her house and come out here, or wherever else I might be at the time. But that was a big *if*, and I would need to know that she wouldn't cave under pressure and tell David where I was. She was just as intimidated by him as she was my father. But, unlike my mother, I didn't think it was OK to stay with a man when he was abusive. Then again, Mom believed in the old school motto, "you made your bed, you lie in it."

My child would learn to be respectful and loving. He or she would learn compassion and free will. There would not be a day that passed when I wasn't going to say, "I love you," or "you are safe with me." If I learned anything about my escape, it was that my resolve to remain free was stronger than I had ever imagined it could be. I also knew, however, that even though my confidence was building everyday, I couldn't yet trust myself not cave under the fear that David instilled in me. I knew I would *fight*, but I didn't know that I wouldn't give in. It killed me to admit that, but when one has had as many beatings as I've experienced, you do whatever it takes to avoid the next pounding. It's impossible to think ahead in the midst of that terror.

That thought made me feel sick inside, and a bit of the defeat I felt with David crept through. *Stop that, Kathryn. Your life is starting. Don't screw it up.* I'd have to try very hard not to.

Chapter Twenty Five

John and I left at 5:30 the next morning. I had woken up three separate times through the night. Actually, I woke myself up twice, and John shook me awake once when I was having a nightmare. John didn't pry when he roused me, but he did ask if I was all right. I lied, of course, and told him that I was fine, but it was the kind of nightmare that stayed with me for most of the day. It was the black hole dream where Gabrielle and I were falling in the black hole. I had that one frequently. And every time, it affected me the same way—with a bone deep grief.

Because of the lack of sleep from the night before, and the emotional stress that hung heavy on my shoulders, I splurged and had a large cup of coffee with actual caffeine. It was so good. I'm a coffee person, and to give up caffeine was pretty difficult. I couldn't wait to be able to enjoy it again. Of course, it would be quite some time, because I planned to nurse the baby. I was eating much healthier and couldn't understand why any mother wouldn't nurse unless there was a medical reason. It was free milk, after all, without having to boil, heat, sterilize, or leave the bed. But most importantly, the bond with the baby.

When Nicolas was born, they knew he wouldn't live, so they encouraged me to nurse him and get closure. I was grateful, of course, but it was also torture. At first, I was afraid to let my perfect little boy latch on for fear that I would never let him go, but once I held him in my hands, I *had* to try. He did nurse very weakly for a few seconds, and then went to sleep. He was so tiny that he fit in one hand. His mouth was so small that the tip of my nipple was just about too big for him to suckle on. I wondered if the yearning might fade a little when this baby came.

John and I drove in silence for a couple of hours. I was reading a book and rubbing my belly. It was getting closer to my due date, so the baby wasn't quite as active as before, but when it did move, half my belly would pop out and stretch to unbelievable proportions. There were times now when one side of my stomach stretched way out, leaving the other side almost flat. It was truly amazing.

John caught one of these movements out of the corner of his eye and looked at my stomach like an alien was about to come out.

"Doesn't that hurt?" he asked.

"Sometimes. Most of the time though, it's just… cool. You know?"

"No."

"Think of it as a really huge muscle twitch. You don't know when it will happen, how long it will happen for, or how big it's going to be." How else could I explain it?

"Uh-huh. Are you sure there's only one in there?" He pointed at my stomach, as if I didn't know where the movement was coming from.

"There's only one. Would you like to feel it?" I turned in my seat at little bit toward him.

"No thanks. I don't think I'm ready for something like that. I'll just think about Jonathon."

"Oh. I'm sorry."

He nodded. "I might want to soon though, if that's OK."

"When you think you might be ready, just let me know," I said and turned back to facing the front.

It was nearly lunchtime, so we decided to stop at the next tourist station to grab a bite to eat and stretch our legs. I had a craving for a steak sub, and John wanted burgers, so we each grabbed our food and met up in the food court. John must have been feeling more comfortable, because he teased me incessantly about how much food I could pack into my small frame.

After lunch, we used the restrooms and bought coffees, this time decaf, and a dozen cookies. I had been yearning for those for a long time and wasn't about to pass up the chance to have something delicious and sweet. John asked me if I wanted to drive for a bit, but I was getting to the climax in *When the Wind Blows* by James Patterson and didn't want to put the book down. Since I left David, I had read four different Patterson books. My favorite so far was *Susanne's Diary for Nicolas*. I picked it up when I saw the title and thought of my own Nicolas.

John only had to stop for me two more times before

we finally arrived at the cottage, but not without him complaining that I had to "pee every two minutes," and "can't you hold it for a while longer?" My reply was simple: "Stop or I will pee in the car. And I can't bend over to clean it." So, he would heave a sigh, and pull over.

Once we arrived, John emptied the car of our stuff while I put the kitchen things away. It was a beautiful place. The cottage itself was a two bedroom with a huge bay window overlooking the lake. Every surface in the cottage was wood, and it was built like a log cabin. Surrounded by the breathtaking scenery, I felt closer to God. When we looked out the back door, there was a fair size deck that had a long set of stairs leading down to the water. To the right was a dock with a small motorboat tied to it.

On the beached part of the water, we were pleased to see a fire pit that we might enjoy sitting around at night, listening to the crackle of wood burning. We would also need a fire inside, because it was chilly enough to need a sweater during the day, so we knew it would be cold at night. Luckily, there was a fireplace to keep us warm inside the cottage while we slept. There was electricity, but we wanted to enjoy the coziness of a natural fire.

John wouldn't be sleeping in most mornings, because he was here to fish. I said I would go fishing with him, but not every morning. I wanted to sleep. I hadn't realized how sleep deprived I actually had been over the years, until I left David. I did offer to cook breakfast on the mornings that I stayed here so when he came back, he could eat a nice meal. He was hoping that he would catch some good fish that he would be able to cook as well.

Once we were finished unpacking, we took a walk down on the beach. Some of the trees were just budding, and a general sense of spring was all around. I would love to come here when spring was in full bloom, to sit by a fire, enveloped by a cool breeze mixed with warmth from the flames, with no other sound save what you would hear in nature--the odd loon, the splash of a fish, and various bird sounds that came throughout the day. Maybe the scamper of a rabbit or a deer. Of course, there would be a muffled barking dog at a distant cottage, maybe trying to catch a fish jumping out of the water. A place like this is heaven, and I felt immediately at peace, like you would expect to feel in heaven. And safe.

I had been to a cottage once when I was little. My grandparents on my mother's side took me the year after Emilia passed. My mother, by that time, had become like a ghost. She was deathly pale and thin, and her eyes were sunken in so much that it looked as if her eyeballs were going to pop out. I remembered being afraid of her during that time, because she didn't look like my mommy anymore.

My grandparents were over for a visit, took one look at my mother, and insisted on taking me to the cottage for a couple of weeks. My mother hesitated, and it took some convincing on my grandparent's part. What cinched it for me was when Daddy came home and made the decision to let me go. So, after dinner that night, (which was nothing special because Mom couldn't bring herself to cook much after Emilia,) she packed my stuff, and gave me a big hug goodbye. I think that hug scared me more than anything, because my mother wasn't the hugging type.

I remember sitting by the fire at night roasting marshmallows. My grandparents would let me have a ton of junk food that my parents would never allow. My grandpa would sit me on his lap to read me stories until I fell asleep. We never went fishing, though, because he just didn't enjoy the sport. I missed them, very much.

They didn't come around often because they traveled a whole bunch, but when they did, it was like taking a break from a grueling, emotionally draining job. They both passed away within six months of each other the following year. My mom always said that they wouldn't do anything apart, so it wasn't surprising that it had included death. It was really hard on Mom, because I knew from a very young age that my grandparents' visits were like a vacation for her, too. Of course, they never knew what my parent's lives had been like. They didn't know that Daddy was an alcoholic, and they certainly didn't know that Dad hit my mom. It was very infrequently, but it still happened. When grandma and grandpa were visiting, all was well, and Dad was on his best behavior.

The scenery here reminded me of that time, and I felt a very strong yearning to be comforted by my grandparents. They would never have let my father push me into marrying David, and if they knew about Mom, they would have put a stop to it. They weren't too happy about the marriage, but Dad had been a good provider, and Mom was relentless in her persistence. I wondered if Mom would still have married Dad if she knew what would happen. She had been intelligent and vibrant once. It was plain to see in older pictures of her. But

Emilia's death and my father's abuse took a toll on her, and she no longer cared about much.

And here I was, adding more pain and worry to her life. I knew she would be falling apart with concern, and I felt the knife twist in my heart with guilt. I had been gone for a month. God, had it really been that long? How unfair and selfish could I be? I just couldn't take the chance of calling her. She would not understand, nor would she keep it from David. Of that, I was certain. *I'm sorry Mom. I will call soon.*

"What are you thinking about, Princess?" John wasn't being insulting now, when he called me "Princess." It was a sweet nickname.

"Um…just thinking about my grandparents. They brought me to a cottage once, when I was little. It wasn't nearly as nice as this," I waved my arm in an arc, "but it was fun."

"Your granddad didn't take you fishing?" he asked with a grin. Man, his grin was sexy.

"No," I smiled back wistfully. "He didn't like to fish. He did, however, like to sit by the water and *watch* the fish."

"Well, you are in for a treat tomorrow morning," he said. "Do you think that you'll be able to get into the boat? You're pretty front heavy," He teased.

"Yes, I can get into the boat," I said evenly. "I'll just sit on the dock and *roll* in."

John laughed. I had to admit that in the last couple of days I had gone through a growth spurt. John even had to tie my shoes for me this morning. I was absolutely horrified. What could I do? If I couldn't reach my feet, I needed help. I was feeling very much like Moby Dick and thought bitterly that maybe I should just beach myself for the week.

"What are you scowling about?" John scrunched up his face in a mock grimace to imitate me.

No way was he going to mock *me* and get away with it, so I smacked him in the arm. "Don't," I said through clenched teeth, "I can't be held responsible for what I might do."

"Ha! That's what my wi…" He stopped dead. Went as white as a sheet, actually.

"I'm sorry, John." I put my hand gently on his arm. He probably couldn't even feel it under his heavy sweatshirt, because I was afraid to touch him. He just looked at me and tiredly smiled. It was in that moment when I recognized exhaustion as deep as my own, that I felt utterly heartbroken for this beautiful man.

You can't live through that kind of abuse whether it's self inflicted or not, year after year, without it draining all your energy. Not to mention your self worth and self-esteem. It never occurred to me that John might be feeling the same worthlessness and self-loathing that I lived with on a day to day basis. I was beginning to think that maybe we could become friends. Yeah, right! A friend, that I desperately wanted to kiss.

He really was extremely attractive. He had these crinkles in the corner of his eyes that were really sexy, and the way the corners of his mouth curved up drove me mad, and I desperately wanted to kiss him there. I could not stop thinking about him, and I found myself innocently brushing myself up against him while we walked or just plain staring at him so I could watch the way his muscles moved and how he carried himself. *Lord! Why don't I just throw myself at him?*

I remembered frequently what he looked like without a shirt when he came to Mrs. Graham's apartment the first time I saw him. He had broad shoulders and a six-pack to die for. Although John kept his brown hair short and was clean-shaven, I wondered what he might look like with a goatee. His jaw line was severe and exactly what you would picture a male model looking like. I couldn't even look at him without blushing.

After about a half hour, I needed to go back to the cottage to lie down and stretch. My lower back was throbbing and it was starting to radiate into my legs. John offered to massage my back for me, but I was terrified that I would lose control of myself and tackle him. Not that I would be able to do anything but bounce my belly off of him, but hey, a girl could dream, right?

We worked our way back to the cottage and John helped me labor up the hill, and then he went back out for a longer, more exerting hike. He had lit a fire in the fireplace before we left for our walk, so it was nice and cozy throughout the place. I grabbed a peanut butter sandwich and some milk, and sat in front of the fire to warm my cool skin. The air up here was crisp and clean, and I felt a little heady. Once again I thanked God for the miracles he had bestowed upon me since I left David.

After finishing my snack, I brushed my teeth and went to lie down with a warm and fluffy blanket that was as soft as a baby chick. It also smelled of John, which made me think that maybe this comforting blanket may have been his son's. My initial thought about John was that he was a bully and a grumpy man. But no, if anything,

FREE

he was turning into one of the most generous and thoughtful people I had ever met. It scared me to think about how strong and sudden my feelings for him were after only a couple of weeks. I knew that these feelings were a decade of a bone deep yearning for unconditional love and gentleness. I knew I could not get close to this man and the more I thought about it, the more worked up I became.

What was I really doing here? How could I endanger the life of another human being just because I was totally infatuated with him? Especially, I thought, a person with a past just as deep and dark as my own. I know with every fiber of my being that David would kill John first and ask questions later if he found us together. The only way to prevent that was to leave when John and I got back to the apartment. The thought left me feeling crushed and caused me to fall into a fitful sleep.

Chapter Twenty Six

John was skimming small pebbles across the glassy surface of the still, spring water. The ripple effect was something that always amazed him, and he loved to watch as the tiny rings of waves expanded, one after another. Funny that nature's course in any form, whether it was human, animal, plant or insect, was full of ripples. Of course, not all ripples are as smooth as the ones he was looking at over the water.

That's what was happening with Kathleen, John thought. A ripple effect on his emotions, (and better judgment) was in full progress. It started in the pit of his stomach and was flowing through him, expanding like the water. Every time he looked at her or saw her belly move with the life within, he felt the pebble hit his core.

Being here at the cottage, secluded from the outside world, was a gift and a curse for John. When Evelyn died, he vowed that he would never love another woman again. Every time Charles introduced him to someone, he was so offended that he merely barked his disapproval and stomped off. Yet here he was, experiencing feelings of joy and longing to be around Kathleen and stirrings in his body when she stood next to him, or when he touched her hand. He also felt guilt.

Yes, Kathleen looked like his wife, and it had nearly tipped him over the edge. But now, when he looked at Kathleen, he saw only Kathleen. She was beautiful in her own way. Her eyes were so large and her lashes long and black. Her skin was so soft, and she had the kind of beauty that was only hindered by make-up. She wore only the smallest amount, so she still looked natural. John wasn't blind to the deep, dark circles under her eyes, and knew they weren't just from the pregnancy. And he certainly noticed how she stiffened up when confronted. But she was a fighter. That was obvious. It drove him crazy, actually, the way she defiantly stood up to him. He smiled at the thought of this tiny creature, who had stood in front of him, with her hands on her hips, tilting her head way up to look him in the eye.

She had courage, and that was extremely attractive to John. Courageous women tend to give a man a run for his money, and although some men like their women docile, John preferred a strong woman. He was far more attracted to Kathleen than he wanted to admit, and the thought of her aroused him.

After staying out for a long while, John headed back for the cottage. It was still quiet when he went in, and he knew Kathleen was still asleep. She had left the door to her room open, and he could see her snuggled up in his blanket. John stood looking at her for a moment and wondered what demons she was battling in her sleep. Her brows were knit together, and she was softly moaning through a grimace. If nothing else, he would like to help her with some of her grief, and didn't realize until he learned of the death of her child, that he needed some help with his.

He suddenly felt like a peeping tom and closed the door before she woke up and saw him watching her. She had said her married life wasn't a good one, so maybe that's what her dreams were about. They had both lost a child. And that is a nightmare that does not go away. Ever.

After closing the door, John decided to go into town to get the groceries. He left a note on the table and his cell number in case there was anything else she wanted him to pick up if she woke before he returned. By the time he got back, it would be well into dinnertime, and he knew that they would both be starved. Locking the door behind him, he made his way to the car and back out onto the dirt road that lead to the main road and into town.

Chapter Twenty Seven

I must have been asleep for a long time, because when I woke up, it was to the aroma of food. Wonderful! This hunger thing while pregnant was incredible. I knew that I could eat a horse, if one presented itself to me. My mouth watered and my stomach growled very loudly at the smells and kitchen noises. I wondered where the food came from and then realized that John must have gone shopping while I slept.

"That smells so good," I exclaimed when I walked out of my room. "What is it?"

John turned to smile at me, and I nearly forgot I was hungry for food when I saw him. "I made steak and corn on the cob. Have you ever had it on the barbeque before? The corn, I mean."

"Once. My mother put them on the grill while they were still in the husks, but left them on too long, so half the cob was burnt to a crisp and the other half was still hard."

"Ah. Well, you'll like the way I've done them. Perfect timing, by the way. I hope you like your steak done medium well." He turned back to the stove and took out the food that he had placed in there to keep warm.

"I honestly can't remember the last time I had steak." I never did end up making it for John at his place and had put them in the freezer. "My husband would hardly buy it. He said it was too expensive, but he always had a case of beer." I knew as soon as it came out of my mouth that I had said too much. There was no mistaking the bitterness in my tone. To divert any questions, I busied myself with setting the table. I knew that he was watching me. I could feel his stare boring into my back, but thankfully he let it go.

"What would you like to drink, John?" I asked.

"Not beer." He saw me flinch when he said it and realized his mistake. "I'm sorry," he rushed. "I blurt things out sometimes. Sorry." John moved toward me with his hand outstretched. I just looked at it for a moment, then went with my gut and took it.

He merely held it between his for a moment and then led me to the table to sit down. He had lit a few candles, which gave the room a beautiful glow. He even held my chair out for me, which is something that only my grandfather had ever done before. I wondered about his mother, and what his childhood must have been like after she passed. It didn't seem to have been very bad, because he clearly chose to stay close to the step-father that raised him.

To change the subject again, I asked, "What was your childhood like, John?"

"It was wonderful. Charles did everything any kid

could want his dad to do." John seemed to relax a bit more as well. Thank God.

"Why did you stay with Charles and not go back to your dad? Was he gone?" I saw John's face cloud over when I asked, and then remembered Charles saying something about John's father leaving when he found out his mother was expecting. I mentally shoved my foot in my mouth. *Dumbass.*

"My father has been in prison for most of my life." He said this without any emotion on his face or in his voice, and I wondered if he had ever met his father.

"Again, I'm sorry, John. I just can't seem to say or ask anything intelligent."

"No it's OK. He's the reason I wanted to be a cop. My biological father was a predator and lured some eight-year old twin girls into his shed where he raped and killed them. He buried them under the shed, beneath the floor. He didn't bury them deeply enough and was caught when one of the neighbor's dogs kept getting into the shed to scratch and whine at the floor." He stopped and looked at me to make sure I could handle the rest of the story. I nodded and he continued. "When my father was arrested, they...the cops, I mean, discovered a dungeon that he had built in the forest behind our farmhouse. There were three other girls dead in there. They ranged from five to nine."

John served our dinner while telling me the grim details of the arrest and how his father's DNA was found in all five victims. There is no death penalty in Canada, so John's father was convicted of five counts of murder, five counts of child rape, confinement, and kidnapping. He had been given five life sentences without the chance of parole. There wasn't a defense lawyer anywhere in North America that would appeal his case, and he had been kept in solitary confinement ever since he was hauled off to prison.

"Charles had said that your father left…" I said

"Yes, he did. My mom begged him to come home, and he eventually did."

"Oh. I see."

"I have never gone to see him, but I know my mother went a few times." He shook his head. "When I was a kid I couldn't understand why she went, but when I got older I realized it was for closure. My mother couldn't believe that it was real for a very long, long time. Eventually she met Charles and understood very quickly that my father had never been a good man, but she hadn't known better because she married him when she was only fifteen."

"I know what that's like. I was fourteen when I met my husband, and we were married when I was seventeen." I looked at John who had now sat down across from me.

"Really? That must have been difficult. Anyway, Charles treated her like she deserved to be treated, with gentleness and respect, and he treated me like his son right from day one. I love and respect that man very much. I just wish my mother had gotten more than eight years with him. Theirs was the kind of love that you read about in a romance novel. Within six weeks of meeting Charles, she had filed for divorce from my father, and within six months, she was married to him. Neither one of us ever spoke of my father again." John looked nostalgic for a moment before continuing. "Charles adopted me after the first year."

"He was a good father, then?" I was so envious of

other people having good fathers because I often felt ripped off about the whole family thing.

"He's amazing. It was very difficult for both of us when Mom died. She was a loving, caring person who touched many lives. I know that the pain of what my father did stayed with her throughout her life, but I also know that Charles helped to heal the part that made her blame herself for not knowing." He picked up his fork and knife and cut in to the steak.

After a few bites, I started to wonder about how the arrest and incarceration of his father affected John. It must have caused him to question his own morality while he was growing up. Perhaps even his sanity. How could it not? Although, he was clearly taught well under Charles's influence. Charles turned out to be a godsend not only for his mother, but also for John. Charles had turned out to be a godsend for me, too. Had he not allowed me to sublet Mrs. Graham's apartment, I would not be sitting in this beautiful cottage by a breathtaking lake, with a strange man that was consuming my every thought. I silently thanked God.

I also realized that I might not have to abandon John when we went back. I was no expert on men and attracting them, but I could have sworn a couple of times that John was watching me and feeling something.

My thoughts were interrupted by John's laughter. "You are scowling again," he said.

"I am? Just lost in my head," I replied.

We ate in silence for a bit then John got up to get a salad out of the fridge. He drizzled olive oil and balsamic vinegar over it, and tossed it before plopping some down on our plates.

"Oh. Thank you. John, this steak is delicious! I honestly have not had a meal this good in…forever." Now I was sounding like a twelve year old. *Like, you know, for-eva,* I thought to myself. *Why don't you just ask him to cut your steak?*

"Wow. You must be really hard on yourself." John was just standing there looking at me with a smirk on his face. "Every time I look at you, you're scowling. It's really pretty cute."

I knew my face was about to explode from the blood rushing into it, and John noticed too, because he outright laughed at me. A hearty, deep rumbling that bubbled over into a laugh.

"Do you enjoy picking on pregnant women? You're embarrassing me and my head is going to pop off," I said with as much poise as I could manage.

John must really be enjoying this, I thought, because he laughed until his eyes watered. It was infectious because suddenly, I couldn't keep from giggling either. We sat there for a good five minutes laughing and crying, and every time we stopped, one of us started up again in a sputtering fit. During one of these moments, John stopped laughing long enough to take a drink, but ended up spitting it all over his plate because I started up again and he couldn't help himself. It was quite possibly one of the happiest nights of my life.

Eventually, we managed to finish our dinner. John sat quietly for a moment then looked at me from across the table. It had grown dark now, and the light from the candles was dancing on his face. My heart stopped. I couldn't draw a breath and I thought that I might just die from *wanting* him. We stared at each other for a few more minutes and then he seemed to grow uncomfortable, and distracted himself then by clearing the dishes.

"Oh, let me do that, John," I said. "You cooked the meal; I'll clean up after it."

"How about we clean up together, and then we'll play cards, or go for a walk."

I nodded and in about fifteen minutes, we were pulling on our shoes to go for another stroll by the water. John grabbed a couple of flashlights so we could see where we were going. The sky was crystal clear and the moon was full, but John didn't want me to trip on something I couldn't see. I had to agree.

It was close to my due date and I was feeling a great deal of pressure in my lower abdomen. I put my hand there affectionately and whispered to the baby that we would meet soon. I was starting to feel nervous about the birth and hoped that nothing would go wrong.

John noticed me rubbing my belly. "Are you ok?" he asked.

"I'm fine." I smiled up at him.

"I remember. Evelyn used to get pretty pissed at me when she got to the end of her pregnancy. One time, she was in a particularly bad mood, and when I got up to go to the bathroom, she jumped up and sucker punched me in the lower gut." He laughed that hearty, deep laugh of his.

"When I asked her why she did it, she said it was so that I would know what it felt like to be hit in the stomach when your bladder was full." He said this with a note of longing, humor, and grief in his voice, and I knew without a doubt that his wife meant everything to him.

"I think I would have liked Evelyn very much." I was laughing now, too. "I promise I won't punch you."

"Good, because I really didn't like it," said John, through his chuckles.

We walked in silence until we got to the lake, John holding my hand to keep me steady. I loved the way his large hand wrapped around my small one. He had big, thick fingers. They were so huge that my thumb was half the size of his and my pinky in comparison looked like a baby's. His hands were strong and warm, and I imagined getting to hold them for eternity. He let go when we were on even ground, though, and I sighed in disappointment.

"It's beautiful out here," he said.

"I could live here. Easy." And I could.

"I could, too. Charles and I are thinking about buying a cottage together up here. He wants to have a place for all of his kids to go for a break. He also wants to be able to take the grandkids fishing." John was scuffing his shoes at the edge of the water.

"It's so peaceful. If I had the money, I think I would buy a cottage to live in permanently. You can't beat clean air and the chance to see this every day." I spread my arms wide.

"Well, if we buy that cottage, you will definitely be welcome anytime you want."

"Thanks. I still can't believe I'm here at all," I said.

"Why is that? Where are you from? I mean, I know you're from B.C., but is that where you came from?" John asked. He turned to face me fully, and I looked up into his eyes wondering if I could trust him with the truth.

Finally, I decided that I could at least tell him about my marriage, but not the name of my husband.

"Yes," I said, and hesitated before continuing. "My husband was very cruel and kept me locked up in our apartment. It was his abuse that caused me to lose my babies." I stopped for a moment to look at his face for a glimpse of what he was thinking, but he was guarding his thoughts. I was nervous telling him too much, but once I started it was like pure freedom and I couldn't stop.

"I have lost two children. The first was Nicolas. The second was a girl that I named Gabrielle. I didn't get to see her, because I was unconscious for three days, and they said that she was deformed from the trauma of the miscarriage." I had to stop again to collect myself. When I looked back up at John, he was watching my face and reached out to wipe a big fat rolling tear off my cheek. I sniffled and wiped my nose on the sleeve of my jacket before continuing.

"I didn't experience the love you had with your wife, John. My husband was an adult when I met him. My father had this weird kind of obsession about him being like a son and pushed me into marriage. I mean, I had a schoolgirl crush on him, but I was a kid. He was a monster.

"My father died of a heart attack on our wedding day. And my mother is useless because she was so brainwashed by my father that she pretended not to see.

I was openly sobbing now, and John looked crushed when I looked up at him again. He gathered me in his arms and pressed my head into his solid chest. We stood there for a long time while I cried my eyes out, and John just kept murmuring consoling little phrases to me, while gently stroking my head.

I suddenly felt foolish and pulled away. John seemed hurt by my sudden reaction, but didn't say anything. He just let go and turned to look at the water. After a moment, I touched his arm and he turned to look at me.

"I'm sorry, John. I don't know what has come over me. You're a complete stranger, and here I am with you pouring out my heart," I wiped the back of my hand under my nose, before quietly adding, "I feel like a fool."

"What are you possibly sorry for?" he asked. "Besides that, what do you feel foolish about?

"Before you came into my life, I pushed everyone and everything from it. I resented Charles for any interference, even though I knew he was trying to help me. You know what I was doing when I banged on the door of Mrs. Graham's apartment that first night I saw you?" he asked.

"No," I whispered.

"I was blubbering like a baby myself, holding a picture of my family in one hand, and my gun in my other hand." John stopped to catch his breath and looked up at the moon. He sighed heavily and looked back at me with a sorrow so deep that I thought my heart would break.

"What kind of a coward would kill himself? It would have destroyed Charles to find me like that. How selfish could I have possibly been?" He choked off the last part. "Kathleen, I went over because you were crying out, and I was pissed that someone was disturbing my plans." John turned toward me and grabbed me by the shoulders turning me to face him fully. He looked utterly destroyed, and I lifted my hands to grab onto his elbows.

"John, you don't have to tell me about this," I said as gently as I could, although I did want to hear it. I wanted desperately to be close to him.

"I do, Kathleen. I do have to tell you. I want to, and I have never gotten this off my chest before. It's like, now that I got started--" he took a breath. "How many times I walked in the front door when Evelyn was pregnant, looking like you did that night. It made my heart stop. When I saw you, my world crashed around me and I was so *stunned*, I couldn't even remember who I was. Time stopped in those few seconds. I wanted desperately to grab you and hold you. But I knew you weren't Evelyn."

"I didn't know. I just thought you were being rude. I don't even know what to say to you right now. I *can* understand the need to end it all," I said, and meant it. "But for different reasons. In the end, I wasn't going to give David that kind of power over me."

"Kathleen, listen to me." John pleaded. "When I saw you, for the split second that I thought you were somehow my wife, I lived again. I haven't lived since the second I found my family dead on my front lawn. I am living *now,* and I'm not seeing Evelyn, I'm seeing you."

"John," I hedged tentatively, "what happened to Jonathon and Evelyn?"

He didn't say anything at first, than began his story. A look of total anguish and something far off shone bright in his eyes.

After finding the six body bags on his lawn, he had gone berserk and had been sedated. When he awoke, he was in a hospital bed. There was a uniform at the door and the captain was sitting in a chair at the foot of the bed. John was confused and it took a few seconds to remember what had happened. What did happen? Before he could ask, the captain told him. He spoke in a soft voice, a calming voice. The same voice John had heard him use on a disgruntled middle aged man who had been fired from a McDonald's for taking cash out of the drawer, and had decided to hold the inhabitants hostage.

He listened in disbelief as the captain started talking about the pimp and child porn and the prostitution ring. What the hell did this have to do with his wife and son? John remembered burying his face under his big hands, which still smelled of burnt flesh and blood. He remembered the dry heaves. The captain remained calm throughout his explanation, as John listened in silent horror as the story of his family's death was told.

Trina had vowed to destroy John's life the way he had destroyed her family, they had surmised. She had a mental disorder, and snapped when her beloved Trevor was shot in the courtroom. She befriended Evelyn and waited for a time when she and her children would be in the home alone. Once John left the house that fateful day, Trina shot her own three children, along with Evelyn and little Jonathon, killing them all and piling their bodies in the living room, where she poured gasoline on the mound of bodies and then on herself. The second she lit the match, she was aflame, and she threw herself onto the pile. Evelyn and Jonathon were on the bottom and were spared being disfigured by the fire, aside from singed hair and a few heat blisters.

John was paralyzed when the captain finished speaking. He couldn't think, breathe, talk, or cry. He remained catatonic for more than a week, blissfully sedated for long periods of time. Evelyn's family buried her and the baby together and took turns sitting with John in the hospital. John's step-father came and offered some relief to Evelyn's family. About a week and a half after the fire, he opened his eyes and saw his mother-in-law sitting, holding his hand, and he began to sob. Loud, racking sobs that took his breath away and left him with the hiccups. He cried until he passed out from exhaustion, but still he spent the next sixth months crying and tried several times to end his life. It did not take long for him to be institutionalized, and after extensive therapy, he was finally able to manage on his own again.

The captain came to visit often, but John couldn't talk to him or anyone from his former life as a police officer. Eventually, he came to this quiet little neighborhood where he had grown up so he could be close to his step-father. John would never be a cop again. He was a contractor now, and aside from speaking to people out of absolute necessity, he worked only a few days a week and spent most of his time alone.

And now here he was, sitting on his sofa, holding the gun and the pictures, thinking of all the anguish, pain, and loneliness he lived and breathed every day. All he could think about was ending his life. Why shouldn't he? There was nothing left. It wasn't that he needed strength to go through with it. He needed strength *not* to go through with it.

His thoughts were consumed with Evelyn and Jonathon. He obsessively replayed that day long ago, over and over in his mind. He never wanted to forget how he let his guard down and how it cost them their lives. He would always punish himself, even when nobody else blamed him. He would never find happiness again. Even as John continued to sit with the gun to his head, he knew that he wouldn't pull the trigger. As much as he wanted and wished for it, he wouldn't give himself a way out. His ultimate punishment was living. Remembering.

We stood there looking into each other's eyes. What could I say? How could I tell him that I was happy that he saw *me,* now? Was that selfish? The blood was rushing through my body in surges, and I began to feel dizzy and swayed. John became alarmed.

"Are you OK, Princess?" he asked me affectionately.

"Yes, I'm OK. Are you?"

"As long as I am here with you, I am. Why don't we go back and we'll sit and relax by the fire?" John turned to go, and I took hold of his large hand, immediately feeling safe and that all was right with the world.

We got back and John stoked the fire. He turned on the portable radio that we had brought with us, and soothing music filled the air. I went to my room and changed into some comfortable track pants and a sweatshirt. I came out, stood in front of the sofa, and put my hands on my lower back to arch and stretch. This pushed my belly out to monstrous proportions, and suddenly, John's good mood was back, because he couldn't help teasing me.

"You better stop doing that before you hurt somebody," he chided.

"You better stop doing *that* before you are the

'somebody.'" I pointed a finger at him. He put his hands up as if to protect himself.

"I'm only saying." He smiled up at me and patted the sofa beside him.

He put his hands on my lower back and started to rub. This time, I welcomed the closeness of his touch. I hadn't realized how much my back was hurting me. He worked his fingers deeply into the muscles, and soon, the tension that had been building up my whole life was melting away under his warm, large hands.

I felt John's hands move up to my shoulders, and he worked the tension out there as well. I sighed blissfully and let myself relax completely. After about ten minutes, John gently tugged my shoulders back to lean on him. I tensed, but his gentle prodding allowed me to relax again and I rested against his solid body. Another minute went by, and I decided to throw caution to the wind and tilted my head back to rest against his shoulder. I could feel his jaw resting on the side of my head, and we began to breathe slowly and deeply together.

John's hands were still at his sides resting on the sofa, so I reached for them and brought them around to rest on my belly. He hesitated at first, but then also gave in to his reservations and allowed me to hold his hands there. I could feel his heart beating fiercely on my back, matching the pounding of my own. It wasn't long before he started tracing the roundness of my belly under his fingertips. He was making slow and gentle circles around my belly button, and eventually the baby started kicking.

The first kick John felt startled him, and he snatched his hands away as if they were being burned, but then almost immediately put them back and waited for the next kick. We both sat there like that in complete silence for the better part of an hour, feeling the languid movement of my baby and being enveloped in the illusion that we were the only two people on the planet.

I nodded off in the comfort of John's strong arms. He smelled of the woods and smoke from the fire, and when I inhaled his scent it crept down into my bones, causing my body to feel like liquid molding into his chest. He was so solid. Against my back, I could feel the curve of his upper body and the dip where the hard muscle cut into his chest.

I snuggled a little closer, if that was possible, and stroked his hands and fingers mindlessly. He instinctively closed his fingers around mine and stroked my hands with his thick thumbs. I marveled at how smooth his hands were, considering the construction work he did. They were not rough in any way. Of course the skin was thick and weathered, but his hands on a whole were beautifully sculpted, and I found myself tracing the silvery lines of scars here and there. One in particular stood out. It was a half circle shape, raised higher than the others, and I wondered where it had come from.

"Where did you get this scar, John?" I asked, quietly.

I felt him smile before he answered. "I was fifteen and very rebellious. Charles had been asking me to clean my room and I was telling him off, so to teach me a lesson, Charles told me to put my boxing gloves on and we would settle it in a man's way, seeing as I was such a tough guy. Charles used to teach boxing at the local gym, and I went with him almost every night to work out.

"Anyway, he was sick of me being disrespectful and

lippy, so he was going to teach me a lesson, and boy, oh boy, that's what he did."

"We were standing in the living room, both of us in a fighting stance. At that age, I was already two inches taller than Charles, and I know my reach was about that much longer, so I wasn't concerned in the least that he would actually connect." John lifted his hand to scratch his chin, so I took the opportunity to sit up and turn to look at him.

"I was seething mad," continued John, "and could not believe he was going up against me. In my eyes, he was an old man already at the same age that I am now. Man, I was dumb. The second I put my hands down in my cocky state he got me square on the jaw. I was so stunned that I did nothing at first, but when I recovered from the blow, I retaliated and began a really good sparring match.

"Had my mother been there, I think she would have had a heart attack with all the pictures and trinkets all over the place. In fact, I know she would have." John's face lit up like a boy. He was shaking with mirth.

"Anyway, Charles and I were going at it, and my best friend, Steve, walked in and started egging me on. Steve used to fight, and he was a member of the Golden Gloves Boxing Team. A real good fighter.

"Anyway, Charles and I were sparring, and I was getting hit every time he threw a punch, so I was getting really pissed, and then I just started throwing my punches with everything I had. I finally landed one right on his mouth, but by this time I had thrown my gloves off because he was getting in some good shots and pretty much bludgeoning my face. When he spit out his front tooth, we both stood and stared at it like idiots, with Steve saying over and over, 'holy shit, man. You're dead!'

"Charles threw off his gloves and got back into his fighting stance." John stopped for a moment.

"Oh, my. What happened next?" I felt like a kid hearing a big secret.

"Well, Charles piped up and said, 'You're going to have to mow a whole lot of lawn to pay for a new tooth for me,' then he jabbed at me, hit me in the chest and knocked me flat on my ass. I was scared out of my shorts, and I hightailed it out of there. Steve and I went to his house, and I stayed there for a few days to let Charles simmer down before I went home."

"And that's how you got the scar on your finger? From sparring with your father…" I laughed. I picked up the hand to look at the scar and to rub my thumb along it.

"Yes. That is exactly how I got the scar," he said triumphantly.

I had to smile at him. "What happened when you went home?"

"Well, Charles had gone to the dentist and had been fitted for a new tooth. When the bill came in, because his insurance didn't cover the cost, he taped the bill to my bedroom door, and every penny I made went to pay the cost. Charles didn't really speak to me much during the month it took me to mow enough lawns to pay the bill, but once it was paid, he simply said, 'John, you've tried me to the limit, but I think we're square now,' and we continued with our lives as if nothing ever happened.

"I learned what respect was in that very moment, and I was never disrespectful toward him again. Defiant and stubborn, I'll admit." John finished his story and sat there smiling at the memory of it all.

"Wow. Charles doesn't seem like the type to resort to violence to teach someone a lesson. You must have really pissed him off," I mused.

"Oh, I did. But you're right, that's not the way he would normally handle me, but I had gotten to the point where I needed a very strong and final lesson, and Charles gave me exactly that." He tilted his head and looked at me quizzically. "Do you know how to box?"

"Me? God no! I wish I did though, because I could have protected myself and my children. Honestly John, I have led an extremely sheltered life. I wasn't even allowed to bring friends over when I was little. Actually, I shouldn't say that. I was too embarrassed by my father and he barked at anyone who came over, so I didn't bother." I let his hand go and turned my back to him so I could snuggle some more.

It didn't turn out to be for long, however, because I had to get up to use the bathroom. When I came out, John was fumbling through his fishing gear. He had brought two poles with him, and I was looking forward to the chance to try it.

"Are you going to come with me in the morning?" he asked.

"Yes. I promise not to be noisy and scare the fish away." I stood with my back to the counter in the kitchen and leaned on it.

"OK, then. We better get to bed because we'll be getting up at 5:30."

"5:30? In the morning? Isn't there fishing later in the day?" I moaned.

"Yes, in the morning. But if you *can't* Princess, you could stay here and cook me a man's breakfast." He ended the sentence with raised brows and I took a slap at him. He dodged it, of course, and grabbed both my wrists.

I stood there looking up into his eyes as they twinkled brightly. His whole face relaxed when he grinned, and I wondered how long it had been since he had last smiled. Before I could ask him, though, he bent down and gently pressed the side of his face against the side of mine. There was an old song playing on the radio, and he started moving us slowly from side to side, edging our way into the family room.

I rested my cheek on his chest and he circled one arm behind me and kept my other hand in his. We swayed back and forth, just inhaling each other's scent and feeling the heat from each other's bodies. A cheesy love song played out while we danced.   I brought my hand up behind him and hooked it on his shoulder. John was stroking my back and pressed closer to me. OK, he pressed as close to me as my frontal load would allow. I looked up at him and smiled. "Do you sing, or just hum?"

"I sing." And he started to. He really had a beautiful voice. It was deep and smooth like velvet. A voice I could listen to for the rest of my life. John sang to me and I could feel his voice rumble through his chest.

Another song began, so we kept on dancing. We were holding each other and stroking each other. He brought my fingers to his lips and brushed them gently across. His breath was warm and his lips were unbelievably soft, and I felt myself melt. God, how did I get here? *Please,*

please don't let it end. Please don't take this dream away, I prayed.

I was stirring in places I hadn't stirred in a very long time. Without realizing I was doing it, I tilted my head up toward his and opened my eyes to see him looking into my face. John brought his hand up and gently stroked my cheek.

"Do you know how beautiful you are?" he asked me softly.

"No," I whispered back. Nobody had ever told me that before.

I smiled up at John, and he bent down to kiss the tip of my nose. It sent chills down my body and my knees almost buckled. I reached up my arms and encircled his neck, twirling his hair in my fingers. Both his hands went around my back and he rested his arms on my hips. A *large* supply of hips, let me tell you.

We danced and swayed and John kissed me again on the tip of my nose and then planted soft little brushes with his lips over my face, finally coming to my mouth. At first he just faintly touched me, but then he began to kiss me deeply and I was surprised at my response to him. I could feel his hardness against my belly, driving me crazy with want. I kissed him back hungrily.

"I can't do this, John." I jumped back as if scorched by him.

"What's wrong, Princess?" John reached out to touch me.

"I'm pregnant, John. I'm going to have a baby in a few weeks, and I shouldn't have come here with you." I began pacing the length of the room.

"Kathleen, I don't want to hurt you. That is not my

intention. We'll take it slow, OK?" he said. He reached out to stop me and I let him take my hand. Looking at my fingers, John said, "If you want to just talk, that's fine. If you want to just sit that's fine, too. I don't want to do anything if it frightens you in any way. Kathleen, you've made me feel alive again." John reached out and brushed my cheek with the back of his large, warm hand.

"You make me feel alive, too." I managed to choke out. "I'm just really afraid. I have never experienced this before. My husband was…he was a brute and a bully." I was stammering and my eyes were filling with hot tears.

John gathered me in his arms and shushed me gently. "I'm one of the good guys, remember? You will always be protected with me. I will never hurt you in any way. Ever. I care about you a great deal and I'm not about to let you go. You're the first thing in my life that feels real in a very long time. I want to do whatever I can to help you."

"I want to. *God knows*, I want to. But I need to think about things for a while. I can't tell you everything right now. I will though. I promise. Right now, I'm just really tired and I want to go to bed." I stood on my tiptoes and kissed him on the cheek. "Thank you, John. For understanding, and not pushing me." I didn't give him a chance to respond and walked to my bedroom.

Once I started crying, I couldn't stop, and I didn't want to do that in front of John. I was grieving a relationship with him that I desperately wanted, but couldn't let happen. I could not bring him into my life and still protect my baby. The baby and I were fugitives and if David found me, I knew that he would try to kill me. If he found John with me, he would try to kill him.

Cop or not, David was brutal and I didn't want anything to happen to John. I was falling for him hard, and the best thing would be for me to leave as soon as possible.

Exhaustion caused me to tilt too far over when I bent to take off my pants. I steadied myself and awkwardly pulled off my socks, and finally, my shirt and bra. As I stood there naked, I began to examine myself in the full-length mirror on the back of the door.

There weren't too many purple streaks decorating my belly, but there were a few. Ugly little things, they were. I couldn't decide which was worse, the purple tiger stripes, or the spidery veins that popped out on my belly and breast. My hips, thighs, and arms remained in pretty good form. Thank God for small miracles, yet I couldn't see why this strange man I was falling in love with would want me.

The late stages of pregnancy were gangly and clumsy, and I contained very little grace, even when I wasn't carrying around an extra twenty five pounds. Now, I was like a blob of flesh waddling to and fro. *I* thought pregnancy was beautiful, but I had never known that a man might think so, especially on any other woman than his own mate. John was showing me that not all men were like David and my father, however. And I knew in my heart that I could trust him with my life and the baby's.

But, what of the baby? Was I prepared to let a man into my new life with my new baby? I had not planned on any kind of relationship with anyone, especially a romantic one. This whole situation hit me like a bomb. I was experiencing emotions that I had never experienced for another man before. Sure, when I was young I thought

I was in love with David, but now I know that wasn't so. I had only known John for a few weeks, and I felt like my life wouldn't be worth living if he was not in it.

Would he mind the purple streaks, I wondered while I traced each one with the tip of my finger. What about the breasts filled with nourishment for the baby? I reached up and cupped a breast in each hand, idly circling the nipples. They were soft and large and reddish brown in color. I sighed heavily, dropping my hands to my sides and crawled under the cool sheets, falling asleep with John on my mind.

Chapter Twenty Eight

Sploosh! The baited hook hit the water and sank. Fishing had always been relaxing to John, but this morning he could barely keep an eye focused on the sinking worm and hardly noticed when he started getting a hit. He snapped out of it just in time to give a jig, a snap of the wrist, and voila! His line stretched and…broke.

"The first one, John. Nice job," he said to himself. "Let's try this again."

He lined another hook, expertly tying the right kind of knots on the end of the line, and snaked another slimy worm onto the new hook. *Sploosh!*

This time, John paid attention and looked around. The sun was starting to crest over the water, and the morning mist was still covering everything like a blanket. Distant trees and hills were eerily shadowed in the blue haze, but it was breathtaking. In a few minutes everything would be covered in gold, and the mist would clear as the day began. The few trees that had any budding leaves would sparkle with crystal clear dewdrops.

When John had left the cabin, Kathleen had been sleeping soundly, and though she had said she wanted to come fishing this morning, John had decided not to wake her. Instead, he came out alone and to be alone with his thoughts. It was still pretty chilly, and John could still see his breath. The temperature was near frigid out here, actually, and he wondered how long he would stay out in the boat. He enjoyed all the seasons, but spring was his favorite. Every day was a day of growth and newness. Before Evelyn died, she used to ask everyday when he came home from work, 'John, did you notice the trees today? If you forget to look and watch, the next time you remember to look up, all the trees will have leaves on them.' Of course, she was always right, and every time he remembered to look up and notice the trees, he was shocked that they would be full of lush leaves, when only yesterday, it seemed, they were empty and full of snow.

Now that Evelyn was gone, he made a point of watching. That was one of the reasons he went for a hike most days by the apartment building.

That was exactly what he had been doing when he saw Kathleen by the creek, after that awful night when he bashed on the door and then stood there gaping at her like she was the ghost of his dead wife. *Dumb-ass*, he thought.

It took days for the effect of seeing Kathleen for the first time to fade. Once reality set in, John and Charles had it out because John knew good and well that Charles had let this woman rent the apartment because of her resemblance to Evelyn. Charles's wish was to rock John out of his self-destruction of the last two and a half years. Charles knew John well, though, and was right on about Kathleen and the effect she would have on him. Pissed John off in a big way, too.

Lost in thought about the night before with Kathleen, he was startled when he got a big hit on his line. *Gotcha!* John began the reel and fight with the large mouth bass at the end of the line. It was a distraction that lasted about ten minutes, before he released the fish back into the water, and placed a new worm on the end of his hook.

The night before had woken up a slumbering bear in John. Kathleen aroused in him a hunger and a *need* that he hadn't felt since he had been with Evelyn. He never thought another woman could do that to him, but she did. Being so close to her and touching her the night before while they danced was torture. He could barely contain himself and almost lost it a couple of times. She was driving him mad and he was being assaulted by a surge of emotion that had been buried deep inside.

He so badly wanted to be alive again. He was knocked over the head with it, actually. He *wanted* Kathleen. John wanted to do what he could to hang on to her and keep her safe.

It was strange that she seemed so afraid, now that her husband was dead. He had seen his share of battered women while he was on the force, but she was definitely not the kind of victim that would be a serial victim. She had fire and strength. He would just have to show her that she could trust him, give her a sense of confidence. In his heart, John knew that she was tentative and afraid of all men on some level.

He had always loved children and the more he thought

about Kathleen's pregnancy and a possible relationship, the more he would love to have the chance to have a child in his life again. At first, the thought felt like a betrayal to his beloved Jonathan, but Charles was right, John had to get on with his life. Having feelings for another family did not mean that he would ever forget his wife and son. They would live forever in his heart. He just wondered if he was strong enough to love freely again. It scared the hell out of him, but it was a chance he would have to take, and he knew that he wanted to take the chance with Kathleen.

Never in John's life had he ever believed in love at first sight. He always thought of it as a girly, mushy sort of fantasy that unhappy women or teenage girls had. But now, he seriously doubted his beliefs. If love at first sight was possible, he was sure he was feeling it now. It was like he had been waiting for Kathleen without knowing that she ever existed.

The sun was coming up, so John decided to bring his pole into the small motorboat he had rented for the week. He pushed his baseball cap forward and leaned back onto his duffel bag as a makeshift pillow. Lying back with his cap covering his eyes, he started thinking about the night before for the thousandth time. He and Kathleen definitely had chemistry together. When he looked into those green doe-like eyes, he could almost drown in them. They were captivating and intense. When John looked into them he could see an intelligence that most men would find intimidating in a woman. Not John. He liked intelligent women, always had.

He remembered the feel of her tiny hands in his, and how they felt soft and delicate. He loved that she was a whole head height shorter than he was. John didn't like skinny women, but he did appreciate a delicate creature. Not to say that he wanted a wimp either and he knew without a doubt that Kathleen had suffered tremendous losses and was probably stronger than most people. So far, she was everything that John had ever imagined that he could want in a woman.

He was getting ravenously hungry and decided to pack it in for the day. Maybe Kathleen would wake up tomorrow and come with him. The motor on the boat sputtered to life, and in ten minutes he was tying the boat to the dock and climbing the hill to the cottage. The smell of freshly brewed coffee hit him in the face about halfway up the hill, and he smiled at the thought that Kathleen was awake. It was a bonus that coffee would be waiting for him.

John entered the cottage and breakfast smells, mixed with the aroma of the coffee, made his mouth water instantly. Kathleen was standing at the stove, one hand on her lower back, and the other flipping pancakes and sausages. When she heard him come in, she turned and smiled warmly at him.

"Good morning, Princess," he said in greeting.

"Will you ever stop calling me that?" She was blowing a string of hair that dangled in front of her eye, and she looked so innocent that he had to laugh.

"Oh man! You are cute." John walked up and wrapped his arms around her front. Kathleen leaned back against him and John idly rubbed her belly.

He noticed her crinkle her nose and sniff the air. "You smell like fish," she said.

"That's because I went fishing."

"Well, I can't eat this wonderful breakfast if you smell like fish." Kathleen admonished him.

"Fine," sighed John, "I'll go jump in the shower. Don't start without me." By the time he finished, Kathleen had set the table and was pouring coffee. He served each of them some pancakes and sausage and poured a generous dollop of maple syrup on the food. Kathleen packed her plate nearly as high as his own and glared at him as he was about to comment.

"Don't you dare say a word. I am well aware that I can eat an entire horse, and I don't need any lip from you," she said testily, although the corners of her beautiful, full mouth curved up. The sight tugged at his heartstrings and he smiled innocently at her.

After breakfast, they wandered around. The day was crisp, cool and clean. John always enjoyed taking deep breaths in this kind of element. It made him feel clean and pure. This was the one and only time that he had felt any true joy since Evelyn and Jonathon. It somehow made him feel closer to them without the oppression of smog and pollution.

It had taken him a year to come back up here after the funerals because he was afraid the memories of all of them here would have been too much for him to handle. It was painful to be up here without them, but he couldn't *not* come. Being up North in a cottage like this one, was something that was a cherished memory. He wanted to make it a good memory with Kathleen as well.

Every time he looked at her or listened to her chatter away about this plant and that flower, he knew with her, he was home. Kathleen still had innocence, despite whatever hell she had gone through. There was no question about the shadow John saw cross her face, but there was also an excitement for life and nature that poured out of her. Every minute that passed while he was with her, filled him with a growing sense to learn and live again.

John walked over to where Kathleen was inspecting an overturned bird's nest, and she held it out to him for inspection.

"Do you think this family of birds will come back to find their home gone, or do you think they will somehow know, and just build a new one?" She squinted up at him in the glare of the sun, and he couldn't help but to bend down and kiss the furrows between her brows until they were smooth again.

"I don't know, Princess. I suppose they might just start a new life and make a new home," he answered.

"Like us?" Kathleen held her hand up near her brow to shield her eyes from the sun so he could look into them.

The sight took his breath away. In the sun, her eyes had flecks of gold here and there and the green was like looking into a glass marble. The sun danced off her strawberry blond hair and gold reflected in all directions, making her glow. Her cheeks and nose were rosy from the cool air, and her skin was soaking up some rays, because there was a faint bronzing of her skin that wasn't there yesterday.

"Is that what you would like, Kathleen? A new life with me?" John knew that he couldn't push her, but he wanted to know what she meant.

"I am thinking about that. It doesn't seem fair to come into your life unexpectedly, especially with a baby due in a few weeks. We don't even really know each other."

"What would you like to know?" he asked.

"When is your birthday, and how old are you?"

"I'm thirty-six and my birthday is December 15th. How old are you? And, when is your birthday?"

"I just turned twenty four on March 30th." She squinted up at him.

"Happy Birthday, Princess." He smiled down at her and took her hand. "Your fingers are cold. Do you want to go back?"

"No way! I've been locked up for years. This cold, fresh air is heaven for me and the baby." Kathleen laughed and brought his hands up to her mouth to kiss the back of his knuckles.

"And as for our future together, why don't you let me worry about whether you are being fair or not? All I know is that you make me feel alive, and I hope that I do that for you. They say that the best kind of friendship is an unexpected one." John wanted her to be comfortable.

She must have liked his response because she smiled up at him warmly and turned to inspect more of the forest around her and whatever living creatures she could find near the water. Today, life was good and John tilted his head up to silently thank Evelyn for bringing this unexpected treasure.

Chapter Twenty Nine

John and I spent the next few days getting to know each other more and I surprised myself with the honesty in which I told him about my childhood and life with David. I think it was a mixture of needing to get a whole lot of stuff off my chest and knowing deep in my heart that I could trust John. The one thing I left out, well two things was the fact that David was still alive and that my real name wasn't Kathleen. I would need to do a lot of thinking on those things.

What I knew for sure was that I was falling in love with John. I was engulfed with radiance from within. He made me feel intelligent and beautiful. With him, I was worth something, and I knew I made him feel the same way. I loved to watch his every move, to see the muscles in his arms work when he did simple little everyday things.

The last few days had been beautiful, and we were both sun kissed and healthy looking. One morning after fishing, we went back to the cottage with slight sunburns on our noses and across our cheeks. It had been such a good fishing day, my second day out with him, that we had stayed out longer than we had planned.

John had to help me into and out of the boat, which was not easy, but was fun. Of course he teased me about not sinking the boat, so I showed him how nasty a pregnant woman could be when teased, and took a swing at his shoulder with the oar. He didn't tease me again.

That night before dinner, John went into town to rent a couple of movies, so I had a shower while he was gone. I stood under the steaming hot water for a long while, and was too hot to dress right away, so I wrapped my body in a very large bath towel. I didn't think John would be back, but when I stepped out of the bathroom I ran smack into him.

He caught me easily. "Whoa," he said. "You're going to knock me over."

I stood there dripping and rosy from the heat of the shower, and John's hands were cool on my shoulders.

I looked up at him and smiled, still holding my towel in place. "Sorry."

"You're dripping." He turned serious and his gaze was intense as he raked his eyes over my face, down to my feet (what he could see of my feet), and back up to my face again.

The pulsing had started already between my legs and I inched closer, tilting my head up. John bent down and kissed me deeply, wrapping his arms around me. I brought my hands up and pushed his jacket off, all the while kissing him back with so much passion, we had to pull back to get a breath.

John started pushing me back toward his bedroom door, kissing me and pulling his shirt off at the same time. I reached down and unbuttoned his jeans, then traced the curve of his hips stopping on his bottom. The roundness of his backside in my hands was a real turn-on, and his thighs were hard and strong.

He sat me on the bed and knelt on the floor in front of me, reaching up to entangle my wet hair in his hands. He tilted my head back and kissed the hollow of my throat, making his way down toward my breasts. One hand freed itself from my hair and he reached down to tug on the towel that was wrapped around my naked body. I let him.

The initial self-consciousness I felt was lost now in hunger and passion. I wrapped my hands up in his hair, cupping the back of his head while he flicked his tongue closer to my breasts. I was intensely aware of the urgency with which my body was responding to him.

John kissed one breast, coming to the nipple and licked and suckled it, driving me to madness with need. He turned to the next one then gently pushed me back onto the bed. His tongue traced my navel, and dipped down to tracing the curve below my belly to where my need was strongest.

It was electrifying!! I had never experienced pleasure like this before, expertly being brought to the edge of insanity over and over. I gasped and squealed each time John took me over.

I *had to have him!* "Come to me John," I whispered, holding my arms out to fold him into.

"Will I hurt you?" he asked.

"No." I breathed heavily. "Come to me." I pulled him on the bed with me.

He lay down beside me and I rolled onto my side so

I could work at his jeans. I decided to return the favor and bent to tickle his chest and stomach with the barest touch from my mouth. The tip of my tongue, traced the feathery line of hair from his navel down. John drew in a sharp breath when I reached my destination, teasing and stroking until I knew he could stand no more.

He moaned in ecstasy.

After a few minutes, John put his hand on my head and murmured, "Come up here. I want to be with you."

He put his hands on my shoulders and rolled me away from him, where he climbed behind me so we were spooning. I was so slippery that the second his hardness slid between my legs, he entered me. I gasped at the shock of him coming in.

I yelped in pleasure with each thrust. He knew what he was doing. He wrapped his hand around my front, cupping my breast as we made love, taking me over the edge again and again.

"John!" I cried. "John!"

"Yes! Yes!" And together we reached our peak, panting with exertion.

We lay there like that for a long time. John gently stroked my belly until it relaxed, before moving to my back, arms and legs. I could completely lose myself in his arms. There was not a time in my life that I felt so safe and loved. His very presence encompassed me with a growing sense of possibility, and I knew without a doubt that for the first time in my life, I was home.

I couldn't help but feel a small pang of guilt at the thought that he had poured out his soul to me, and I had kept some things away from him. I would have to tell him the truth before we could move forward and think about a future. I just didn't know how I was going to do that.

We dozed for a bit, and I was woken up to the pressure of John's excitement gently prodding me. His fingers were stroking me in the front and I arched my hips forward, moaning in pleasure.

"Lay on your back, Princess." He said as he got up and kneeled down on the floor in front of me again. The bed was low so I let my buttocks dip slightly off the bed, while John supported my legs.

This time, he was slow and gentle, until once again I was shuddering from John's continued and practiced movement inside of me. I lay there with my eyes closed. The heat from John's body washed over me in waves of ecstasy.

When John was done, he flopped himself down beside me in exhaustion and kissed me slowly. His mouth was sensuous and hot, and he kissed me softly, moving his lips over my eyes and forehead.

He took my hand with his and brought it to his lips. "Are you OK?" he asked.

"I've never been more OK in all of my life," I replied and tiredly smiled up at him.

"Me neither," was his reply. "Are you hungry, Princess?"

"I'm famished. Let me go start dinner," I said, and slowly started to get up.

"No. I'm going to take you out for dinner."

"Boy, what did I do to deserve that?" I asked mischievously .

"You couldn't tell?" John laughed. "I thought it was

obvious. Maybe I'll have to try again later." He slapped my rear affectionately and got up.

"Oh, I could tell. But I think you're right. You better try again later." I giggled and balled up my towel to throw at him, then got up to get ready. OK, I didn't *get up*, I rolled off the bed, which made John laugh at me even more, so I grabbed his discarded shirt and threw it over his head.

We went to a quiet little family restaurant near the grocery store. We both dined on chicken, roasted veggies and salad. John had some white wine with his meal, while I stuck to mineral water. It was delicious. The chicken was sautéed in a rosemary wine sauce, and the veggies were mixed with sesame oil and seasoned just right.

I suggested that John go to the grocery store for a few items we still needed, while I popped my head into the bookstore. I knew there was a pay phone in the back of the store, and I needed to make a dreaded call. John didn't know I was doing anything other than looking for some new books, and I hated being sneaky about it, but I still didn't know how I was going to tell him the whole truth. I needed to find out what David was up to.

The shop was empty except for the elderly woman who owned the overfilled new and used bookstore. She smiled warmly at me, and I told her that I needed to use the pay phone. She pointed me to the back of the shop where the phone was. I pulled a bunch of quarters out of my wallet and dialed the number.

She answered on the third ring. "Hello, Mother."

"Kathryn? Kathryn, is that you? Oh, Kathryn where are you?" My mother's voice came at me in a frantic blur of words.

"I can't tell you where I am, Mom. I'm sorry I haven't called you. I needed to make sure David wasn't going to find me," I told her.

"Kathryn, David is going out of his mind with worry," she said.

I'm sure he is, I thought. "No Mom. David is not worried. He wants to hurt me and the baby, and I won't let that happen again." I was starting to get angry with her. Would she ever really see what was in front of her?

"No, Kathryn. He was crying and everything. He says he's sorry for hurting you. He told me that himself," she said triumphantly.

In the background, I heard a door slam shut, and then my mother said, "David. Oh, thank God you're here. Kathryn is on the phone."

"Give me that phone!" I heard David bellow, and then I was back in our stinking apartment. Back in that reeking prison I had lived in year after year, being tortured and raped. Where my babies died violent, meaningless deaths.

"Where are you, bitch?" The instant I heard the voice, the blood drained from my head and my world started to spin. "I'm going to find you, bitch, and when I do, you will be sorry! Do you hear me? You stole my fucking money," he screamed into the phone.

With as much force as I could evoke, I spoke into the phone. "No, you will do nothing to me ever again! I am never coming home!" I hung up.

I was shaking uncontrollably and each limb felt like rubber. The storeowner rushed to my side and put an arm around me to help me over to a chair.

"Are you alright, hun?" she asked with concern.

"Yes I'm fine, thank you," I lied. I wasn't fine at all.

"I'll get you a glass of water," the woman said and rushed off.

When she came back, I thanked her, took a few sips, and some deep breaths. I didn't want John to see me so shaken. I didn't know that I could keep the secret while I was so upset. At least, I knew now what I needed to know. David was trying to find me, and my mother was just as oblivious as she had always been. That meant two things: one, I will probably never see my mother again, and two, I could not stay in Niagara Falls with John.

My heart sank and the old exhaustion crept into my bones. I heard the bell over the door and shakily stood up. I knew it was John, and I didn't want him to see how upset I was. Too late. *Damn!* He took one look at me and rushed to my side.

"Princess, are you OK? You don't look so good," he asked. His face was rigid with alarm.

"I'm fine. I just got dizzy and needed to sit down." I tried to smile up at him, but I knew it looked forced.

"Let's get you home, Princess, and I'll make you some cocoa. You can lie down on the couch, and I'll rub your feet." John grabbed my hands and gently helped me up.

When I looked up at him, I was startled to see guilt so plainly etched on his face. I reached up and cupped his cheek in my hand.

"John, you didn't cause me to feel sick. I'm just tired." This time I did smile at him, and we went out to the car.

By the time we got back to the cottage, I was feeling much better, and we snuggled together to watch the movies John had rented. Both were comedies, so after a couple of hours of laughing, I was feeling much better. I knew that John still felt guilty. He said he was sorry, what seemed like a thousand times.

"John, it wasn't anything you did. I just felt faint and had to sit down," I said. Thankfully, the woman didn't tell John that I was using the phone when I got dizzy. I would have had to lie to him, and it was killing me to lie. He did not deserve that.

After the movies ended, we went to bed. This time, we went to bed together. We slept in John's bed, and he spooned with me for most of the night. I felt so safe with his arm wrapped around me and his hand protectively draped over my belly. The baby was kicking and moving around for most of the night, and I noticed that even in his sleep, when the baby kicked, John rubbed the spot.

I lay there thanking God and the Saints for John. I also prayed for the strength to tell him the truth. He was giving me everything he had inside of him, and I simply was not. John gave me respect and trusted me with his deepest secrets and pain, but I couldn't return the gift. And I felt guilty down to every fiber in my body.

Finally I fell asleep, but not peacefully.

Chapter Thirty

John and I were walking through the forest holding hands and giggling like school kids. I was feeling safe and happy. The sun was shining, the trees were all in bloom and to our delight, a family of deer crossed our path. They were grazing in the newly grown grass and didn't stir or scare when we came upon them.

We were petting the deer and enjoying the sun, when suddenly, a blacker than black cloud swept across the crystalline sky, engulfing us in dread and bleakness. The deer took off in fright, and John grabbed onto me, pulling me away from the darkness.

The wind was picking up to hurricane proportions and sleeting rain was soaking us through to the bone. I tried to run fast enough to keep up with John, but he got ahead of me. I don't remember letting go of his hand, but somehow he was suddenly gone. I stood in the middle of the forest, not knowing where to go, or how I was going to get out of there. Leaves and tree branches were whipping by, slapping me in the face.

I screamed for John over and over. I could hear him

calling for me, but I didn't know where he was because the wind was slamming into me from every direction. I blindly stumbled forward, hoping that I was going in the right direction. I could taste blood in my mouth from a cut on my lip. I knew that my face and arms had been slashed in a few places from the slapping branches.

Finally, John found me and grabbed my hand, but when I opened my eyes, it wasn't John. It was David.

"Gotcha!" David's face was dark and grotesquely stretched with tendons and muscles. Horns had ripped through the skin on his forehead, and his eyes were blazing red.

"Noooo!!!" I screamed and tried to pull away. I was frantically scratching at him and fiercely fighting for my life. I screamed for John, over and over. I could hear him, but he couldn't find me.

David smiled his evil smile and laughed. The laugh made me wince, and I screamed when he opened his mouth. It was full of shark's teeth, dripping with saliva. His fingertips were like razors and he began ripping through my stomach, pulling my baby out, tearing through a chunk of tender flesh with his teeth. His fangs dripped with blood, and the baby was screeching and trying to wiggle free as David held it roughly in his claw-like hands. I kept screaming over and over, as David laughed and dangled the baby out of my reach.

"KATHLEEN!!!"

I jumped up, flailing and fighting.

"Kathleen, it's me! It's John!" he said urgently and gathered me up in his arms.

"John..." I sobbed. I crumpled in his arms and kept crying. My body convulsed with hiccups and I gulped for air. John soothingly stroked my hair and back, telling me reassuring nothings until I calmed down.

"It's alright, Princess. I'm here with you. You're safe, now," he crooned.

"No! It's not all right. There are things that you don't know John," I cried.

"It's OK. Whatever it is, I'll help you. I won't let anything happen to you." I knew he was serious. John would protect the baby and me with everything he had. "Kathleen, I'm not going anywhere. You just have to trust me."

I started sobbing all over again. Exhausted and drained, I finally fell asleep in John's protective arms. We didn't go fishing the next morning, opting instead to stay in bed. We slept until noon, and John made love to me slowly when we woke. It lasted for a long time, and when we were finished, I felt warm inside. I stretched my body and relished in the pull of my sore, used muscles.

A while later, John got up, bent to kiss the tip of my nose, and went to have a shower. Despite the previous night, I felt rested. I couldn't help but to feel better with John by my side, and I knew that I couldn't leave him. I had made the decision when I woke that I wasn't going to let David take anything else from me. John had become my life these last few weeks. David would not take him away from me any more than I would let him take the baby from me.

After John finished his shower, I got up to have a steaming hot one myself, and he offered to make breakfast. When I came out, he had cooked omelets with peppers, leftover ham from the day before, and cheese. It was delicious. John obviously knew his way around a kitchen, because he was constantly making wonderful food. It was everything a pregnant woman could want in a man.

"You know, I wanted to be a chef before I became a cop," he said when I asked him how he knew how to cook so well.

"Wow! You just keep surprising me, John," I said.

He smiled. "I'm afraid if I don't feed you, you'll hurt me. What was it that you said, 'I could eat half a cow'?"

"Well, now you're being mean." I feigned hurt feelings.

He laughed and kissed me on the forehead. "Believe me, I know better than to mess with a pregnant woman and her food. When Evelyn was expecting Jonathon, she would eat everything in sight." He grinned at the memory.

I smiled back up at him. He loved his family well, and I felt so blessed to have him in my life.

John's expression turned serious. "Kathleen, I know all of this is going very fast, but I wondered if you were going to go back to Mrs. Graham's when we go back tomorrow?" he asked, looking down at me with a hopeful expression.

"I don't know, John. I haven't thought about it." I didn't know what to say. Of course I wanted to stay with him, but I still needed to think things through. "Are you saying you want me and a newborn baby to live with you?" I asked.

"Yes, Princess. That's exactly what I'm saying. I want you with me, if you'll have me. I want to take care of you and the baby." He paused for a moment. "I know you have some things that you haven't told me about your life, but that's fine. You'll tell me when you are comfortable." He knelt on the floor before me.

"Kathleen, you have taken over my life. I was dead to the bone before I met you. I didn't *want* to live. I pushed it away. You've saved me, Princess, and I don't want to let you go. You or the baby." John was looking at me with such love in his eyes, it brought tears to mine.

I sat there sniffling, my hand in his, and my heart full. I didn't need to be anywhere but here. The nightmare from the night before was still with me, but I was determined not to let it ruin what was building between us.

John and I spent the rest of the day just lounging around, marveling at how many leaves had grown on the trees during the last week and the sheer beauty of being in nature. We were both sad to have to leave the place, but John had already booked us the first weekend in July to come back. By then, the baby would be here, all the trees would be in full bloom, and we would be able to swim and sunbathe. I couldn't wait to come back. I bid God goodbye for now, and at the end of the day, we packed to leave in the morning.

John got up early to go fishing one last time, but I stayed in bed. I hadn't yet decided if I was going to move in with John or if I was going to go back to Mrs. Graham's until the lease was up. It didn't seem right not to finish out the lease. I doubted Charles would be able to find someone else when there was only a few more months left. My final decision would be made when we got back to the apartment.

After John returned from fishing, he cleaned up, packed the car, and we left to get breakfast on the way out of town. We went to the same restaurant as the night before and took our time eating from the buffet of breakfast foods. It was only Friday after all; I didn't have to be anywhere until my appointment with Dr. Smart on Tuesday, and John didn't have any construction jobs until the middle of the following week. He thought we might even stop for the weekend at a bed and breakfast on the way home. So, in the end, we decided that we wanted to have a couple more days with only each other.

We stopped in the town of Barrie at a five bedroom bed and breakfast in an old Victorian house remodeled for accommodations. The owners were a lovely retired couple whose kids were all grown up and busy with their own lives. Mr. and Mrs. Beard were their names. Mrs. Beard apparently loved to bake because there were fresh apple and blueberry pies cooling on the dining room table when they gave us a tour of the place. I couldn't wait to get my hands on one of those pies and my mouth watered at the thought of it.

John and I had a wonderful, home cooked meal of roast beef, potatoes and steamed veggies, finished with the best coffee I've ever had and a slice of apple pie. The rest of the weekend was spent eating, sleeping, wandering around town, and making love. Sunday came far too quickly, and we were both going to miss Mrs. Beard's cooking, but I had to admit I was anxious to get back.

All the fresh air was good for us and we were both positively glowing. When we stumbled into the apartment on Sunday evening, Charles came out as we walked by. He could hear our giggles and wanted to know who was out there.

"So the week didn't kill you both after all, I see," Charles said suspiciously.

John took his adoptive father's shoulders in his big hands, shook him, and kissed him on the cheek. "No, it didn't kill us, Charles. It brought us back to life." He beamed.

Charles shot a smile back at John, and there was a great deal of affection and lifted tension in those eyes. "I'm glad to hear it, son." He patted John on the back heartily, and then turned his attention to give me a hug and a peck on the cheek.

John and I thanked him, and bid him goodnight. I had decided to keep Mrs. Graham's apartment until the lease was up. John wasn't too happy about it, put he didn't push. He gruffly admitted it would be a good idea so he could get his spare room ready for the baby.

"Kathleen, tomorrow I'm going to the cemetery. Would you like to come?" He surprised me with the request.

"Are you sure you want me to come?" I asked.

"Yes, I'm sure. I think it's time for me to say goodbye to Evelyn, and I would like you to be there when I do." I was so moved by the fact that he wanted to include me in something that was, no doubt, extremely painful. Saying goodbye meant that he was accepting she was gone for good. Moving on with his life.

"Thank you, John. I would love to come." I gave him a lingering good night kiss, and went to Mrs. Graham's apartment.

All the work that had been done while John and I were away was finished and the apartment was sparkling when I went inside. It smelled of cleaning supplies and paint. Every nook and cranny had been polished, as well as all the furniture. Mrs. Graham was going to be thrilled to come home to such a clean apartment and a sparkling bathroom installed with new plumbing.

After unpacking, I cut up some fruit and had a nice hot bubble bath, with candles all around. Mrs. Graham's new bathtub was huge. It was very deep and had Jacuzzi jets for massage. John and I could easily fit in this tub together, I thought. I lay my head back, closed my eyes, and thought about what we could do in this Jacuzzi tub. As if he could read my mind through the walls, I was startled to hear a soft rap on the bathroom door, and John softly calling me.

I laughed. "How did you get in here?" I asked as he came into the bathroom.

"I do all the maintenance in the building, so I have a key. Can I join you?" He started undressing before I answered, but my wide smile was invitation enough.

"You must have been reading my mind." I splashed him in the face when he sat down across from me. We both lay our heads back for a while and just breathed in the scent of the bubbles and candles. John turned the jets on low, and I relaxed completely with a gentle massage on my lower back and shoulders.

About fifteen minutes later, I opened my eyes to see John watching me. He was pink with heat, and I had to touch him right then, so I leaned on his knees to steady myself and kissed him thoroughly.

His eyes were dancing with mischief, and he brought his hands up and cupped my rear. I scooped a handful of bubbles and plopped them on his head, then gave him a bubble beard. Then I put my hands on his head and heaved myself up so I could dunk him. He came up laughing and splashed water in my face.

"That's not fair! I'm defenseless against a pregnant woman," he complained.

"Good, then you will do what I want you to do." It was my turn to be mischievous, and I straddled him.

I brought my arms up around his shoulders and entwined my fingers in his hair. Roughly, I yanked his head back and pressed my lips to his, searching for his tongue. I could feel his hardness against the insides of my thighs and lifted myself slightly. He had to lay back a bit, because my huge tummy was a little in the way.

"Talk about mission impossible." I laughed, and then wiggled myself around until he slid up inside of me.

We both gasped at the heat between us, and I moved my hips back and forth, and then side to side. John kissed me urgently and moved his mouth over my breasts, taking turns expertly swirling his tongue around each nipple, then back to my waiting mouth. We splashed water on the floor and were both flushed from our passion, but couldn't help giggling with the intoxication of being together.

"Princess, you've outdone yourself." John laid his head back on the edge of the tub and closed his eyes. The smile stayed on his lips, though.

"My pleasure." I lifted myself off of him and he moaned.

"I'm battered," he teased.

"I am too." I went quiet for a moment. "I've never experienced it like this before."

"I will never hurt you, in any way. I only want to love you, and to be loved by you." John reached out his hand so we could clasp our fingers together. We lay there in silence until the water got cool, then reluctantly got out.

John cleaned the water from the floor, than kissed me good night and left. I went to bed that night with a smile on my face and warmth in my belly.

Chapter Thirty One

John couldn't believe what was happening to him. His life had taken a complete turn around in the last week. He never would have believed it, if someone told him he would love again. It was a love so unexpected and deep that it left him positively buzzing. He was giddy and happy, constantly smiling to himself. The guilt he initially felt while he struggled with his feelings for Kathleen was now gone.

It was time to say goodbye to Evelyn, and that was OK. He doubted that he would ever be able to accept the death of Jonathon, but he would work on it. John still felt that he needed to be punished in some small way for the death of his son, so he would not allow himself to be totally happy.

Back in his own apartment, he grabbed a book and tried desperately not to think about Kathleen for a while. Picking up the book made him think about how she looked the other day when he went to meet her at the bookstore, and how she had seemed to be in some kind of shock. He remembered the pay phone behind her, and suddenly recalled that her wallet had been sitting on the phone, along with a whole lot of change. Had she been making a phone call? If so, who was she trying to call, and why had it upset her so much? Troubled, he wondered about what kind of secret Kathleen was afraid to tell him. He would give her time, though, and when he knew she felt more secure, he would ask her about it.

Chapter Thirty Two

It was night and I was wandering around in the forest again. The wind had picked up, and I had to shield my face from being hit by flying debris. I was blindly searching for John again, but couldn't find him.

A shriek of evil laughter broke out behind me, and I knew that David was after us. The baby and me. I took off running, but exhausted quickly from the extra thirty pounds of baby weight and fat I had put on over the last seven and a half months. Both my hands were cupped under my belly to keep if from bouncing up and down, but that slowed me even more. I could feel the baby bouncing anyway, and I was deathly afraid that I was hurting it somehow. But it was nothing compared to what David was going to do when he caught up to us.

Suddenly, I stopped short, almost slamming into a huge wooden door suspended in the forest. There was nothing before or after it. It just hung there. I didn't even think about it. I used both hands to turn the enormous door handle and used all my strength to push the door inward.

Before I had even the chance to step through, I was

sucked in, and when I looked behind me, the forest was gone, as well as the door. I stood there in nothingness and looked around. There was no sound, no air, no light, no dark. Just...nothing.

I started calling for help. My voice caught in my throat and wouldn't carry, because there was no air. Panicked now, I spun on my heel and ran. It seemed like I had been trying to run for hours in this nothingness, when suddenly there was a light in front of me. It led down a hall with another huge door.

When I came to the door, I pressed my ear against it to see if I could hear any sounds coming from the other side. Nothing. This time, I held tight to the door handle, so when the door swung in, I wasn't sucked into another empty space.

Sitting at a huge wooden table was my sister, Emilia.

I ran to her and put my arms around her. "Emilia!" I screeched. When I pulled back to look at her, she was reaching out to me, but her eye sockets were empty and blood flowed out and down her cheeks. I screamed and jumped back. She stood up and came at me, her mouth moving in an effort to speak, but nothing would come out.

I backed up as fast as I could, banging my hip on the table. Emilia was moving slowly, but somehow she was upon me in a heartbeat. She put her hands around my throat and squeezed. The stench coming from her was vile and made my stomach coil. She smelled of blood and rot. Behind her, I noticed a large, antique mirror, and all my blood ran cold, forming a ball of electric ice heavy in the pit of my stomach. I hadn't noticed it before, but when I saw our reflection in the mirror, Emilia was hanging off me. She was choking the life out of me as we stood there, but was grotesquely severed from the waist down, with stringy bits of flesh and mucous hanging from her torso.

I became aware of splats of blood and flesh hitting my bare feet. Abstractly wondering where my shoes had gone. Emilia kept choking me and I forced myself to look at her face. A stringy mass of torn flesh and rot made up what used to be my beautiful sister. I forced myself to look into her face, and belatedly noticed her eyeballs weren't gone at all. They had been pushed into the back of her skull.

This wasn't my sister! I fought back, kicking and screaming. I raked her face and clawed at her hands. Finally, she let go. I smashed her in the face with my elbow as hard as I could, which sent her flying back. I spun on my heels to run in the opposite direction. There was another light and another hallway. I ran down it, still protectively holding my belly, which was now slimy from gore and blood..

When I went through the third door, there, to my relief sat John. This room was brighter, and warm. There were no corpses without legs coming at me, and John rushed up to gather me in his arms. Before he made it to me, though, he stopped dead, instantly going pale and looking clammy.

"John." I cried. "What's the matter?" I moved toward him, my arms outstretched.

He just stood there, not moving. After a moment, ever so slowly, he lowered his eyes to meet mine. In that instant, I knew he was dying. Also in that instant, David moved up behind John from out of nowhere, wrapping his left arm around him, as his right arm swiftly moved across John's throat. So swiftly, in fact, that I only caught a glimpse of sparkling silver. As quickly as the snap of a finger, John's limp body fell to the floor. I looked at David in horror and shock, while he stood there smiling that evil smile and laughing that evil laugh.

Chapter Thirty Three

I was screaming. Screaming until John woke me up. I must have looked horrified, because John had tears in his eyes and was completely stricken with panic. My throat hurt a great deal and it took me a few seconds to realize that I was back in Mrs. Graham's room.

I lunged for him, and wrapped my arms around his neck as if he were saving me from a sinking ship. I clung to him, sobbing and shaking violently. He just kept shushing me and stroking my back. Gently, John laid me down, and then lowered himself down beside me, holding me tight.

"Go back to sleep, Princess. I'm here with you," he whispered into my hair. He also planted soft kisses on my ear lobe and my wet cheek.

"I—it—wa-was so *real* an-and *gruesome*!" I choked with anguish. "M-m-my sister was trying to k—k-ill me. An—and you were dead!"

"No, Princess. I'm not dead. I'm holding you close and staying here with you. OK?"

I nodded and turned around to face him so I could

snuggle my face in the crook of his neck. He smelled safe. He smelled like the man I had come to love so completely in just a short time. I fell asleep

Chapter Thirty Four

IN THE MORNING, JOHN WAS gone, but left a note on the table telling me that he would see me later that afternoon; he had some errands to run. I needed to shower and get ready for my appointment with Dr. Smart at the clinic. I knew I couldn't go far from home now, because my due date was just around the corner. There was the chance, also, that I would deliver quickly when labor started, because I had already had two pregnancies.

I gobbled down some toast and coffee and ran out the door. Well, *ran* is an overstatement, but I did move *quickly*. My intention was to walk to the clinic, even though it was three blocks away. Charles stopped me in the lobby to offer me a ride, but let me be when I insisted on the fresh air and exercise. I also needed to stop at the pharmacy on the way home to get some more hair color, to cover my re-growth. Had it really been almost eight weeks since I'd been gone? Time was flying, and I was definitely having fun. The most fun I'd ever had.

By the time I reached the clinic, my bladder was about to rip open wide. I hated when my bladder got this full, because it always made me think about the years I had spent hiding in the closet from David, waiting for him to finally pass out in a drunken stupor. At the same time, however, that was becoming someone else's life. I was no longer that timid, fearful, battered girl. I was free and strong. I felt like whooping with laughter. *I'm free!*

"Kathleen Lockhart," a nurse called from behind her station.

"Yes. That's me," I said and got up to follow her to Dr. Smart's office.

"Hello, Kathleen. How are you doing?" she asked as I walked through the door.

"I'm doing wonderful!" I was gushing, but I didn't care.

"You look fabulous! Very healthy, actually. I see you've also put on some weight," she observed.

"I've been eating well." I was a little abashed and let a giggle slip.

"All good food, I hope?"

"All good. Everything."

"Good, now lie on the table, so I can take your measurements and check to see if you're dilating yet." She patted the table and took out her measuring tape.

After measuring my belly, I stepped onto the scale. Dr. Smart beamed her approval of my healthy state. "Kathleen, you're doing great! What's so different? You don't even have the exhaustion showing on your face that you had two weeks ago."

"I'm just very, very happy," I simply stated.

"I'll be back in a few minutes. I'd like you to take your pants off and put the gown on." She turned and left the room, so I could change.

I hopped up onto the table, covered myself with the paper sheet, and waited for her to come back. On the walls, there were several posters of animated drawings of the inside of a womb during different stages of pregnancy. I looked at the one that showed the last eight or so weeks and imagined what my baby would look like.

I pictured the tiny fingers and toes and the fuzzy mass of hair the baby may, or may not, have. What color eyes would it have? How much would he or she weigh? As I imagined all of this, my thoughts constantly went to John, and how he was turning his life upside down for me and this strange baby that wasn't his. It took a different kind of person to love another's child with complete abandon. Yet I knew in my heart, like I knew I would never be David's prisoner again, that John was already in love with me and the baby. John did not want me to wait to move in with him. He was going to get his son's baby furniture that he had never brought himself to part with, for us to put in the spare bedroom.

Excited that we were in his life, John wanted to get out the crib, buy a new mattress for it, and go shopping together for baby stuff. I still had a large sum of money left, so John didn't need to buy anything, but he wanted to. He was everything I ever imagined a lover and expectant father could be. Actually, he was more, because I wasn't capable of imagining nearly as much as he was already.

All of his enthusiasm was wonderful, and it filled me with gratitude and joy, but I couldn't help but feel guilty as well. I was still keeping secrets from John. At first, I was terrified that he would turn me in for kidnapping if I told him the truth, but now, I was terrified that he wouldn't want to keep me with him or be appalled that I would take a child away from his father. Even though I told him what the baby's father had done to me.

John wants you and the baby, Kathryn, I thought to myself, and to my surprise, tears sprang to my eyes. *He doesn't even know my real name.* All the happiness I was feeling turned to dread in an instant. *You have to tell him, Kathryn. You have to tell him everything.* My mind was made up. That night, I would tell John the whole truth. He deserved at the very least, the truth. I didn't want our new love to be tainted by lies.

After giving a soft rap on the door, Dr. Smart came back into the room. The rest of the exam lasted about ten minutes, and then she instructed me to get dressed and go into the adjoining room so she could discuss some options with me.

"Well, Kathleen. You're doing great and the baby's head is down, getting ready to engage," she said in her pleasant, reassuring voice.

"What does it mean that the baby's head is engaged?" I asked. I hadn't gotten that far in the first two pregnancies.

"It means that the baby is getting into position, and now we just wait for the baby to drop and labor to begin. I don't expect that to be long, however, because you are two centimeters dilated. Of course, it's still early, but not so early that you couldn't go into labor. Don't be alarmed that you're already dilating. It's perfectly normal. " she smiled as she said this.

"I've been getting cramps." I said.

"Kathleen, we need to decide the option of where you want to give birth. Here, at the clinic, or at home."

I was surprised. I didn't know anyone still had children at home, and I said as much.

"Most don't, but we're a non-profit organization with more options, so we can cater to different preferences or religious beliefs. Think about it, and let me know when you're in next week."

"OK. Goodbye, Dr. Smart. Thank you." On my way out, I stopped at the nurse's station to set up my next appointment.

When I went outside, John was sitting at the curb, waiting for me in the car. He smiled, waved, and beckoned me over.

"What are you doing here?" I asked as I squeezed into the front seat.

"I thought I would take you out to lunch, and we could go shopping for some things."

"That sounds wonderful. I have a craving for hot dogs."

"Uh…I was thinking more along the lines of chicken salad or tuna salad. Maybe even fruit salad." He raised one eyebrow.

"Only salad? Boy, you sure know how to crush a girl's dreams," I teased.

"I'll make it up to you. But, does it have to be with food?" he asked suggestively, which made me giggle.

We opted for the mall, grabbed chicken salad, and he treated me to some chocolate frozen yogurt (every woman needs chocolate), and then we went into the baby store. There were so many things to buy. One could go crazy trying to decide between all the little sleepers and other outfits, the tiny socks, and bonnets. We ended up spending almost an hour picking out new bedding for the crib, lamps, nightlights, and window coverings.

"John, you're doing too much for me," I said quietly when he took out his credit card. "I can pay for all this stuff."

"Look. I've made up my mind that you and the little gaffer in there," he said as he pointed to my belly, "are going to be with me. I get the impression that you kind of like me, so stop complaining and let me pay for this stuff."

"If you put it that way," I said, and then relented and let him pay. "But that's it. I'm paying for my own stuff." I demanded.

We played around at the mall some more before heading to the cemetery. John picked up a small bouquet of flowers at the corner store and drove the scenic route to where his wife and son were buried. He became somber almost as soon as we drove onto the property. We drove slowly in silence around all the different bends in the single lane road. John pulled over to the side about halfway through the cemetery.

It was a beautifully landscaped piece of land, and as far as you could see, there were all kinds of different headstones planted in the earth. We got out, and John took my hand to lead me to his family. On the way, I think to break the silence, he pointed out a far off corner that was put in place over two hundred years ago. The little section still had the original rough wood fence, and within its structure, there stood about twenty crudely made headstones. It was utterly beautiful. I had always had a fascination with old cemeteries, and thought that some other day, I might come here to walk around and read the headstones.

We stopped at a headstone that read, "Here lay a Mother and her Child taken into the Embrace of Heaven. In Loving Memory of Evelyn Joyce Sullivan and Jonathon James Sullivan." Below the inscription were the dates of their births and deaths. The headstone itself was in the shape of a cross, with a small picture of each engraved on either side of the cross, with the inscription in between the faces. It was breathtaking.

John knelt on the ground near Evelyn's picture and laid the flowers down gently beneath her etched face. I moved behind him and put my hand softly on his shoulder. He brought his hand up to meet mine and we stayed like that for a long while. I think John was trying to find the courage to speak, because when he finally did, there was a quaver in his voice.

"Hello Evie," he whispered. After a pause, he added, "I came here to say goodbye, Baby." John lifted his hand and ran it across his nose, and I knew he was silently crying.

"I've met a wonderful woman, whom I know that you would love." Another sniffle, another pause. "Her name is Kathleen."

I think I felt my heart break in that moment and I felt the hot flow of my own tears roll down my cheeks. *No John, I'm not Kathleen.* John didn't notice my tears, though, but he did squeeze my hand for support.

After another long pause, John kissed his fingers and placed them on Evelyn's beautiful face, then turned slightly to face his beloved child's cherubic portrait.

"Hey, Sport. Daddy misses you." That was it. The

anguish that poured out of him was too much to bear. I knelt down beside him, and pulled his head onto my shoulder.

We both sobbed for a long, long time, both feeling the grief that was so deep, it ripped chunks out of our souls. No parent lost a child and still kept their spirit in one solid mass. The unimaginable pain of such a loss crept into the cracks of your skin, tearing out your heart here, ripping out laughter there, threatening to dissolve every good memory there was.

Every birthday that would have been. Every park where you heard a child's laughter. Every schoolyard and swimming pool where children played. Every McDonald's Playland, or Walt Disney movie. And Christmas. Christmas was the most excruciating, with imagined giggles and presents that would never be opened; the imagined gift you would never receive. Teenaged angst and rebellion. Prom, college, and marriage.

We cried in each other's arms until there were no more tears, using the sleeves on our jackets to catch our running noses.

"Daddy will see you soon, Sport. When I come back, I will be bringing a baby brother or sister for you to meet." He looked up at me with the question in his eyes. I nodded and smiled. "But, I will always love you."

John stood and took my hand to help me up, and we lingered for another moment before we turned to go.

"Thank you, John," I said. "They are beautiful, and they were lucky to have you." I paused then added, "And you were lucky to have them."

"And now, I'm lucky to have you," he said before

planting a kiss on my forehead. Like every other kiss, it felt like home.

John seemed to relax greatly after our visit to the cemetery, and his mood lifted once we left. We decided to go see a movie. Why not get as many in as you can, right? This time, he let me pay, and we saw the latest Jackie Chan action/comedy. After the show, John thought it would be nice to go for a walk along the Falls. I had only glimpsed them once, on the day that I had finally arrived here on the bus, so I was all for seeing them in the evening light.

As we walked, I told him about the doctor's visit, and what my options were.

"Kathleen, I would like to ask you a question, and I hope you don't think I'm being too forward." He paused and took a deep breath before continuing. "I was kind of hoping that I might be able to be there with you, when you have the baby."

"Really?" Of course, I had been thinking about it myself. "Oh, John! Really? I've wanted to ask you, but didn't know how." I was beaming, and he beamed right back at me.

"I have something else to tell you, or rather, to ask you," he said. "Charles's oldest grandson, Steven, just finished college, and wants to come to stay here for the rest of the spring and the summer before he starts his job placement." I nodded for him to continue.

"Well, Charles and I were thinking that he could take over Mrs. Graham's lease until she comes back, and you could come and stay with me." John stopped walking and looked straight into my eyes

"If you still don't feel comfortable doing that, Steven

can just stay with me. But I thought that since we've already talked about it…" His voice trailed off as he shrugged his shoulders with a boyish innocence that made me smile.

"John, there are still some things that you don't know about," I began in a shaky voice.

"What is it, Princess?" he asked. He said 'Princess' with such affection, that it nearly tore me apart.

"I'm afraid to tell you," I whispered.

"Don't cry, honey. You can tell me. I understand why you might be unable to fully trust me. You've had a shitty deal with men, but I'm not like that, and you have to know that I would never hurt you." John remained as gentle as ever with me.

I had to tell him at least my real name. "My name is Kathryn."

He didn't say anything for a moment. "Kathryn is a great name."

"Kathryn McKenna is my maiden name." I held his gaze for a moment. "Please forgive me, John, but I can't tell you any more right now. I still need more time."

"That's fine Kathle-Kathryn. Whatever you've gone through is obviously very painful and scary. Like I said before, I'll wait until you're ready." He was so reassuring, that I knew he wouldn't press me for more information for the time being.

I desperately wanted to try to contact my mother again, but I couldn't risk it. After speaking to her from Muskoka, I knew without a doubt that David was controlling her. It broke my heart because my father had restrained her for years. God helped me get this far. Maybe He would help her, I prayed.

We walked in silence for a time, enjoying the sheer wonder of Niagara Falls, while getting sprayed by the mist. Our hands were clasped tightly together and our thighs bumped each other constantly (I had a major waddle going on) in our effort to be as close as we could to each other.

It was dark, and the beginning of the week, but that didn't stop the area from overflowing with tourists and local teenagers hanging around. We stopped at one of the spots where we could see the rushing water spill over the side of the cliff. There were huge lights of different colors dancing over the water, giving it a mystical feeling. It was refreshing to feel the water tickle our faces and to breathe in the clean, crisp air.

John put his arm around my shoulders and I leaned back against him to feel his warmth.

"You're shivering, Princess. Let's get you home."

"OK," I said, reaching up to touch his cheek, looking lovingly into his eyes.

He dipped his head down to kiss me softly.

When we got back to my apartment, it was too late, and I was too sore from walking around, for us to worry about moving my things over to John's. I didn't have much, just a duffel bag and a few groceries, but I just wanted to go to bed, wrapped in John's arms. He helped me undress and then rubbed my swollen feet between his large hands. My feet were cold from the lack of circulation that so often happens near the end of a pregnancy, but the constant heat from John's hands warmed them quickly. Weariness crept over me like a blanket, and I fell asleep while John was still massaging my feet.

Chapter Thirty Five

In the mist of the Falls I could see the silhouette of a man. Just barely, but I knew he was there. It was very dark, and I was completely alone, except for the man in the mist. Standing there watching the shape, I felt oppressed, like I needed to be somewhere, but was unable to move to get there. I spun around to see what was behind me and found myself in a deserted, dark hallway. The hall went on forever in both directions, and about every ten feet, there was a door.

Each door was numbered, and to the right of each door, there were brass candleholders with thick, white candles, burning high flames. At least, they seemed to be white, but everything was covered in what appeared to be half an inch of dust. The wax from the candles hardened in big goopy mounds on the candles themselves and down the walls. There were even clumps of wax on the carpet beneath the candles.

I looked down at the carpet to see that it was a rich, blood red carpet that had a gold paisley design embroidered throughout. Next, I looked at the door to my right. The number on it read 664; the one on my left, 663. Not knowing where I was, or what to do, I started walking down the hall, speeding past the door that had 666 on it.

I began to hear noise coming from farther down the hallway and realized that the sound was John's voice. I opened the first door that I thought it came from, but the room was empty, save for a bed and nightstand. Then I opened the next and the next, coming to each door, knowing he was behind it, only to find him gone when the door was opened.

I was getting panicky and frustrated. I sped by another twenty doors, and another twenty empty rooms. I could hear another sound creeping up behind me. It seemed to follow me into each room, just behind my head. Every time I jerked my head around to see where the sound was coming from, there was nothing there. Fear was starting to grip me deep in my stomach and I started running to each door. I threw myself from one door to the next, and so forth.

Although John's voice came from behind each door, I was deathly afraid to open any of them. Behind me, the sound turned to a hissing, and when I turned to look, there was a large snake forming from the gold paisley design, rising from the threads of the carpet. It loomed before me. The snake's eyes were David's. It smiled at me, sticking out its tongue, flicking my face. The eyes were the blood red of the carpet, and it had fangs that were long and curved, dripping with acid and venom. Each drop leaving a sizzling hole in the carpet.

Rigid with terror, I couldn't move. The snake kept flicking my face with its tongue. Finally, I turned to run. But the more I tried to get away, the more I realized I couldn't move, and I began to panic.

The David-Snake kept snapping its head forward,

as if to bite me, and I squealed each time, dodging from right to left. I was running at full speed, but I wasn't going anywhere, and the floor beneath my feet started to feel like I was running in water. When I looked down, I didn't see water. It was blood. The carpet was full of blood, squishing between my toes. I noticed that I had lost my shoes.

At last, I slipped and started to fall. I screamed for John, but he didn't come. The snake bore down on me digging its fangs…

"*Kathryn!* Wake up!" John was shaking me, just roughly enough to rouse me.

I looked at him in confusion, blinking my eyes until I realized that I had been having a nightmare again. "I'm sorry," I croaked.

"What were you dreaming about?" he gently asked me.

I was exhausted and the dream was already starting to fade. "Mmmmh…?" My lids were heavy.

"It's OK. Just go back to sleep."

So, I did.

Chapter Thirty Six

John was deeply disturbed by the obviously traumatic nightmares that Kathleen...*Kathryn*, was having. Nightmares like that were usually caused by horrific experiences, and he doubted that they were just the result of her miscarriages. He had been a cop long enough to know Post Traumatic Stress when he saw it. Hell, he suffered from it, himself. Half the police force suffered from it.

For the hundredth time, John wondered just how bad the abuse had been for Kathryn. John could protect her, but not as well if he didn't know what he was up against. She had told him that her husband died in a car accident right before she found out she was pregnant. And yet...one didn't have to be a rocket scientist to know that something else was going on here.

She said her name was Kathryn McKenna. An Irish name. She *looked* Irish, with the green eyes and the fair skin, with a splash of freckles here and there. The freckles were almost too light to see, and spread across her nose and cheekbones. They were very attractive, and gave her a certain innocence. Some might say she was too young for him, and he felt a twinge of that himself, but whatever she had gone through, had given her a maturity that far surpassed her age. It saddened him to think that her innocence had been lost at such an early age. He had witnessed too much of that on the force, especially on his final case.

Why would she not have told him her married name? he wondered. In John's experience as a cop, that usually meant that there was a kidnapping involved, although this time, the child in question was still in the womb. He only knew that she had been married, that her mother was still alive, but Kathryn didn't have contact with her.

John wanted to help Kathryn any way he could, but he knew he would have to do a little digging around, use some of his old contacts, to find out a little more. Lying to Kathryn wasn't something he wanted to do, but some situations required lies to get the information.

She said she was from the British Columbia area, so he could only go on that and the name she had given him. That day, John put a call in to one of his former colleagues from the force in Victoria and asked for a favor. In return, John agreed to visit in the winter, to enjoy some R & R on the ski slopes.

The next morning, his friend called him back with the information John was seeking. Kathryn was her name, but she was definitely harboring a secret. His buddy faxed him all the information he could find, along with driver's license pictures, social insurance numbers, and a copy of a marriage license. There were also copies of her children's death certificates.

John's guilt grew steadily. The more he read, the

worse he felt for going behind Kathryn's back to find out about her life and what she ran away from. He was certain almost from the beginning that she was running from something, or someone, and this confirmed it. Her husband had an arrest record for various incidences of violence and drug charges. Nothing too big, but enough to paint a picture of the kind of guy he was. One thing John knew now with certainty: Kathryn's husband was alive. Otherwise, there would have been a death certificate.

As John sat and stared at the latest mug shot of David, he felt his anger bubble to the surface. This was the guy that had beaten Kathryn. This was the guy she suffered nightmares about almost every night. *What did you do to her?* John thought.

David didn't seem the kind of person that Kathryn would match up with, but then again, perhaps John didn't know Kathryn. Maybe he only knew Kathleen. It was strange to think that he was in love with a stranger, yet he could not deny loving her. John was going to make sure this guy didn't come back, and if he did, John would take care of him.

John asked his buddy to put a tail on David, to see if there was something he might be doing to try to locate Kathryn. Men like David didn't just let it lie when their women ran out on them. He did know that David didn't call the police to report her missing. That only increased John's sense of unease about the situation, and he felt better knowing that Kathryn was going to stay with him, in his apartment.

The rest of David's information was about his growing up in foster care in different parts of British Columbia.

It didn't appear that David was very lucky when it came to the foster parents. Not all foster parents took children in out of love. John knew from experience that if a child grew up in shitty foster care, there could be issues of possessiveness and controlling behaviors as an adult. The child grew up feeling abandoned and out of control of their own lives, which often led to aggressive personality disorders as they grew older. It appeared that David had grown up with all the constraints that would lead to a life of ill opportunity and the need to find a partner he could control.

That had been Kathle...*damn*, Kathryn. She was simply a victim of domestic abuse. Not that domestic abuse was simple. Obviously, the degree of abuse ranged from mild emotional jabs, right up to agonizing physical and mental torment. Kathryn had clearly been on the receiving end of torturous cruelty.

David's mental instability was also clear in the photo before John's eyes. The picture was taken after an arrest for a DUI, which resulted in an accident where an elderly woman suffered a fractured hip, requiring surgery.

David's face stared back at John, with an evil smile curling over his teeth. It sent shivers down John's spine to think that Kathryn had suffered at the hands of this creep. It brought out a primitive need to protect what was his and that was exactly what John was going to do.

He locked the papers away in the vault under the carpet in the floor of his study. He kept the bonds that he had inherited from Evelyn and some other important documents in there. It was safe in there and fireproof. Not even Charles knew it existed.

John had never felt truly secure leaving his personal

things in a safety deposit box at some bank. He supposed that was the cop in him, still wriggling its way into his life in one form or another. Hopefully, he wouldn't have to resort to his protective means, but he took out his gun, checked it, and decided to tuck it away in the ankle strap that he used to wear to house an extra weapon when he was on active duty.

He also vowed to make sure Kathryn didn't leave his sight until he knew what exactly David was up to.

CHAPTER THIRTY SEVEN

WHILE JOHN WAS AT WORK, I rearranged our things together in his room. I had finally decided that I wasn't going to fight my feelings of what was right or wrong, or inappropriate. I wanted to be with him, plain and simple. Of course, when I thought of how much time had actually gone by, my stomach fluttered with butterflies. John was such an unexpected gift in my life, and the more time I spent with him, the more secure I felt.

John did not own as much clothing and things as some people did. He was a much simpler person than that. His collections were more in the area of books and antiques. In the study, he had an old, rustic looking desk of great value and quality, lamps and a throw rug. There were also rows of books of all kinds, neatly stacked on oak bookshelves that John had lovingly crafted by hand. The upstairs bathroom had an old claw-foot bathtub, and the armoire for the bathroom things looked so simple that it could have come straight out of 'Little House on the Prairie.'

His bedroom was a little more modern in décor,

but he had a beautiful throw rug at the foot of the bed, covering the dark hard wood flooring that he had so masterfully refinished. His natural ability with wood was something to be proud of and just looking at his work unveiled his love of creating something with his own hands. Even when he dusted his furniture, I noticed that he took his time, making sure each and every grain in the wood surface was stroked with protective oil. Like me, he was passionate about nature and what could be created from it.

John had bought me some more clothes against my will. He said that most of my clothes looked like they were a decade old, which they were, so he insisted on going on a shopping spree. He purchased a few pairs of jeans, some tops and a few pair of sneakers and sandals, because summer was just around the corner. I also splurged a little, buying myself some new, better fitting undergarments. Nothing made a woman feel sexier than sensual lingerie.

When I modeled one of my new purchases for John, he slipped his pinky finger under the strap of my bra, following the curve of my breast to lovingly caress the nipple. Of course, the bra didn't stay on for long. Neither did the panties, and I couldn't help but smile to myself at the thought of that little romp. I still found it hard to believe that he truly found me desirable in this late stage of pregnancy.

Every night since we got back from the cottage, John would lay his head on my lap and stay there until he felt the baby kicking. Or he would cup his hands over my belly and talk softly to the baby. He said all kinds of little endearments, as if this child was truly his. For the first time in my life, I was happier than I could have ever hoped to be, and I knew that happiness would only grow when the baby came.

When my next appointment with Dr. Smart came, the baby's head had dropped into position. According to her, it was still safe to have sex, and John was always careful with me. He was a very considerate and gentle lover.

For us, our lovemaking grew more electrifying every day, and every day we hungered even more. We simply could not keep our hands off each other. And every day, my old life drifted farther into the back of my mind.

John had two dressers in his room, and gave me the empty one, yet when I got to the third drawer down, it wasn't empty. It had a photo album in it. At first, I didn't think that I should look through it, but in the end decided that we had felt our pasts were behind us, so I flipped open the cover.

The very first picture was a larger version of the family picture I had seen already, when they were down in the Gorge. I traced my finger along Jonathon's small face and smiled at the thought of how John must have been with him. Then I drew my attention to Evelyn. Her face was beautiful and her eyes were full of life and love. She was laughing at something Jonathon had said or done, and it looked as if her smiles came easy. There was no tension in her face at all, and I knew that John had loved her completely.

John's face was also relaxed and full of love. The way his eyes lingered on Evelyn was a clear window of his feelings. It pulled on my heartstrings to know that such a loving and happy family had suffered the way they had.

I wondered how much time Evelyn had before she and Jonathon were killed, to know what was happening. Did she have to watch her child being killed? What had she done to try to stop it? Or maybe she had no clue at all that any of it was going to happen, and had died instantly. John hadn't mentioned if there appeared to be any kind of struggle or if she had been holding her boy close.

So sad, yet I couldn't help but to be happy that I was going to be John's new life. How could I not be? I was terribly upset at the fact that a mother and a child had died, and I did feel guilty about being happy that John was with me, but I couldn't lie about my feelings either. If John and I weren't meant to meet and fall in love, then we wouldn't have. Just as I was meant to eventually get away from David.

I sat down on the king size bed in our room. It was a wonderfully comfortable bed with a pillow top mattress. When I lay down, I was engulfed in warmth and safety. It felt like I was lying on a cloud, it was so soft. My lower back was aching quite a bit from doing the household chores, so I rolled over on my side and tucked my knees up as far as I could.

"Ah-h-h," I sighed. My hand went to the mound of my belly, feeling the rolling movement of my baby. The baby had been moving around and stretching for the last little while, and I wanted to revel in the sensation of his little bum or knee pressing against the palm of my hand.

"Are you ready to come out yet, baby?" I whispered to my belly. "We are not going to be alone, like I thought."

The baby kicked a fierce one into my ribcage. "Oh!

Don't kick me too hard, baby." I laughed. As if he or she could hear me, it settled into some more subtle stretches.

Sometime later in the day, I woke with John beside me. I looked into his soft brown eyes, and studied the lines on his face. He smiled at me and traced his finger down the length of my nose.

"Hi, Princess," he said.

"Hi."

"Do you feel rested?"

I smiled a little wickedly at him, and he laughed at me. "Not for that, as much as I would like to," he said.

I leaned up on an elbow to look down into his face. "For what?"

"A real show," he said excitedly.

"What kind of a 'real show'?" I was intrigued now.

"The kind that you dress up for, and there are people singing and dancing."

"Ooooh! I've never seen a show like that before." Now, I was excited.

"I even bought you a dress." He beamed. Rather like a little boy getting his first bike.

"You bought me a dress? What kind of dress?"

"A flowing, dark red one, with tiny little sparkling straps," John said confidently.

"But I don't have shoes." I pointed in the direction of my feet, although I was probably pointing at the floor.

"But, you do." He reached behind himself, and picked up a pair of sparkling, strappy sandals. They had a three-inch heel and a string of rhinestones to wrap around my ankle.

"Oh, John. They're beautiful! Can I see the dress?"

I bounced off the bed and snatched the sandals out of his hand.

"You can put the dress on. We have to leave in twenty minutes." John got off the bed and sauntered into his walk-in closet, pulling out a tux.

"You have a tux?" I asked.

He smiled and nodded. "Get dressed. I'll use the other room and the main bathroom. You can get ready in here."

The dress was truly beautiful. It was blood red in color, made out of a chiffon material. The bodice fit snuggly, dipping down a little in between my breasts to show off some cleavage. There was a string of rhinestone that traced the bodice on the top, and again around the bottom. From the seam that encircled me under my breasts, layers of chiffon emerged, hanging softly to about two inches above my knees.

Normally, I would never have picked something this racy for myself, but I had to admit that I looked stunning. I ran my fingers through my hair and chose to do a simple upsweep, piling it high on my head, leaving some tendrils hanging down. I applied my makeup slightly darker than what I was used to in the last couple of months, and I felt a little self conscious, but tucked those feelings deep inside.

I gave myself a quick once over, then grabbed the sandals and entered the hall. John came out of the bathroom at the same time, and he stood there gaping at me. He didn't say anything. Instead he reached my side in two strides and took me up in a deep kiss. After a few moments, he pulled away and held me by the shoulders.

"You look stunning," he breathed.

"Thank you," I said a little shyly. "Can you help me put my sandals on?"

I handed them over to him, and he motioned for me to sit in the chair that was propped against the corner at the top of the stairs. His large hands slid the sandals on my feet and he strapped them up. I got up, took an exploratory step, than balanced myself to walk. Not too bad. By the time I reached the stairs, I was perfectly fine in them. I didn't even waddle too much.

"My god, you have great legs!" John said from behind me on the stairs.

I turned to smile up at him. I had never in my life worn a dress like this, and I felt like royalty. I stood in front of the mirror at the bottom of the stairs and twisted my body left and right to make the skirt flare out. John slid behind me and put his hand on my shoulder. He looked at my reflection for a moment.

"I have one other thing, Princess." He dangled a gold necklace in front of my throat and draped it around my neck, expertly clasping it closed.

Hanging from the necklace was a simple diamond. It was elegant and sparkly, just reaching my cleavage. I felt my eyes sting with hot tears, and I turned to hug John closely.

"Thank you." I choked. "Thank you so much."

"You're welcome, Princess. Now, let's go." He plucked a shawl from the closet, (another gift), and hung it around my bare shoulders. It was soft gold and brown, made out of faux fur, and fastened at the throat with a single ivory button. It wasn't cold enough to need anything more.

John looked gorgeous in his tux, and he had gotten

a hair cut, so he looked like he should be walking on the red carpet, instead of beside me, then quickly admonished myself for the negative thought.

We went downtown, to see a Cirque de Soleil type of show, which was immensely entertaining, and then went to a beautiful little Italian restaurant for a very late dinner. John and I looked across at each other with our hands clasped while we sipped drinks after a scrumptious dinner of blackened salmon, with roasted zucchini, broccoli and mushrooms drizzled in garlic butter.

"Is this OK?" he asked, pointing at his glass, opting for Scotch, rather than tea.

"Yes. I trust you, John. Thank you for asking." He was very considerate about my feelings.

We finished our drinks and went home. By this time, my ankles were pretty swollen, not having worn high heels in a very long time, plus the extra baby weight.

I sat down on the sofa and laid my head back, closing my eyes. I had a smile on my face and opened one eye to see what John was doing. A man had gone around the restaurant taking pictures of celebrating couples and parties of people. He had taken one of us, and John took it out of the inside pocket of his tux jacket, looked at it thoughtfully, and placed it on the kitchen table.

"I have the perfect frame," he said as he took his jacket off.

"Speaking of pictures," I thought I should tell him about the photo album that I found. "I found a photo album in one of the drawers while I was putting my clothes away." I looked at him a little guiltily.

A puzzled look crossed his face for a second, then it

cleared and he nodded. "Yes, I forgot that I had put it in there."

"That's fine. I hope you don't mind that I looked through it," I asked.

"No. I don't mind. It's still very painful for me to see pictures of them." He spoke low and a wistful expression crossed his face. "Especially my boy. I meant to look at them a few times, but could never get past the first page." He tilted his head sideways and grinned a little ruefully.

John then took my feet onto his lap and absently began massaging my swollen, tired feet.

"When you feel ready, I will look through them with you, if you would like that," I said. I only had one picture of Nicolas that was taken moments after he was born, which I had often held close to my heart while hiding from David. It gave me strength and courage.

"For now, John, why don't we just keep it in the drawer, and when you're ready, you know where it is," I offered.

"Do you mind much? I mean, that it's still hard for me?" he asked.

"No! I'm very thankful that I got to see the love you all shared. I'm thankful that you have allowed me into that part of your life. When Nicolas died, I wanted to hold him tight in my heart and not share his memory with another living soul."

"I know what you mean," John said. "It was like if I spoke of them, the parts that were trapped within me," he pointed to where his heart was, "would somehow seep out, and I would lose that last bit of oneness with them."

"Yes. That's exactly what I mean. My husband wasn't

there when Nicolas was born, so I was alone, and I sucked the experience in and vowed to never let it out. He, my husband, never asked about the baby anyway, and my mother and I buried Nicolas."

John looked horrified at the thought that a father might miss his own son's birth, let alone his son's funeral. I was grateful for it, though. David would have ruined the magic that took place when Nicolas was laid in my arms, and the next little while he lived. I fell in love with my baby boy, without the presence of his abusive father.

John turned to me then and looked me deeply in the eye. Gently, he said, "You help with the pain and I am living again. The pain is still there, of course, but so is my love for you."

I just looked at him for a few minutes. My heart was, yet again, filling with gladness, love, trust and fear. "I love you, too," I managed to whisper. "Like I never knew was possible." And like a broken dam, the floodgates opened up and I lunged at John.

He buried his face in my hair, and held me tight. "I never thought it was possible to love again either, Princess," he said with passion.

"No, John. I've *never* loved before! I never loved my husband. I had a crush on him, in the beginning, and I *thought* I loved him. But, I couldn't. Not until now, have I ever *known* love. Expect for my babies." I reached for a tissue and gingerly wiped my nose and dabbed at the tears running down my face. God, I hoped I didn't look ridiculous with raccoon eyes from my mascara.

John laughed through his own tears. "Don't," he grabbed my Kleenex, "you look beautiful."

We both sniffed and laughed, and went up to bed.

John had to get up early to finish the remodeling of a bathroom at a house a few blocks away, so we undressed and fell asleep. Sometime in the middle of the night, however, despite how tired we were, we made love slowly and passionately, and then fell asleep in each other's arms.

I woke at around ten o'clock the next morning, had a shower, ate breakfast, and ventured out to find Charles. It had been a few days since I'd seen him and I was hungry for his company.

"There you are!" I exclaimed when I finally found him pruning the rose bushes. "Can I help?"

"Good morning, dear. Yes, you can help an old man in his garden. But, I'll do the bending, because I suspect that you won't be able to get up, and I can't help you," said Charles, and put his hands on his back to stretch. "These old bones are creaky."

"How about I rake then, and you prune," I offered.

"Perfect!" Charles nodded to my house of a belly, and said, "You're about ready to pop, I see. How long? A week or two?"

I looked down and smiled at him, patting my belly. "More like five or six." I had gone through a major growth spurt in the last couple of weeks.

We worked in silence for awhile, and then sat down at the patio table in the soon-to-be garden, to enjoy a glass of iced tea and cucumber sandwiches.

Charles looked at me thoughtfully. "John tells me that you have decided to have him in the delivery room."

I smiled. "Yes I have. Is that OK?" I was suddenly concerned.

A look of alarm passed his face. "Oh, yes, my dear.

I'm happy for you both. My son is mighty stubborn, and it took a long time to even get him out of his apartment, let alone fall in love again." Charles winked at me as he said this. "You are everything and more than I ever hoped for him."

"Thank you. I'm just as surprised about how things have turned out as anyone," I assured him. "I only thought I was renting an apartment from an older, traveling woman. Not falling madly in love, and having my life turn upside down in two months." I stood up and bent to kiss Charles on his forehead. My hands were on either side and I held his face in my hands and said, "Thank you. If it weren't for you, I would never have been so happy. It's so unbelievable, don't you think?" I asked.

"It is, but then that's how I fell in love with John's mother. It was love at first sight." He stared off in the distance, remembering.

"John was just a little mite then and barely able to walk." He paused. "When his mother died, I thought I would stop living, but that little boy kept me alive, and eventually I met and married another wonderful woman. I wanted to return the favor, you see."

I looked at him, confused.

"John saved me from myself, all those years ago, and when I saw you, I knew without a doubt that you were that woman for him.

"Sure, Evie was a wonderful woman, wife and mother, and I miss her terribly. But, I knew that there was a little spark missing, that you don't ever know is missing, until one day, you find it." He stopped for a moment to collect his thoughts.

"As bad as it is to say, I don't think that John would have mourned the death of Evelyn so severely, had he not blamed himself for it. It destroyed him; the fire, Jonathon and how everything happened. But, it wasn't Evie that destroyed him. It was his guilt. Ate him up alive.

"This is between you and me," he said, with another wink.

I nodded, and he continued.

"John's guilt for what happened almost caused him to end his own life."

I felt a pang of guilt, because I knew that John had come close a few times.

"He and Evelyn loved each other, but their lives were separate. She had hers, and he had his. It worked for them, and that's why they were so happy. And of course, they shared love and pride for their son."

Charles paused to take another long drink of his iced tea.

"When I saw you, my first thought was that you would awaken that spark in my son. I also saw in you, the need for the spark." Like an owl, he blinked, and I smiled.

"Yes. That's certainly what happened with me," I said.

"Yes," said Charles, smiling. "My son is happy, for the first time, in a very long time. Thank you."

We finished the rest of the gardening, and then I went in to have a nap.

Chapter Thirty Eight

"Push! Push! Come on, Kathryn. You can do this."
"No! I can't!" I sobbed.
"You have to! Now, push!" The doctor urged me on.
I screamed and writhed in pain. I pushed with all my might. Pushed until I physically could not do it anymore.
"That's it, Kathryn. We're almost there! One more push."
"Ugh!!!" One last push and out slid my baby boy.
"He doesn't look right," I heard a nurse say.
"What's wrong with him?" I cried. "Please! Someone tell me what's wrong with him!" I tried to push myself up from the bed, but someone held me down, blocking my view from what they were doing with my baby.
"He's got a pulse!" Someone else said. "I'm losing it!."
"NO! No! No!" I cried, over and over.
"Kathryn, you need to calm down. He is premature, and there's a lot of trauma. Kathryn, I'm sorry, but...he won't live." It was the doctor, but I only vaguely heard him.
"I want to hold him," I said in a meek whisper.
"That's not a good id-"

"I want to hold my baby!!!!" I screamed.

After a few minutes of discussion, they let me hold him.

I took my tiny Nicolas in my hands, and looked at his face so intently, to burn his image into my memory for all time. His nose was tiny and he was all scrunched up. His skin was red and raw from not being fully developed, and he mewed like a kitten.

It broke my heart, and I had to keep clearing tears from my eyes to see his face clearly. I kissed his tiny face and his tiny fingers and opened the blanket he was swathed in so I could see his miniature knees, feet, and toes. I kissed his feet and felt the tiny toes flex around my lip.

When I brushed his cheek, he rooted for some food, so I brought his lips to my nipple, willing my nourishment to somehow let him live. My nipple barely fit into his mouth, but after a few tries, he got on and suckled.

How could this perfect little baby not live? I thought. The tips of my fingers gently stroked the fuzz on his perfectly round head.

Suddenly, he was gone. Just like that. The perfect rosebud mouth, pursed in a kiss, and his unbelievably tiny fingers wrapped around mine. They were so small; I could barely feel the touch.

I bolted up, sweating and sobbing. I lay back down and hugged John's pillow, to draw in his scent, and fell back asleep.

Sometime later, a banging at the door woke me. It could only be Charles, so I hurried down and pulled the door open, ready with a smile. I felt every drop of blood drain from my body, shooting ice streaks, pooling in the pit of my stomach. I swayed, but his hand snatched out to grab me.

"Hello, Bitch." David smiled in the doorway. "Gotcha."

Chapter Thirty Nine

John was finishing up at the job he was working on, humming to himself with Kathryn and the baby on his mind. He couldn't stop smiling, and the elderly couple he was doing work for commented on it several times. That just made him happier.

The thought of having a baby around again was intoxicating. *A baby!* How had he gotten so lucky? He wondered. A new woman. *The* woman and a baby. Kathryn was opening up to him, and despite the fact that he knew David was still alive, it didn't change the way he felt about her. She was sharing her most treasured possession with him. Her child. John knew without a doubt that he would love this baby just as much as he loved his own Jonathon.

While John cleaned up the mess from laying ceramic tile, he was thinking about whether the baby was a boy or a girl and all the different things he was going to do with that child. He couldn't wait to splash in the water at bath time, or go to the cottage and swim. He couldn't wait to change a diaper, or to watch Kathryn fall in love with the child while she nursed. John couldn't wait to smell the smell of a newborn baby and to know that his body heat would warm the child against his skin. Yes. Life was good. Finally.

A small shadow crossed his mind, though, when he considered what he needed to do about David. Of course, he had to tell Kathryn that he knew David lived. He only hoped that Kathryn would understand that he just wanted to protect her, not control her. John should hear from his buddy in Victoria today. His distant friend was going to report weekly as to the whereabouts of David, and what, if anything, David was doing to find Kathryn.

Enough of that thought. The last thing John was going to do was to let this David character mar his good mood and excitement about seeing Kathryn in the next half hour. John finished loading the last of his tools into his work van and bid the elderly couple goodbye, telling them that he would see them on Monday morning. Today was Friday, and John was looking forward to spending the weekend alone with Kathryn.

He stopped at the flower shop on the way home and picked up a dozen roses. He picked four each of red, white, and yellow. Each color was meant to signify passion, growing love, and friendship. He parked his van in his spot in the apartment lot and made his way to the back door of the building. John thought he would stop in for a second to say hello to Charles and to let him know that he and Kathryn would be lying low this weekend. The baby was due soon and John knew that all the walks and hikes were getting too difficult for Kathryn.

Charles wasn't in his apartment. *Must be doing something for someone,* thought John. He would just call on him later, maybe invite him over for dinner the following evening. John made his way to get the mail and was sauntering up the stairs, when suddenly he heard a blood-curdling scream.

John bolted up the rest of the stairs and stopped. A second later, he heard the scream again and knew it came from his apartment. He dropped everything on the floor and ran for his door. He opened it, lunged through the door and froze on the spot. It took a millisecond for his mind to catch up to the image before him, then there was a second of sheer terror, before the cop in him kicked in and instinct took over.

In those two, maybe three, seconds from opening the door, he took in the scene. On the floor, just on the inside of the door, Charles lay in a crumpled heap, knocked out with an obvious head wound. Kathryn was tied up to a kitchen chair, head hanging low, blood dripping from her mouth and a gash on her forehead.

Terror ripped through his gut for another second, because he thought that Kathryn was dead. John fought hard not to lose sight of what was going on, and he fought hard to keep himself detached so he could try to save their lives. Kathryn lifted her head slightly, but let it drop again. She was too weak to hold it up. She was losing a fair amount of blood. It was running down her face and onto the front of her shirt. John noticed a slash across her belly as well and felt himself blaze with a murderous rage.

David turned his head at the interruption. He stood looming over Kathryn, a large kitchen knife in one hand and a .38 caliber Smith and Wesson in the other. Not the best gun at a distance, but perfect for close range killing.

David stared John down then pulled his lips back from his teeth, looking like the devil himself.

"Are you the new man in my wife's life?" David asked. His tone was so casual that John felt the blood leave his head, and a cold electric shock pierced his spine, causing him to almost vomit.

"That would be me," John said, somehow managing to match David's casualness.

"Well now, we have a problem then, because she's mine and I intend to take her home with me."

Kathryn moaned, and rocked her head back. She managed to croak, "John…"

John said, "There is a problem because Kathryn is staying here with me, and if you leave now, I won't press charges."

David threw back his head and laughed. He then looked down at the gun in his hand and arched his brow at John. "No. That won't do. That bitch is mine." He pointed the gun at Kathryn's head. "And the kid is mine." David then pointed the gun at Kathryn's belly, digging the muzzle in hard enough for Kathryn to let out a strangled scream.

David flicked his wrist and delivered another blow with the butt of the gun to her face, causing her head to snap back. She started sobbing then and struggled against the restraints around her wrists.

"Shut up, you stupid bitch!" David snarled.

"I think if I were you, David, you might stop doing that," John said, coolly.

David laughed again. "Do you love this whore?" he asked John.

"More than my own life." John took a step forward,

and David jumped back and sideways, so he was standing behind Kathryn.

"Stop!" David hissed, while simultaneously grabbing a handful of Kathryn's hair and wrenching her head back so he could place the knife on her throat.

John took a step back then and threw his hands up. "OK! OK!" He spat out desperately. "Maybe we could make a deal." John's mind was going a mile a minute, flicking through memories of different scenarios in similar situations, when he was on active duty.

"No deal. It's simple. Kathryn is my wife, and she is leaving with me. The only other option is I slit her throat." David pressed the knife hard enough to penetrate the skin on the tip of the blade and a drop of blood emerged from the wound. She whimpered, and John winced from the physical pain of seeing her like that.

In desperation, John said, "I'll pay you. I have money."

"I don't want your money, slick, I want my wife. Don't want to be held down by a brat though." David replied, while sliding the knife down and poking the tip of it into her belly.

Kathryn panicked again, and yelled, "No David! *Please, no!* Please, please no, David!" she sobbed.

John's heart was breaking. He felt desperate and impotent.

David chuckled again. "See? She wants to come back with me," he said triumphantly. David was still holding Kathryn's hair. It was gathered in the hand that had the gun, and John thought that maybe he could lunge at David and disarm him, but David might still have time to shoot or stab her.

John kept glancing from David to Kathryn and the

panic was rising to the surface. He drew in some sharp breaths, gaining control of his emotions again. In the corner, he could hear Charles stirring and struggling to rise. John dared the split second to look over at Charles. The man had managed to roll onto his side and was facing the scene before him. John's stomach lurched at the site of his father's face being bludgeoned like that.

"How did you find Kathryn?" John asked, in an effort to distract David.

"Well, I'm sure you noticed that she's not the smartest in the bunch. Did you know she called her mother from Muskoka?" David asked.

"No, I didn't." John couldn't figure out when she could have called anyone, then belatedly remembered the pay phone at the bookstore, her wallet on it, and how shaken up she had been.

"She's lying to you, already?" David arched his brows in inquiry before continuing. "Like I said, she phoned her mother and I had the call traced to Muskoka, jumped on a plane and rented a car to drive out there. It didn't take long to find out about the two of you, and where you were staying. I have to admit, I was very surprised to find out that she was with a man. I happen to have connections, and found the two of you easily.

"I'll ask again," John began, "can we settle this business with cash?" John took an ever so slightly step forward and to the side toward Charles.

David raised the muzzle of the gun and rested it on his forehead. "Let me think on that. Umm…no."

John shifted from one foot to the other and managed another step toward Charles. John had a plan and all he had to do was brush his ankle up against Charles's hand. He held his hands up and slowly took his jacket off. David watched carefully, but didn't say anything.

John stepped sideways again, bringing his foot right up against Charles's hand, while leaning over to throw his jacket onto the floor, then bent to put it gently under Charles's head, looking down briefly enough to see the comprehension on Charles's face. He gave Charles an almost imperceptible nod.

"You might stop moving around, *John,*" David warned with vehemence in his tone.

Again, John put his hands up. He needed to get David to look the other way. Charles brought his hand up to his face, almost immediately letting it flop back down to rest beside John's right foot. *Good Charles. Good.* Charles understood John's plan. John nudged Charles's hand ever so slightly.

"Well, I think our little party needs to come to an end. So, I'll be taking my wife out of here." David stepped to Kathryn's side and beckoned John over. Holding the gun to Kathryn's head, he said, "Come untie the bitch."

"I will not," John said calmly.

David lowered the gun, shooting Kathryn in the thigh. Kathryn screamed in agony and she bent over as far as she could. At the same moment, Charles reached up John's pant leg and grabbed the gun from its ankle strap.

David and Charles pointed the guns at each other in the same moment. It all happened in a split second, but that was enough time for John to lunge at David.

John grabbed David's wrist, just as David and Charles shot their weapons. David and John were both thrown back from the shots. David's shot hit John in the shoulder, and Charles's shot hit David in the arm, halfway between shoulder and elbow, causing David to drop his gun.

Kathryn screamed and writhed. *"John! John!* Please, John!"

David didn't stick around. He bolted out the door and out the fire escape at the end of the hall. Charles took another shot, but missed, hitting the doorframe instead. He then dropped his hand in failure, an anguished cry leaving his throat.

"It's OK, Pop." John's voice was reassuring.

"John!" Kathryn yelled.

John spun on his heel and knelt on the floor before Kathryn, frantically untying her bonds. In his haste, he couldn't get them off.

"Princess! Princess, I'm here! God, I'm here," he cried.

"Untie me, John. Please." Kathryn was almost hysterical, and she suddenly threw her head back and screamed in agony.

John jumped in surprise and turned to look for something to cut through the rope. Remembering the knife David had, he snatched it and cut through the rope.

"John, the baby's coming!" Kathryn exclaimed in a frenzy. She struggled off the chair and crawled away from it as if it were alive, despite the gunshot wound in her leg. Charles labored to get up, throwing himself by her side.

"John!" Charles was in a near panic as well. "Her water just broke!"

"Hold on, Princess. I'm coming." John ripped off his belt, and wrapped it around her thigh, just above the gunshot wound. She winced as he fastened the buckle as tight as it would go, but he wasn't sure if the pain was from the wound, or from the intensity of the sudden onset of labor.

He wasn't concerned about the pain in his shoulder. It wasn't too bad. The bullet had just grazed it.

Kathryn was in bad shape, screaming and writhing in pain. She was alarmingly pale from blood loss, and John's worry was growing rapidly. He ran as quickly as he could to the linen closet and grabbed a handful of towels. He threw a couple at Charles. "Go wet those and call an ambulance!" John demanded.

Charles got up, surprisingly fast and steady, and ran to wet the towels. He picked the phone off its base as he ran by and dialed 911. By the time he got back to Kathryn's side, John had already cut her pants off and tucked some towels beneath her bottom.

With every contraction she screamed, and the hardening of her belly caused the slash in her stomach to ooze fresh blood.

"Charles. Apply pressure to the wound." John barked in panic.

Kathryn grabbed John by the arm, "John," she gasped. "John. The baby is coming. John, you have to save the baby." She began to sob.

"Shhh. I will save the baby, Princess. Just do what I say. OK?" He leaned over her face and pushed her hair from her bleeding, sweating brow.

She nodded and lay her head back down. Almost immediately, she convulsed with the unimaginable pain of a contraction. John put his hands under her knees and lifted them up, so he could see the opening.

There was a gush of blood and amniotic fluid with the next contraction and he could see the top of the baby's head. Just a little bit of fuzz showed, but he could also see that she was indeed ready to push. Being a cop meant that you had to know how to deliver a baby in an emergency, and he remembered clearly what Evelyn had looked like when she was ready to push. He wondered just how long David had been here, for her to be this far along in labor. For all he knew, David could have been here for eight hours, and he felt sick at the thought of Kathryn being tortured all day.

"OK, baby," he said. "When the next contraction starts, I want you to bear down. Can you do that for me?" He looked up at her, and she nodded. Charles looked alarmed, but he also knew that John could handle the situation.

John could hear the faint whine of sirens in the distance and breathed a sigh of relief. Kathryn's next contraction came, and Charles pushed her up from behind her shoulders.

"OK, Kathryn! Push!" cried John. "That's it! Push! One, two, three…" John counted to ten, and Kathryn collapsed onto Charles in exhaustion until the next contraction.

On it went for another ten minutes, until finally Kathryn screamed again, and on the last push, the baby slid out in a gush. John took the wet towel and wiped the baby's face, then swept the tiny mouth with his pinky before blowing a couple of small puffs into the baby's mouth. A shriek ensued, and they collectively laughed in elation. She was fine.

"A girl? It's a girl?" Kathryn was reaching out to take the baby, and John had never been filled with so much gratitude.

FREE

They were all laughing and crying at the same time, and John took the rope that was tied around Kathryn's wrist, and tied off the umbilical cord about four inches from the baby's belly. Charles handed Kathryn one of the softer towels so she could swaddle the baby. She tensed again as another contraction hit.

"OK, Princess. It's time to push out the placenta."

"We'll handle that, sir," a paramedic said as he walked through the door.

"Oh. Thank God!" John breathed, and the tension of the last hour seeped out of him in a wave of emotion. He leaned down over Kathryn's face, kissing her, then the baby, and then her again. Charles patted John on the back, causing John to draw in a sharp breath, but he laughed and cupped his adopted father's head and bent to kiss it, right beside where he was hit with the butt of David's gun.

"Are you alright?" he asked Charles.

"Better than I've ever been." Charles reached up a hand to where the gash on his head was. It had stopped bleeding, but there was a very large lump. "I've a bit of a headache." He smiled at John.

The room was filling up with paramedics and police, while other residents of the building gathered in the hall, where they were soon ushered away by the police.

In the midst of all the chaos, John and Kathryn managed to see only each other and the baby. Kathryn couldn't stop crying and kept saying over and over, "Thank you."

Chapter Forty

I was in my hospital bed nursing my new daughter, when Charles came in bearing a very large bouquet of flowers. There was a pink balloon sticking out of the top, with the inscription, "It's A Girl!" In his other hand, he held a box of chocolate cigars, wrapped in pink foil. I smiled up at him.

"Hello, my dear." He bent to kiss my cheek, which was the only place on my face that wasn't bruised or cut, and I kissed him back.

"Hello, Charles." I lifted my hand to caress his pudgy cheek. "How are you feeling?" I was harboring a great deal of guilt about his wounds.

"Not bad, for an old guy," he said. "Where's my son?" he inquired, looking around the room.

"Right here," answered John, as he entered.

John winked at me and came to my bedside. After a lingering kiss on my lips, he brushed his lips on the baby's forehead.

"How's our baby girl, today?" he asked.

"She's wonderful. How are you?" I asked John. He

pulled one of the chairs over and sat beside me to clasp my hand in his.

"I'm fine, Princess. How are *you,* mom?" John brought my fingers up to his lips and held them there for a moment.

"Fine. Especially now that I know we'll all be OK," I said. It had been a difficult three days since David had found me. Getting shot in the leg had been excruciating, but the bullet had only bitten into the flesh on the side of my thigh, and I would be able to walk normally again after some therapy.

We all sat there watching the baby's small movements, staring in utter amazement at how innocent she was. She would never know that her biological father had almost killed her, too. This perfect little creature had the love and support of a new daddy that would always be careful, gentle, and protective.

"Do you have a name for this little angel?" asked Charles after a few moments.

"Well, we've been thinking of a few names," said John, thoughtfully.

"You were as much a part of saving us as John was," I said to Charles. "I will be forever grateful to you both for giving me my life back." I started crying.

John looked from Charles to me and I nodded. "We are going to call her Charlene Evelyn Sullivan."

Charles's smile widened. "Well, how about that?" He beamed.

"And I would like to make Kathryn's name Sullivan," said John.

I looked at him in astonishment when he pulled a simple, yet beautiful diamond ring out of his pocket. He held the ring out in front of me and I just stared at it. And of course, cried even more.

"Oh, John," I managed through a breath.

"Will you marry me?" John raised his eyebrows in question, taking my hand and slipping the ring onto the tip of my finger. He held it there until I sputtered, "*yes!*"

Fresh tears and laughter commenced after that, with painful slaps on John's back from Charles, who kept forgetting that John had been shot in the shoulder. John cringed, but didn't mind. He was beaming with happiness.

Charlene and I stayed in the hospital for another week, while I built up my strength. I had needed a transfusion from all the blood loss and still felt weak and dizzy. While we were in the hospital, John and Charles hired some people to clean up the apartment and finish a few last minute baby preparations. Charles wasn't letting his son out of his sight, and by the end of the week they were bickering like an old married couple.

Charlene was perfect. She had a head full of golden red fuzz and her eyes were pale gray, with a hint of green in them. She weighed in at six pounds, eight ounces, so she was a tiny little thing. Her perfect little fingers wrapped around mine, while she suckled her meal out of my breast. Her lips formed a perfect rosebud pout when I pulled her off to change sides.

"You're such a little piggy," I said, smiling down at her. Charlene's protests reached hysterical proportions in the seconds it took to switch sides.

"Are you starving her again?" John said as he came in. I picked up a roll of socks off the bed and threw them at him.

FREE

"Unlikely. She's gained two pounds in the last week alone," I said.

"Daddy's girl. A hearty appetite will get you everywhere. Speaking of that, how about we get out of this place?"

I looked up at him excitedly. "I can leave?"

"Yes, you can. Charles is bringing up the baby seat. Although, I think he's trying to hustle the nurse that's getting the wheelchair." John chuckled.

Charlene, full now, fell asleep and I handed her up to John. He took his daughter and snuggled her close to the crook in his neck.

"She smells like you," he said, and leaned down to smell my cheek.

He planted a small kiss on my lips. "Are you alright?" whispered John. I knew what he meant. I was deathly afraid that David would get me or Charlene, despite all the security measures John had put in place and the bodyguards hovering about.

It was also time for me to call my mother. I knew that she would have seen what happened on the news. A crime of this magnitude could have possibly made headlines across Canada. It was unfair of me not to have called her, but it was a call that made my stomach churn. I was positive that she would make this hard for me. I knew that she would accuse me of sinning and chastise me for the events that led up to David's escape. My only option was to tell her the whole truth. That seemed a task beyond impossible.

"We don't need to think about it now, Princess. Let's go home and be a family." John said and put Charlene in her hospital crib.

At this time, the nurse Charles was accosting blew into the room in a huff, with Charles at her heel.

She looked to John. "Could you call off your father?" She hooked her thumb over her shoulder in Charles's direction.

"Sorry. Once he has something in his mind, there's no stopping him," John said apologetically, and we all laughed.

The ride home was slow and wonderful. I sat in the back with Charlene, while Charles drove. John still couldn't handle much movement of his arm and wanted to be able to turn easily in his seat, if he had to.

We all went up to the apartment and stopped outside the door. I was rooted on the spot and couldn't bring myself to go inside. I knew that I would have nightmares about what happened for years to come, and I was really struggling with a great deal of guilt over John and Charles's injuries.

John felt me tense up and put an arm around my shoulders. "Why don't we go sit in the garden for a while?" he suggested.

"That sounds perfect." I smiled up at him, and he brushed a tear from my battered face with his thumb. "Don't cry, love. It will be all over soon. We'll find David."

"I know," I whispered.

"Why don't you two go outside and I'll put your things away," Charles said.

"OK. Thanks Pop." John handed me the baby and we took the elevator down. I was still limping and my leg hurt like hell, but I felt comfortable carrying Charlene.

We sat on the stone bench. I took a look around and

was amazed at how much nature had progressed in the last week. There were leaves on all the trees and some of the flowers were blooming. I took a deep, healing breath and felt alive again. The exhaustion that John and I were both feeling was bone deep, but neither one of us had to be anywhere. I had some money left, and John had invested much of the money from his house and from Evelyn's death.

We planned on going to the cottage in a few weeks, and I couldn't wait to be in that environment again. Charles was going to come up with us. He couldn't stand to be away from his new granddaughter for more than a day at a time. We didn't mind though. Charles was also alive and feeling the rush of new freedom.

New freedom.

There was a time when I thought I would never be free. I hoped that when I talked to my mother, she would understand. My long term hope was that she would sell her house and come out here to live with John and me. I knew of a small bungalow down the street that was for sale. John said it needed some work, but that was something he could do. There were also plenty of apartment buildings in the area, with all the amenities one could need.

I couldn't plan a wedding or my new life without coming clean with my Mom.

"Let's go in," I sighed.

John nodded and handed Charlene back to me after I stood. Once inside the building, I hesitated at the apartment door, but took a deep breath and entered. What John had done took my breath away.

He'd bought all new furniture. Everything was different. It was beautiful!

"John!" I cried. "This is amazing!" John replaced the browns and golds with soft, smoky blues and greens. It was very earthy in tone and texture. He also changed the way everything was placed throughout the main floor.

"I knew that if it looked different in here, it would be easier to forget," he said.

"What did you do with all the other furniture?" I asked, while I walked around the room, picking up this and that. Finally, I sat on the new sofa.

"I had it all shipped up to Muskoka." He smiled and joined me on the couch.

I just gaped at him. He laughed, and got up to get a picture from the kitchen counter. He placed the photo of a large log cabin cottage in my hands. I remembered the cabin immediately. John and I had walked through it while we were up there. It had been listed the week we went up. The week we fell in love.

The cabin was a five bedroom, with two large fireplaces and huge windows on each side. There was a large deck off the back that had stairs leading to the water's edge. I had been in awe of the place when we walked through. I never imagined he would own it.

"How?" I knew John hadn't been up to Muskoka.

"My step-brother, Steven, went up for me and handled all the preliminaries," He said.

"It's yours?" I asked. I was still in awe.

"No. It's ours."

"Oh, John!" I cried. "It's beautiful!" Then, being the mother of a newborn, I stifled a yawn.

Chapter Forty One

ANOTHER WEEK HAD GONE BY and John, Charles, and I were healing. The gunshot wounds, thank God, hadn't been too serious, and surprisingly, weren't giving us too much difficulty. The pain was manageable at least. All the bruises were getting to the yellow stage, and I now had a few new scars on my lip and forehead, not to mention the slash across my stomach where David slid his knife. Every few hours John came over to me and gently kissed my wounds, as if his kiss alone would heal them. He would say, "My kisses are full of love and love heals everything." It was very endearing.

The baby seemed to sense that we were all hurting and hardly cried at all. She was already sleeping for a full six hours through the night, though I felt that I should be waking her up after four to nurse. Dr. Smart said that if she slept for six hours, let her sleep. That was fine with me. The constant threat of David coming back, not to mention the guilt I felt because John and Charles were seriously injured by my deranged husband, induced a little more than mere exhaustion. I took little naps with

Charlene, managing to eat small meals while awake, but the toll of the whole situation was severe and I wondered how the overall effect would change things.

John would not leave me under any circumstances and hired his step-brother, Steven, to do our errands for us so as not to be out in case David was lurking around. Since David's escape, John had called in every favor he could from former colleagues in British Columbia and here in Niagara Falls. There were also twenty-four hour guards outside our door, Charles's door, and around the perimeter of the building. John wasn't taking any chances and was attempting everything in his power to find and catch David.

I was terrified, yet I knew that John would protect Charlene and me. In the two weeks since Charlene had been born, John was doting on her as if she truly were born from the new love we shared with each other. Despite everything, we were a family. John changed diapers and bathed our tiny daughter. He cuddled her when she cried and basically couldn't put her down. He had fallen in love with her just as much as I had.

When David slashed my belly, I thought that he would kill this baby. The whole time he beat me, all I could do was curl up as much as possible to protect my child. I felt sick thinking about it, and shivered at the memory. But, John was here, and David would never beat me again.

Charles, of course, blamed himself for what happened, despite the fact that he couldn't have possibly known that David wasn't the brother he claimed to be. Charles had tried to stop David, but when David pistol-whipped Charles on the top of his head, he went down like a load of bricks. I had been so grief stricken, thinking he was dead. If anyone was to blame, it was me. I should have been honest with John, so he and Charles could have been prepared. They would have known what David looked like, so Charles wouldn't have been tricked.

It was also time to call my mother. John had purchased a plane ticket for her that would be waiting at the airport in B.C. for tomorrow's four thirty flight. I was very nervous at the thought of my mother coming here and not understanding why I had to leave. The mere idea of it all was draining. John sat beside me on the bed while I dialed my mother's phone number.

"Hello, Mother," I said when she answered her phone.

"Oh my God, Kathryn! I've been so worried about you! I didn't know where to call you to tell you that David was looking for you," she gushed.

"Yes. David found me. Mother, I need you to hear me out. It's very important." I prayed that she would listen, and that I could get through to the part of her mind that hadn't been brainwashed by David and my father.

"Mom?"

"I'm here. Where are you, Kathryn? You've been gone for so long, and I've been worried sick." She was calmer. Good.

"Mom. I'm sorry for making you worry, but you need to listen to me, and when you get here tomorrow, I will tell you everything."

"When I get where?" she asked.

"To Niagara Falls. That's where I've been. There is a plane ticket for you at the airport for a flight tomorrow at four thirty in the afternoon. The flight will take you to the Buffalo Airport, where I will be waiting." I held my breath, waiting for her to answer.

"Alright."

I was stunned. "That's it? You aren't going to argue with me?"

"No. I know something bad happened and I need to see you, Kathryn. I want to help you." My mother had never in my life acknowledged any of the bad stuff. Not with my dad, nor with my husband, and I wondered what the sudden change was. I was actually uneasy about how this was going with my mother.

John sensed my nervousness and gently squeezed my hand in encouragement. I nodded and took a deep breath.

"OK, then. I'll see you at the airport tomorrow," I said and bid her goodbye.

"Are you sure you want to drive to the airport tomorrow, Kathryn? You're still in rough shape," said John. "I don't want you to overdo it."

"Yes. I have to go or she won't leave the terminal. Besides, you are going to be with me." I smiled weakly up at him and he bent to kiss my nose.

"I will always be with you. I will not leave your side as long as David is alive and loose." John reassured me.

Charles rapped quietly on the bedroom door just then, to deliver Charlene to us so that I could nurse her. He was just as much in love with her as John and I, already claiming his grandfatherly rights. It made me smile at the thought. I also wondered how my mother would react to all of this. She still didn't know that I had given birth, and she certainly didn't know that I had a new life with another man. It was going to be challenging to change her mind about David. Not to mention that I was wearing an engagement ring from John, and I had no intention of taking it off or hiding the fact that John and I were in love.

Since our apartment had been a crime scene, and David was on the loose, I knew that I had to tell John all there was to know about David, myself, and our life together. As I nursed Charlene, I revealed everything. It was difficult to bare all my horrible secrets to the man that I had grown to love more than life itself, especially since I had kept it secret and they had almost died because of it. He had had an extremely difficult time with his emotions, ranging from sadness, rage and helplessness. We both cried. John held me for a long time, rocking me gently back and forth, crooning sweet nothings in my ear when I was finished.

"That will never happen to you again," he told me. "You will always be safe with me, Princess."

"I know, John. I'm just really sorry that you and Charles got hurt," I cried. "David could have killed you both. *Tried* to kill you both."

"But, we're not dead, and we will heal. Besides," he laughed, "do you have any idea how hard Charles's head is?"

We laughed together and Charles walked back into the room at that moment.

"I heard that," he said. But we kept laughing. "Are the two of you hungry?"

Actually, I hadn't realized just how hungry I was until Charles mentioned it. "Yes. Famished."

"I could eat," piped in John.

"You could always eat, John," admonished Charles.
"I'm a growing boy, Pop."
"You stopped growing a very long time ago."
"Are you implying that I'm old?" John asked.
"No. I'm implying that you have a hollow leg and you eat for the sake of eating, not for the sake of growing." Charles laughed.

John said nothing more and bent to scoop up Charlene. "Come here, little one."

I followed the men out and down the stairs to the wonderful smell of omelets and fruit salad. The food was delicious and I gobbled it down as if I hadn't eaten in a long time. Nursing took a great deal of energy, I had explained to John when he teased me about my never ending appetite. We then decided that we needed some fresh air and dressed to go out for a walk. I was nervous about being out in the open despite the fact that there would be police officers clad as civilians around us. But John reassured me, so we decided to walk to the Farmer's Market to stock up on produce for my mothers arrival tomorrow.

There was this one little booth at the Market that I particularly wanted to go to. Run by a wonderful little Italian man, with such a warm and inviting disposition. His stand always had the most crisp, sweet, juicy apples. I had been craving these apples, and took a moment to show off Charlene after my purchase.

It was a beautiful day. Almost everything was in full bloom, and the sun was shining high and warm. The smell of flowers was in the air, and I immediately felt much more energized. John pushed Charlene's stroller

FREE

and we walked very, very slowly, marveling at how different the world seemed since last week.

We stopped at the park and sat in the garden on a stone bench on our way back from the Market. By then, the pain in my leg was too much and I was grateful to be able to sit. We were surrounded by tulips and pruned rose bushes. The breeze touched our skin in whispered caresses, comforting my uneasiness. I lifted my face to the sun, feeling the warmth of the rays sink beneath my skin. I was beginning to feel energized and hopeful for the future.

John and I sat for a long time in silence before Charlene started to shriek in hunger. Instead of going home, however, I opted to nurse her in the park so we could stay out longer.

"Are you nervous about tomorrow, Princess?" John asked me, although I knew he sensed that I was.

"Yes," I said, pausing for a moment. "My mother has always been so closed-minded. Especially, when it comes to the roles of husband and wife," I said. I extended my hand out before me so I could admire the engagement ring.

"It looks beautiful on your finger."

I smiled up at him. His eyes had flecks of yellow in them in the sun, and when he looked down at me, I was instantly comforted by those intense, beautiful eyes.

"Do you know that I love you?" I asked him.

"Do you know that I'm the luckiest man on the planet?" He kissed me deeply then. "Try not to worry too much about your mother. It will be OK."

I nodded and we got up to leave. I could only pray that John was right. I hated the thought of what it might do to her when my mother finally realized that I had no intention of going back. Of course I wouldn't be going back to David. Afraid as I was, I knew that he would eventually be caught. But that didn't mean that I wanted to go back to British Columbia with my mother and her lonely life. After all, my mother lost two grandchildren, and Charlene would be the first to survive, so hopefully my plan for her to move out here would be appealing.

I had every intention of telling her everything about David. I was not going to sugar coat any of it. As difficult as it would be, she needed to know the hell I had lived. She was thick that way and a strong dose of reality may very well be the only thing that snaps her into normalcy. It is not normal to stay with a man who beat and raped you. Marriage certificate, or not. My mother was living in the stone ages, and it was up to me alone to change her mind.

By the time evening came, there was still no report on any sightings of David and I was exhausted. I took Charlene and went up to bed. I lay her down on a pillow beside me and turned on my side so I could nurse her. She fell asleep almost as soon as she burped, and I drifted off shortly after that.

When I next woke, it was three in the morning. Charlene was crying and John had already gotten up. I went into the nursery to find John changing her diaper as quickly as her squirming body would allow. I laughed over her shrieking.

"She's giving you a run for your money," I said.

"So are you." He turned to smile at me, with those luscious lips.

"When I heal, I'll give you a run for something," I

teased and rubbed up against his body, stopping suddenly because of how much it hurt.

John winced too. "Ouch! I think we both still need healing for a while. How about we get this little one to bed for a feeding before she wakes up the whole neighborhood?"

We had been practically yelling to hear each other above Charlene's wails. "OK. Thanks for changing her."

My milk was really coming in now and I drew in a sharp breath as the flow rushed through the milk ducts. It was a pull that started deep under the armpit and flowed through to the nipple in slices of itchy, engorged pain. The instant the baby began to suckle, the itchiness of the pressure from within was relieved.

After I nursed Charlene back to sleep, despite our tiredness, John and I lay on our sides facing each other. He lifted his hand from Charlene's back and caressed my face.

"You have the most beautiful eyes I have ever seen," he whispered.

I smiled.

"I can't wait to marry you." John ran his hand down to the finger that had the ring.

"Me neither," I said. "But what if we never find David? It could be years before we catch up to him."

"I know it's hard, Kathryn, but I don't want you to worry about that. I was a good cop, and David isn't the type of guy to flee from what he thinks is his. He will try to come back, but this time we're prepared and we will catch him." John was so assuring, I had to believe him, and I nodded.

"Sleep, Princess. We have another rough day ahead of us."

"Yes. I love you." I was falling asleep even as I was saying it and barely heard John's reply.

When I next woke, Charlene's tiny hands were flailing in protest at being hungry, yet again. A smile lit my face, and I caught one of her tiny fists. It felt cool and impossibly frail. Yet, at the same time, there was a physical strength that one could hardly believe from such a small creature. Charlene was only two weeks old and she was already holding her head up while in a fury.

Once changed to a dry diaper, I took the baby downstairs and sat on the sofa with her. She now had a head full of fuzzy, coppery blond hair and her eyes had changed to the same green as mine. I loved the way her head felt in my hand when I held it close to my breast.

She had perfect little rosebud lips, and when her eyes were closed, her long, long lashes rested easily on her round cheeks. The tiny nose was a perfect little ball, and she scrunched it up before she began to cry. It was so cute and innocent. This perfect little baby completely filled my heart.

John handed me a coffee to sip on while I nursed. He put it in a travel mug, so if the baby squirmed, I wouldn't spill on her. When I finished nursing, he took her in his arms, expertly draped the baby blanket over his shoulder, and lifted her up so he could burp her.

"Go eat, Princess. We need to leave soon."

"What's for breakfast?" I asked as I got up.

"Scrambled eggs and toast."

"Yum." I stood up on my tiptoes to kiss him full on the mouth.

"I'll dress the baby," he said, and whisked her upstairs.

Breakfast was good and despite my trepidation about seeing my mother, I felt pretty fine. How could I not, with a new baby, a new man, and a new life? I had so many blessings to count and I did so every minute of the day. Now that I was emotionally stronger, I was able to push my fear of David aside with more force than I ever had.

John also took the time to sow me how to use his gun. Not the .38, but a smaller one. A .22, which was easier for me to handle because of my lack of experience using a weapon. I shivered at the thought of possibly having to use it, but I had decided long ago that I would kill David if I had to. Certainly, now that Charlene was not encumbered in my belly. Her birth made her more vulnerable to harm.

When John came down with the baby, we put a cute little purple sweater on her, a bonnet to cover her ears, and then I buckled her up in her infant seat. I had finally mastered the breast pump, so I was able to pump a few bottles over the last couple of days. John grabbed two of the bottles and put them in the diaper bag with the rest of the baby stuff. We certainly had packed everything but the kitchen sink for the day trip with Charlene.

It didn't take long to get to the airport, but took almost as long as the trip to find parking and walk to the main building. It was the most physical work either one of us had done in the last two weeks and we were both stiff, sore, and tired by the time we made it to the right terminal. I kept lagging behind, even with the stroller to support me, but I was determined to walk, although a mental note to make sure that we took the bus back to the car with my mom.

We sat down to wait, and Charlene needed another feeding and diaper change, so I took her to the restroom for nursing mothers. My mother's plane wouldn't be in for another twenty minutes, so I still had plenty of time. When Charlene had a full belly, she was content to let me change her. Once she was all clean and smelling like baby powder, we emerged to sit with John again to wait.

Finally, the plane arrived and my stomach lurched. I put my hand on my belly, to calm my nervousness. My stomach was still soft from the birth, but it was steadily shrinking, and I was fitting into my pre-baby jeans. Strictly due to stress, I might add. It was a comfort to be held snuggly in the middle after giving birth. It was definitely better than walking around jiggling.

The stitches in my stomach were also being held in with the jeans and that was a relief as well. I wished that I could hide the bruises and cuts on my face so people weren't constantly looking at me when they walked by. They were looking at John, too, but it was more shocking to see a woman with bruises than a man.

A few people even blatantly asked me if my husband beat me, so I murmured 'car accident, willing them to walk on by. After what seemed like an eternity, my mother emerged through the gate looking prim and nervous. She took another couple of steps, scanning the area for me. I lifted my hand to wave. She looked right at me but continued scanning the room.

Then it dawned on me. My hair was different and I wasn't pregnant. Charlene was in her stroller behind me, beside John. I was also wearing make-up. However, I knew the make-up wasn't noticeable against the bruises on my face.

I waved again. "Mom! Over here."

She spotted me and truly looked shocked. My mother came over and hugged me close.

"Kathryn," She breathed, "how are you?" she asked.

"Uh...I'm fine." *Where is my mother and what have you done to her?* I wanted to ask. "Ho...how are you?" I managed to stammer out.

"I'm fine, now that I know you are." She put me at arm's length and looked at me from head to toe. She stared intently at the bruises on my face for a few seconds and reached up to trace the cut on my lip, then continued her gaze down to my toes. She stopped at my belly and a look of grief flooded her face. I realized belatedly what she was thinking.

"Oh! No, Mom." I stepped aside. John pushed the stroller up beside me, and I bent to pick up Charlene. "Mom, this is Charlene."

"Kathryn," my mother wept, "she is so beautiful! She looks just like you." Carefully, she took the baby from my arms, and looked her over the way any grandmother would look at her granddaughter for the first time.

"Mom," I said and motioned John forward, "this is John."

My mother was stunned for a moment, not realizing that there was another person with me, then recovered quickly and smiled at him.

"Hello, John," she said.

"John, this is my mother, Meredith." After the introductions, mom put Charlene back into the stroller, and John suggested that we leave and go somewhere for dinner.

We crossed back into Canada and went to a local Italian restaurant. It was quiet and not too busy, so at our request, we were ushered into a booth for more privacy. Once drinks and appetizers were ordered, we got down to business.

"Mom. There is a lot going on, and I'm sorry I made you worry, but I had to be sure that you wouldn't tell David where I was," I stated flatly.

"Kathryn," she began slowly, "I was very worried, and you could have called." She wasn't giving me shit, she was expressing her concern.

"I know. I called when I could. When I tell you all there is to know about David and me, then you will understand why I couldn't take the chance that any phone call I made home would be traced." Oh, man. This was going to be difficult. My hands were shaking almost uncontrollably.

We hadn't said a word the whole way from the airport to the restaurant, and now there was no turning back. I had to tell her everything. It was only fare.

"Mom. I don't want to get into all the details here, in the restaurant, but I will not be coming home with you. I have made a new home here, with John, and when we can, we will be getting married." *How's that for laying it on thick?* I thought. I also held my breath, waiting for her to say something.

"I don't know what to say to you Kathryn. You've been gone for months, only made one phone call, and now you tell me you're with another man, and you're not coming home. I expected that you wouldn't be coming home, but the rest is a shock," she said.

"I know it's a lot to take in, and I know it's unfair to dump it all in your lap, but we don't have all these bruises on our faces for nothing," I said.

"Kathryn, honey, I'm not trying to attack you. I was very worried, and I know you left because you thought I wouldn't understand." She smiled at me. "Baby, I know I've never been strong and I've ignored the way David treated you, but I am here now." She put her hand on mine, and looked at John.

"So, John. What do you do for a living?" My mother turned her smile on him.

"Well, I used to be a police officer, but now I do construction work. Custom work, actually," John replied.

"A police officer? Why did you leave it?" she inquired.

"It's a lot of hard work and not a lot of pay. It's extremely stressful, as well, and I got sick of it and moved back here to be with my father."

I knew John must have been feeling like a kid on his first date, trying to impress the parents. I hid my smile in the crook of Charlene's neck and then turned to him with a look that said, 'sorry about the twenty questions.'

"So, you love each other." My mother simply stated, as she leaned back in her chair.

"Yes Ma'am. I hope that we can get to know each other, and I can quell any fears you might have. We are going to all be staying in my apartment, and I hope that you will be comfortable. We'll tell you everything, but for now, I think we're all tired and in need of a good meal," John suggested.

"Actually, that does sound wonderful," my mom said.

"Kathryn, please tell me about the birth and exactly how old my granddaughter is."

John and I told her everything about that day, except for the fact that David had tied me to a chair, beaten me to within an inch of my life, and shot John and I both, while leaving Charles in a heap on the floor. We would tell her all of that later.

The three of us laughed while we ate and cooed at the baby. We were all relaxed by the end of our meal, and the ice ball in the pit of my stomach began to melt. After eating, we went home to our apartment. I showed mom up to her room and gave her a tour so she would know where to find everything she would need. While mom unpacked her things, I went down to the kitchen to make us all some tea. We hadn't said anything about the police at the door, but when she came down, she asked about it.

"Kathryn, am I correct to think that the police have something to do with David?" she asked.

"Yes. There's a lot I need to tell you about David," I began slowly.

"I know, dear," she said. "I know that he wasn't the kind of husband that you deserved."

I stood there gaping at her. She had never, ever acknowledged anything wrong in my life. Or in her life, for that matter.

"Why didn't you ever say anything?" I asked. As much as I wanted to stay calm, I could hear the anger creep into my voice. After all, when Daddy died, she could have stopped the wedding. For all these years, she could have helped me. Especially, after the babies died. I wasn't always able to hide the bruises. She had known.

"I didn't know how to say anything. But I want to change that, Kathryn. I don't want to judge you and I don't want you to judge me. I know that I was never there for you, but now I want to be. I need to be." She grabbed my hands and then put them down to reach for my swollen, bruised face.

"Did David do this to you?" She asked while tracing the cut on my mouth, then my forehead.

"Yes." Hot tears started to roll down my cheeks and I pulled back a little, feeling awkward at my mother's sudden affection. It seemed as if I had been waiting my whole life for her to soothe me. She dropped her hands and looked down at them.

"I knew that he bullied you, but I didn't know it was so bad." She sniffled, and I immediately felt guilty.

We sat there completely awkward, yet so much needing each others acceptance. She acknowledged her failures and apologized for not helping me to get away from David. She said she knew that life for me was hell.

"But, Kathryn, I didn't know *how* to help you. I noticed all the long sleeved shirts you wore in the summer, and how often David said you were busy, when I knew that he just wouldn't let you talk to me." She kept sobbing and hastily grabbed a Kleenex to blow her nose.

"I felt so guilty, Kathryn. I *feel* so guilty. I should have protected you." My mother kept saying it over and over, until finally I had to grab her hands and shake them.

"Mom! It's not your fault. I didn't tell you anything and it was stupid not to."

"What else did he do to you? Please tell me, Kathryn. I need to know," she pleaded.

So I told her. Not every gory detail, but almost everything. All the years of abuse and how David was at fault for the deaths of Nicolas and Gabrielle. She sat there listening intently to me. Nodding once in a while and patting my hands at the most difficult parts.

My mother gasped and went as white as a ghost.

"What is it Mom? You look like you're about to faint." I was alarmed.

"David found you because of me." She looked down, refusing to meet my eyes.

"What are you talking about?" It couldn't be her fault. "Mom, I was in Muskoka when I called you." I added.

"Yes, and we didn't know where you were, but I was angry with you, and I told David to go after you." A large tear rolled down her cheek.

"David was coming after me anyway, Mom. And of course you were angry with me." I handed her a tissue. "It was selfish and wrong to have taken off like that, but I needed to know that I was far away and get clear in my mind before I called you. "If it's anyone's fault, it's mine. I should have told John what I was hiding, but I was too afraid. If I had told him, we could have been prepared. I also thought that I had covered my tracks better. I was wrong, and too many people were hurt." My own tears started up again, but I drew in a deep breath, and calmed myself.

John had been standing silently in the doorway of the kitchen, and cut in. "It's nobody's fault but David's. Men like him only want one thing. To have total control over someone." He turned to my mother. "I'll bet he was controlling you in some ways, wasn't he? Maybe blaming you for Kathryn's escape somehow?"

She nodded slowly, looking up at him with shame. It broke my heart to see my mother suffer like that. To think she believed that David finding me and almost killing me was her doing was almost unbearable. I reached over and put my hand on hers, and she covered mine with her free hand.

John brought us back to the main concern. "We need to worry about where David could be and when he might strike again. So far, there haven't been any sightings, but that doesn't mean he went back home. Clearly, as much as I hate to admit it, he seems to have at least some intelligence. He wouldn't go home, knowing that an arrest warrant will be out for him. Not to mention the fact that his face has been plastered all over the news," added John.

"I agree," I said. "I thought I was smart enough to escape without being caught. I didn't know any other way to get out though."

"Kathryn, I don't want you to think I'm going to take David's side. I know I'm set in my ways, but I'm not blind either, and seeing you this way, with so much courage, gives me courage. I've never seen you so strong." My mother looked at me for a moment before continuing.

"Will you forgive my foolishness?"

"There's nothing to forgive. I know that Dad victimized you, just like David with me. Now, you and I are together, and David will never hurt either of us again. I know that in my heart." I said, and prayed to God that I looked convincing.

We smiled at each other, and then Mom got up and

scooped Charlene up from her bassinet. "This little one has a stinky bum. I'll go change her, than maybe we can go for a walk. Show me around a bit."

"Let me have the area checked first," said John, "and Charles and I will go with you."

We didn't end up going for a walk until the next day, because there had been a sighting of a man that fit David's description. So, after lunch the following afternoon, John set out to check for himself that all was safe.

It was half an hour before we were able to leave, which gave me time to nurse Charlene *again*. Then we all went out. I noticed immediately that Charles and my mother tended to lag behind, walking silently side by side. John and I looked at each other and smiled.

We had the diaper bag with extra bottles with us and decided to go to a nearby restaurant for dinner, after having spent the entire afternoon at a nearby park, soaking up the sun. We were relaxed and happy, despite the dangers of being in the open and went back home to get to bed early. John had some inquiries about today's searches and possible sightings, so I went to sleep without him. It wasn't long before he came to bed, however, and we spooned closely until drifting off. We hadn't been asleep for long when the phone woke us both up.

My heart jumped into my throat at the sound, and John picked it up before the second ring.

"Yes?" he said into the receiver. "I'll be right there."

"What is it?" I asked sleepily. "Have they found him?"

John looked at me, trying to decide whether or not to tell me the truth. I raised an eyebrow in question, tilting my head down a bit. He got the hint and smiled.

"Yes. Well, no. There's been a sighting. I'm going to go check it out. You'll be OK?" He leaned over to kiss me before I answered.

"Yes. Please be careful. I love you."

"I love you." He said and left.

Chapter Forty Two

Sitting in the passenger seat, waiting for David to come back to the motel he was staying at, was almost unbearable for John. He was seething mad and knew it would require great restraint to not kill the man while the police made the arrest. John hadn't told Kathryn that he knew David had been spotted a couple of times, somehow managing to elude everyone.

The last thing Kathryn needed to worry about was the fact that, despite David's lifestyle, he was not a stupid man, and kept getting away. There had been four sightings, although none were confirmed that it was David. He was worried about Kathryn and her ability to cope. She was deathly afraid, though she tried to hide it from him. She couldn't hold anything without her hands shaking, and she was pale and ill looking.

Charlene was a joy and a blessing beyond their wildest hopes, but that didn't seem to be enough. Kathryn's resolve was depleting rapidly, and her health with it. John was desperate to catch David, and he was grateful that the police were involving him in the search even though he hadn't been a cop for a few years. His friend back in British Columbia had pulled a lot of strings for him, and John didn't want anything to go awry in the pursuit of David.

The sight of Kathryn tied to a chair, huge belly before her, dripping blood from the gash in her forehead, was still burning in John's mind as vivid as that day. The only other time John had felt fear like that was when he had driven home that fateful day years ago and saw the police, fire, and ambulance vehicles at his house, knowing he couldn't do anything to save his family.

He would be plagued with that image for a long time, he knew. He had already bolted up a few times from a bad dream. Except in his nightmare, David killed Kathryn and Charles, and the baby died in Kathryn's belly.

"There he is." The cop sitting beside him in the car nudged John in the arm, snapping John's attention back to the present.

John's whole body went rigid with a fierce desire to kill the man. He was absolutely vibrating with rage, and the only thing keeping him from jumping out of the car and ripping David's heart out, was Kathryn. He couldn't wait for long, he knew, and he sensed that the cop beside him knew it too, but didn't say anything. John had, after all, been a veteran cop with an impeccable record.

They watched as David, clad in a baseball cap and a black windbreaker with Elvis style glasses, walked toward the motel. It was hard to tell if David noticed anything suspicious, because he kept his head low. On either side of the building, John watched as two undercover officers approached David. One was dressed like a street gang kid and the other like a businessman. Both were behaving like any other person walking down the street. David tensed almost imperceptibly as the street kid walked by, appearing to argue with someone on his cell phone.

Without hesitation, the second cop passed David, turned on him, and lunged, knocking David down. Then chaos ensued. David was quick and jumped up almost as fast as he was knocked down. He lurched forward and plowed through the officer dressed as a businessman, taking off in a sprint.

John and the officer sitting beside him sprang out of the car and everyone started running. John's whole body ached in protest at the physical exertion. It had been a long time since he had to take someone down and it killed him to know that he probably wouldn't be the one to capture David, but there was nothing he could do about it. He was out of practice and injured.

David darted in and around people on the street, knocking some of them down as he rushed past. The police were gaining on him, but were not able to do much without endangering innocent by-standers. They had their weapons out and were screaming for David to stop.

To everyone's horror, David snatched a small, elderly woman as he ran by her and pulled out his own gun. He held her against his body, with the gun pointed at her head. She went dead white with fear and started to scream. At that point, David noticed John and their eyes locked.

"Let her go!" bellowed the street kid cop.

"Not a chance," said David, cool and calm like a snake.

The woman stopped screaming when David threatened her, but kept whimpering. John didn't take his gaze off David, and David gave him a slow, evil smirk. Clearly, the man had no fear, and John felt a surge of panic rush through his blood. The realization that David clearly had no regard for ending a human life sent up a huge red flag in John's mind.

John yelled over the chaos, "Back off!"

The officers both took a step back, and the one in the car crouched behind his open door. Backup started arriving from every direction, encircling David and his hostage. David backed up slowly to a doorway in another building.

"Stop! Put your gun down!" yelled an officer new on the scene.

John pleaded with David, "It's over David. Give yourself up."

"So you can have a nice life with my wife? Nah," said David, shaking his head. "Won't do. I'm going to kill the bitch." And with that, David simultaneously pushed the old woman forward and ruthlessly shot her in the back, before jumping through the doorway and taking off.

Cops started screaming orders and pedestrians started screaming in terror. There were shouts coming from everywhere, only adding to the confusion of the situation. John watched in slow motion, while the horror of the knowledge that David was getting away again built up in him like a volcanic explosion threatening to erupt. Under strict orders to not get physically involved, John took off through the doorway anyway, despite his injuries, taking out his gun as he ran. He was rusty when it came to pursuit, but he was being fuelled by rage and revenge.

He could not go back to Kathryn and tell her that David got away. He couldn't fail her like that.

Other cops followed in pursuit, each taking a different direction, shouting for people to get down. They were in a large office building and despite the police orders, some people panicked and started running all over the place, unintentionally allowing David to get a head start to the other end of the building. John knew that this particular building had more than one entrance and an anguished cry of frustration left his throat as he yelled at the occupants of the building.

David was quick. He was also vicious and violent. Each person that happened to be in his way was plowed over in his quest for escape. John was gaining on him, though, and with only about seven feet between them, John sprang off his feet and hit David square in the back with his uninjured shoulder. They went down and tumbled in a heap of arms and legs. David brought up his gun and smashed John in the side of his head.

The blow knocked John over and he fell onto his side, quickly getting up on his hands and knees. David was scrambling away, but cocking his gun at the same time in an effort to shoot at his pursuer. He wasn't quick enough, because John leapt up and caught David under the jaw with a huge fist. David's hand came up with the gun, but John caught his hand with his foot in a roundhouse, sending the gun flying.

John could hear the other cops behind him and caught David sparing a half-second glance over John's shoulder to see that he was going to be surrounded in a couple of seconds. Panic flitted in David's eyes, but he recovered quickly and threw a shot at John's injured shoulder. The impact took John's breath away and sparks shot in every direction in front of his eyes.

He was going down. He knew he was going down. He fought with every fiber within him to regain control of his senses. One breath. Two. OK. He could see again. And he saw that David was getting away, despite the police close at his heels.

"Nooooo!!!!" he bellowed. "Get him!!!"

But they couldn't. David was too fast and too far ahead. He was an animal, willing to do anything to not be caged, including killing anything that came in his way.

John threw up his arms, and then winced from the pain, causing the volcano to erupt. He lost all control and threw his fist through the nearest wall, ignoring everything else.

"NOOO!!! No! No! No!!" His voice was strange, even to his own ears. It rumbled and came out hoarse, starting deep in his chest, ripping through his throat. He felt desperate and hostile. Somebody needed to pay for this debacle. Never in his career as a cop had he witnessed so much incompetence and disorganization. He *said it!* He told the sergeant at the precinct that there weren't enough men on it. He told them that David would be armed.

"We don't have enough man power," Sergeant Billings had said.

But, what could John do? His hands were tied. They were giving him special privileges, after all.

John's breathing became ragged, and he labored to control himself before smashing one of these incompetent police officers. There were still a couple on foot, and he knew there was a patrol car circling the area, but David was gone. Again.

"Sir?" Someone was tugging on his sleeve, and when he turned to look, a short woman dressed in a paramedic uniform looked up at him, fearful to wake the bear.

John softened his expression a bit. It wasn't this woman's fault David got away. "What?"

"I'm sorry to bother you," she began, "but you're bleeding pretty badly from the wound on your head. We need to get it to stop." She pulled on his arm to lead him to the ambulance. He followed without complaint.

Chapter Forty Three

I was wringing the end of my skirt in my hands to the point where it was stretched to deformity. John had been gone for a few hours and I hadn't heard anything from him. *Please don't let anything happen to him*, I prayed for the thousandth time in the last few hours. I kept going back and forth from being angry for not hearing from him and being worried senseless. Charlene clearly sensed that something was wrong, because she had been crying for the last two hours straight, which only frayed on my nerves further.

Then guilt gripped me in the stomach, because it wasn't her fault, and I knew I needed to calm down if she was going to. I took her from my mother, who had taken the last shift of pacing with Charlene, and went to sit to try nursing her again. After a ten minute struggle of tiny hands and feet flailing around, she finally latched on and alternated between suckling contentedly, to arching her little body in protest.

I couldn't help but smile at her stubbornness and felt myself relax enough to concentrate on Charlene's fierce determination to suck every last drop out of me. I put my hand on her fuzzy head and gently stroked her with my fingertips. Eventually, she changed her mind, deciding finally that she wasn't in a fitful rage and fell asleep.

Almost the moment I put her down, John came in, sporting a fresh gauze dressing on the side of his head, looking grim and a little ill. He stopped in front of me, and we just looked at each other for a moment.

"I'm sorry, Princess. He got away," he said simply.

I couldn't respond. My head swam with a thousand different thoughts. Was he on his way here? How did David get away? Was he the one that hurt my beloved John? On and on it went, and the next thing I knew, John and my mother were standing above me, both expressing a look of utter shock.

"Don't sit up too fast, Kathryn." John laid his hand on my shoulder to keep me down.

I looked around and discovered that I was now lying on the sofa, my feet propped up, with a cool cloth on my forehead. I must have passed out. I hadn't expected David to get away and I was stricken to the bone with the realization. I knew, without a doubt, that I would not be able to take much more. I needed to know David was caught and behind bars, like I needed to breathe. I couldn't live without either.

"What happened?" I asked.

"You passed out, dear," said my mother.

"Yes. I know that," I said a little testily. "I mean, what happened with David?" Looking at John, I sat up slowly.

"He took a hostage, and..." John stopped mid sentence, as if deciding what he should tell me. "He shot the woman, and we had a fight, but he got away." John looked tortured and it broke my heart to see the guilt so clearly etched on his face.

I reached up and gently grazed the bandage on his head. "Are you badly hurt?"

John shook his head. "No. Just a few stitches. I'll be fine."

"I guess we'll have to wait for another opportunity to catch him." I tried to sound reassuring.

"I am sorry, Kathryn. I tried," John said in an anguished voice that was barely audible.

I nodded. "What are the police doing now?"

"They're finally taking me seriously. They've upped the search and the protection around the building. David isn't stupid, but he's not smart enough to leave it undone. He wants you and I don't think he'll stop until he gets you."

My mother looked frightened again and John noticed. "Don't worry, Meredith. I won't let anything happen to her or Charlene."

My mother just nodded, and then got up to put the kettle on for some tea. That was her habit. She only really drank tea when she was worried. I got up, wobbled a little, and went into the kitchen to grab some teacups and biscuits. When the tea was steeped, the three of us sat down to sip it and have a snack.

Despite having the tea to wash them down, my throat was thick, and the biscuits took their merry old time making their way to my stomach. Normally, I enjoyed the treat, but they landed in my stomach in a heavy heap, and I felt nauseous after only a few bites.

"Do you want to go lie down?" John asked me.

"Yes. I don't feel well." I went to scoop up Charlene and took her to bed with me. It wasn't that I didn't trust my mother or John to protect her, but David had killed Nicolas and Gabrielle, and I wanted to feel Charlene's tiny body against mine to know that she was safe. I fell asleep as soon as my head hit the pillow and almost as quickly my mind plunged into nightmares, as always.

Each one was different, ranging from David setting the apartment on fire, trapping us all inside; to his capturing me and torturing me ruthlessly. I woke up several times in a sweat, but fell back to sleep. When I finally did wake up fully, Charlene was screeching in my ear and it was beginning to get dark outside.

I rolled over on my side and Charlene latched on in starvation, drawing in long, deep swallows of nourishment. I winced a little as the milk came in, then sighed in relief as her tiny mouth relieved me of the pressure. I bent my head down to kiss the fuzzy blanket of down on her perfect head, drew in a deep breath, and smelled a mixture of new baby, baby powder, and breast milk.

"It's OK my sweet baby," I said to my precious daughter. "Daddy will protect us. He won't let anything happen to us."

"No, I won't." I looked up to see John come through the door. "I heard her crying. Did you have a good rest?"

"No." I sighed. John slid onto the bed behind me and pressed his body up against mine, wrapping his arm protectively around us.

His large hand cupped Charlene's impossibly small bum, and the three of us lay there quietly for a long time. When Charlene finished nursing, John got up and changed her diaper, then deposited her into her crib with an affectionate kiss on her round, chubby cheek.

He came to lie with me again, but this time we faced each other. We locked hands and pressed our foreheads together. I took another deep breath to take in his scent and my heart quickened at his closeness. My fingertips traced the lines on his face and again went to the bandage on the side of his head.

"How did that happen?" A fresh bruise was creeping from under the bandage and I had the suspicion that John's injury was more serious than he led me to believe. I wasn't going to call him on it, though. He was clearly gripped with guilt

"With the butt of his gun." He reached up to take my hand away and brought my fingers to his mouth. His breath on my hand and face was hot and smelled of tea and biscuits.

"Did the woman die?" I was afraid to know.

"Yes. She was elderly, and even if he hadn't shot her, she probably would have died from the push he gave her in his escape." John was being matter of fact, trying to hide his anger and embarrassment.

"It's not…"

"Don't!" He jumped off the bed, and began pacing the room. "I don't need you to tell me it's not my fault. It *is* my fault, and someone died today because of it."

"I don't believe that!" I spat back, jumping off the bed myself. "It's my fault for not telling you everything! If I had of told you everything nobody would have been hurt!" We were both getting passionate.

"You were afraid to say anything. Anyone in your

situation would be. David will hurt anyone that gets in his way. He wants you, Kathryn, and he won't stop until he gets you. The only thing that telling me ahead of time would have done, would have been to give me a head's up so that I could have planned something."

"Exactly! I didn't say anything, and nobody was prepared when he found us. Not only were you hurt, but so was your father! How am I supposed to live with that? You couldn't have done anything. You're only one man, John. Not an army." I regretted saying it as soon as it left my mouth.

He just stood there, staring at me for a few minutes before continuing slowly. "I'm aware of the fact that I'm out of practice and that I am only one man," he stopped to steady his breathing, "but I am capable of protecting you and Charlene." With that, John turned and strode out of the room, leaving me crying.

I lay on the bed and cried alone for some time, before he come back and sat down gently on the bed beside me.

John's large, warm hand stroked my back before he said, "I'm sorry, Princess. I'm going crazy here. I can't lose you or Charlene, and I'm scared shitless that David is going to come back. I *know* he's going to come back."

I rolled over onto my back and glanced in the crib before turning my attention fully to John. Charlene was asleep again, and I felt confident that she wouldn't wake up for the next little while.

"John. I'm also going crazy, and I can't face losing you, either. But you have to understand that as guilty as you feel, so do I. If I had never come into your life, you and Charles would never have been hurt." I pleaded with him to understand me.

"If you had never come into my life, I would still be dead." John was getting passionate again, but not in an angry way.

"Then why don't we agree to disagree about whose fault it is?" I suggested.

I could see John struggle with the thought, but he finally nodded slowly. "Fine. But, you have to tell me everything, all over again. I know it will be difficult and exhausting, but we need to go over everything again, so I can come up with a better plan."

"OK. Can we eat while we talk?" I asked. My stomach was rumbling loudly and I felt as if I could eat an entire pizza. It's amazing what stress and fear could take out of you, not to mention nursing and caring for a newborn.

We ordered a pizza. And no, I didn't eat the whole thing, but I did down a few slices, and then gulped down a can of Coke. Caffeine free, of course.

I told John everything, but this time my mother added to the information. Thank God she was there, because I completely forgot that David had been in the Army Reserves from the time he was sixteen, until the age of twenty-one.

"Oh, my God! John, I don't know how I forgot that!" I felt so foolish. All the time David had weapons, it never clicked that he had military training.

"People, who are under constant threat of being killed, sometimes overlook the most important facts. Don't worry too much about it, Princess. This gives us an edge now. I just don't know why nobody else figured it out," John said in frustration.

"What kind of an edge?" my mother asked.

"Well, for starters Meredith, we know that he had army training. Kathryn, do you remember what job he was training for?" John looked at me.

"No. He never talked about it to me. It only ever came up a few times in the beginning." I chewed on my lower lip, deep in thought.

"I think it was weapon's control, something or other," said my mother.

"A Weapons Tech?" John asked. My mother nodded.

"That means that his knowledge of weapons and how they work is far more advanced than we thought. But that's a good thing, because now we know exactly what we're up against."

John got up and went into the study to make some phone calls. While he was in there, my mother went upstairs to get Charlene when we heard her crying on the baby monitor. She resigned herself to give up her granddaughter so that I might nurse her again. Did all babies eat this much? I wondered.

"Kathryn, I'm worried about you," my mother said.

"I know, Mom, but it will pass." I smiled tiredly at her.

"Not just about this," she said as she waved her hand to indicate that she wasn't just referring to my getting involved with a strange man and moving in with him after just a few weeks of knowing him. "I'm worried about the effect all of this is having on you. You don't look well, Kathryn. Not like you did last week."

"I'm just tired, Mom. There's a lot going on," I said.

"Yes. I am here with you," she said dryly.

"I'm sorry, Mom. I'm not being fair to you." I needed to make things right with her. She had only had a short time to get used to all this. Everything about me was drastically different, and I didn't need to let my frustrations get in the way of my mother's acceptance of my new life.

"I will admit that meeting John was a shock. But, that's not it. I really like him, and I see the way you look at each other. I see the way he's gentle with you and with Charlene. And, I've actually grown quite fond of Charles." She blushed a little as she said this, and I had to smile.

"I've noticed. He's a wonderful man."

Her hand fluttered up to her throat. Something she did when she was embarrassed, which of course made me smile even more, but this time I tried to hide it.

"Kathryn, have you had your check up at the doctor's, since the baby was born? And, I'm not referring to the week you spent in the hospital recovering."

"Actually, I've been so consumed with everything that's been going on that I missed my last appointment," I said, and vaguely remembered Charles leaving me a note on the table that the clinic had called.

"I think maybe you should go and get a check up. All this stuff going on could interfere with your recuperation. You are pale and exhausted looking."

"I agree with Meredith," John said as he walked from the study.

I threw my free hand up, in acquiescence. "I will go to the clinic."

"When?" They said in unison.

"Tomorrow." Geez. I felt like a kid getting admonished for not cleaning my room and said as much.

"There is no reason for you to forget, then," John said.

I had to admit that I hadn't been feeling well at all. I had been waking up with bruises here and there on my body, without any recollection of how they got there. The exhaustion and weight loss were explainable, I thought. Although overjoyed at having a healthy, beautiful baby against the odds, I was deathly afraid every minute of every day, and I also knew that nursing burned a lot of calories and made you tired. But even I had to admit that I was looking sickly thin and pale. My pre-pregnancy jeans were also getting very loose. Not good.

"I will go with you, Kathryn." John said.

In any event, it was another four days before I got to see a doctor, because the Royal Canadian Mounted Police got involved in the search for David. It turned out that when the police discovered David's belongings in the motel; they were able to match up his prints with a couple of unsolved murder and rape cases from when he was a teen. It was never caught before, because in the military, it's not a requirement to be finger printed. Or, at least, it wasn't when David was in the Canadian Reserves.

"How could it have gone unnoticed?" I asked the R.C.M.P. Officer. "He was arrested for a D.U.I." Officer Spence was standing in the kitchen with us at John's apartment.

"Actually, he wasn't," she said. I liked her immediately upon meeting her. This woman commanded respect, and got it without the slightest hesitation or scorn from the male officer's involved in the search. Officer Spence continued, "Your husband was only held in a cell for the night. He was never finger printed, nor was he arrested. They couldn't arrest him, because he was walking away from his vehicle, and not driving it."

I stood there dumbfounded and felt sick at the thought that he had murdered at least two other people. How had my father ever seen anything other than evil in David? How had I? And, without warning, I threw up. Right at Officer Spence's feet. She jumped back just in time, too. Gently, she guided me to the bathroom where I heaved a few more times, before stopping.

"I'm sorry," I croaked out.

"It's OK, hon." said Officer Spence. "Why don't you splash your face with some cold water? You'll feel better." She left me alone for a moment.

I did dab cold water on my face and rinsed my mouth out before brushing my teeth. I looked in the mirror at my reflection and almost started at the person staring back at me. When was the last time I had looked at myself? I couldn't remember, but the person staring back was *not* me.

She was pathetic and gaunt looking. Her cheeks were sunken in and she had huge dark circles under her eyes. *No wonder everyone keeps looking at me the way they do,* I thought. I looked like a skeleton, and even my collarbones were sticking out grotesquely. I lifted my shirt and balked at the sight of my ribs poking through the skin. I shuddered, and pulled my shirt back down. I thumped my butt down on the toilet seat and began to cry. At first, it came out slow, but quickly built up momentum, causing me to sob loudly and hyperventilate.

John came rushing in, not even bothering to knock on the door. I clung to him as if I were drowning in a sea of grief. He held me tight, but my body began to spasm. I couldn't breathe, and desperately gulped in air, only causing myself to hyperventilate more.

"Calm down, Princess," John was saying, but I barely heard him. "I'm here. I'm here with you."

Darkness was engulfing me. The last I heard was John screaming for someone to call an ambulance. I remembered waking a few times for just the briefest moments to see John sitting beside me. I was aware of movement and somewhere in the back of my mind, I knew I was in an ambulance, but then slipped back to darkness.

I awoke to the sound of Charlene's cries and set myself to go get her from her crib. Something cold and hard met my arm when I raised it to pull the blanket off me, and I became aware of the smell of my surroundings, then the blinking of lights and beeps. Now that I was snapping back to reality, I realized that I was in a hospital bed, hooked up to a few wires and machines with an I.V. sticking out of my arm.

"Hello?" I cried. I was in a private room and absently wondered who paid for it. As if it mattered.

Almost before the word left my mouth, John walked in with my baby in his arms. He was struggling to try to get her to take a pumped bottle, but she must have heard my voice, because she wasn't having any of it.

I held out my arms and John reluctantly handed her down to me.

"I'm OK," I said, and smiled up at him. "Just exhausted."

John relaxed a little when Charlene latched on to her source of food, and we could talk without having to shout over her crying.

"Are you really, ok?" he asked. He put the railing of the bed down, and I scooted over and patted the bed beside me. He sat down, taking my hand and bringing it to his lips. "You had us all worried."

"I know. I'm sorry. I guess I kinda freaked out. I feel better now, so we can go home."

"I'm afraid you can't," said a tall, stern looking doctor. He was an older man, with large rimmed glasses perching halfway down his nose. He looked down that nose at me in a not-so-friendly way, and I felt myself shrink into my pillow.

"I'm Dr. Alder, and I've spoken with Dr. Smart, and she agrees that you should be admitted for a few days for exhaustion and dehydration," he said, in the annoying matter-of-fact way tone some doctors used.

"Oh." It was the only intelligent thing I could come up with. I wondered if I was dehydrated, if that was why Charlene seemed not to be satisfied.

As if reading my mind, Dr. Alder added, "I'm sure you've noticed that the little one hasn't seemed to be filling up?" He ended his statement in question form, and I just nodded.

"We have you on a saline drip and have added some vitamins to it. You'll have to stay here for at least three days. Your husband insisted on a private room." I didn't correct him, that John wasn't my husband. He was to me. "The baby can stay with you, so as not to upset anyone further."

"When will I see Dr. Smart?" I asked. This lacked

bedside manners, and no offense to him, but I wanted my own doctor.

"She will be in to see you tomorrow and she is fully up to date on your status," he answered and turned to leave. He stopped at the door, turned back and said, "There will be a nurse in shortly to draw some blood. We couldn't get it earlier, because of the dehydration. It was almost impossible to get an I.V. in."

After Dr. Alder left, I turned my attention to Charlene for a few minutes. I burped her, than put her on the other breast. I planted a few kisses on her perfectly round cheeks and tiny fingers before I turned my attention to John.

"How long was I out for?" I asked.

He knit his brows together and said, "About three hours. Your body just shut down for a while."

"Where is my mother?"

"She's in the waiting lounge with Charles and Officer Spence. Would you like me to go and get her?" asked John.

"In a minute. I feel like I haven't seen you in a week. I miss you." I looked at him longingly and felt the now familiar flutter in my stomach and heart when I looked at him, or when he touched me.

"I miss you too, Princess." He leaned over and kissed me deeply and slowly. Charlene started to squirm a little and John pulled back laughing. "I guess I'm not allowed to share you at the moment."

"I miss your laugh."

"It will be over soon, Princess. Now that we know what we're up against, I think we'll catch David soon. When that happens, we'll all be free," he said.

"I know. I trust you." I reached up to cup his rough cheek in my hand. I loved to feel the scruff of his unshaven face in the palm of my hand.

I put Charlene down on her back between my legs, and John got up to let my mother and Charles know that they could come in now. He also brought the diaper bag back with him, so I could change Charlene's diaper. Enough people had been doing that for me, I protested vehemently when John wanted to do it.

Charles and Mom took turns doting on Charlene, and I fell back to sleep a few times. John went and got us all subs for dinner, piling mine high with veggies, meat, and cheese. I looked at it as if it would eat me.

"Do you honestly expect me to eat that?" I asked John when he plopped it on the table beside my bed.

"Yes I do, Princess. And you're going to," he demanded. "You need to put some meat on those bones if you're going to be strong enough to leave the hospital."

I looked to my mother for support, but she shook her head and held out her arms in my direction. "Don't look at me, darling. I agree with John. Here," she reached behind her and produced a bottle of orange juice, "drink that, too."

"All right then. I guess I'm outnumbered." I resigned myself to hunkering down with my huge, fattening, submarine sandwich.

Officer Spence came in, then and gave us an update. The plan was to put the word out to any Army Surplus stores in the area and to get in touch with any informants that had any access to illegal gun sellers. There would always be a minimum of two police officers outside my door, and only nurses and doctors specifically given the OK by Officer Spence would be allowed into the room.

John assured me that he wouldn't be leaving the hospital unless Charles or Meredith were there with me, and his step-brother Steven was still doing shopping and what-not for us. I had a shower in my room, the cafeteria was nearby, and a crib from the maternity ward had been rolled in for Charlene, complete with diapers, wipes, breast pads, and Vaseline. I felt like I was staying here for a month, rather than a week.

Mom and Charles left at around seven thirty in the evening, and I couldn't help but notice they were holding hands when they left. I pumped my thumb in their direction when they left. "Do you think there's a budding relationship?" I asked John.

"I think so. They've been spending a great deal of time together, and I know Pop has filled Meredith in on our whole situation," John smiled absently.

"Wouldn't it be wonderful if they got together?" I mused.

"Yes, it would," John agreed. "Your Mom seems nice, and Charles has a good sense of character. Otherwise we would never have met," he added with a grin.

John stayed with me, squeezing onto the bed until Charlene woke us up in the middle of the night, needing my attention. After that, he fell asleep in the recliner chair in the corner of the room. We woke the next morning when Charles and Mom came blowing in, bearing treats of real coffee and muffins. Chocolate-chip muffins.

"How are you feeling this morning deary?" Charles asked me. He bent down to kiss my forehead.

"I'm good, Charles. I already feel more rested. How

is your head? Is it all better now?" I touched his forehead with my fingertip.

"Good as new."

"Good," I said.

The next few days went by that the same, with a few visits from Dr. Smart. Although all of my test results hadn't come in yet, she seemed to think that I could go home the next day and felt satisfied that I was bulking up and re-hydrating. Charlene even seemed more content, although the last time I fed her, it seemed as if one of the milk ducts was a little blocked. Right up under my armpit. Dr. Smart said that it happened sometimes and she would look at it next week if it persisted. In the meantime, I was to see her the day after tomorrow for all my results. She said there was something important we needed to discuss.

That night, after settling once more to my hospital room, John firmly warned the two police on watch that night to keep an even closer eye on me while he went down to the cafeteria and the bookstore, before he needed to go fill out some paperwork for the contractor that he hired to finish the job he had been working on when David first showed up.

With much trepidation, he left the room, with me practically having to shoo him out. Just to feel a little safer because John wasn't there, I wheeled Charlene's crib over and rested it right against my bed so I could keep a hand in there, holding hers.

Sometime in the night, I heard a bit of a commotion in the hall, but quickly decided that it was just the hospital staff. My door was opened a crack, and I could see the tip of a shiny black boot, so I felt certain that the police officer was still at my door. I bent to check the baby and when I was satisfied that she wasn't about to wake up, I went to the bathroom.

While I was doing my business, Charlene started crying. Wailing, in fact. "Oh, great. Now she'll wake the whole hospital." I opened the door to go back into the room.

"OK, baby. Mom-" I stopped dead in my tracks, and I *know* all the blood drained from my head, slamming into my feet. I couldn't move, I couldn't breathe; I couldn't form a complete thought.

There, standing beside the crib, holding my child, was David. He looked at me and smiled. "You've done good Kathryn. It's too bad that you won't be able to keep living in your little fantasy land."

I just stood there gapping. I tried to speak, but only stammered. I tried to call for help, but the words caught in my throat. I froze. Completely froze. How could I *not* move? This monster was holding my baby. My only living baby.

Finally, I managed to squeak out, "How?"

"How did I get in here?" David finished for me. "Oh. That's the easy part." Belatedly, I noticed the police uniform he was wearing. Including the gun.

"I know people, who know people, and one of these bozos guarding the door has a kid on the fourth floor, getting his tonsils out. I had him paged, and voila! A neat smack on the head, a handy pair of cuffs, a strong piece of duct tape, and I have myself a cop's uniform." David puffed out his chest in pride.

Charlene kept wailing. "David. I need to feed her, so she'll stop crying."

He looked from me to Charlene and back again, finally deciding that he'd better let me feed the baby. I nearly choked on my heart when he grabbed her chubby little wrist, dangling her over the bed for me to catch. I did grab her, but barely, and she went blue, holding her breath. Or rather, not being able to catch it.

Thankfully, she started breathing again when I held her against my breast and she could hear my voice. David just stood there with that evil smirk on his face. "Oops," he said, shrugging his shoulders.

I chanced a look at the door and my heart sank when I saw that it was closed all the way. I needed to gather my thoughts. David was on the other side of the bed and I was closer to the door. But, was the second officer outside the door conscious, or even alive? I had no way of knowing.

"Well, are you going to feed it, or not?" demanded David.

"Her," I said. Why did I say it? It didn't matter. "Yes, but I need to sit down." I remembered something.

I didn't want to turn my back on him, but I wouldn't feel safe until Charlene was lying on the pillow so I could feed her football style. Her tiny head fit into the palm of my hand, and her body lay along the pillow. As inconspicuously as I could, I reached under the pillow until I could feel the cold metal of the knife John insisted I keep there. I wrapped my fingers around the hilt.

David moved around to the same side of the bed as me, and I had to let go of the knife so he could see my hand. I pretended to adjust the baby's head, than glanced up at David. He stood there watching me, with a look of hunger on his face, and I could feel the bile rush up into my throat. *Please, please someone come and help me.* I willed my thoughts to reach John somehow. I was desperately trying to stay as calm as I could, because I didn't know what David would do to Charlene if she started crying again.

Thankfully, she fell asleep after about ten minutes, and David came over and picked her up. I reached for her, panicked.

"I'm just putting her in the crib," he said in that snaky voice of his. "We're going to have some fun."

"Please, don't. David, I will leave with you. Please just leave her alone," I pleaded and got up to tug on his sleeve.

He placed Charlene in the crib and whipped around to backhand me in the face. I fell onto the bed with a crash, and David jumped onto me. He pressed his foul mouth onto mine, biting my lip hard. He laughed when I cried out, and I could taste blood on my tongue. I struggled, and managed to push the crib away from my bed.

"Leave the baby you dumb bitch," David hissed in my ear. "Or I will kill her." He then took a gun out of the holster and pointed it at her.

"Noooo!" I sobbed. "Please, no. I'll do what you want!"

"Oh, you know you will." He pulled me to a sitting position and undid his fly.

Think. Think!! I needed to get the knife. If I could just lie back down. Why couldn't I? I flopped back and pushed myself up onto the pillow. He slapped me, hard, forcing me onto my side. *Good!* I reached under my pillow and grabbed the weapon.

He yanked my head back by my hair, hitting me in the face with the butt of the gun. This time, I couldn't hold back the scream, and I seemed to startle David just long enough for me to bring my hand up and plunge the knife deep into his throat.

He stared at me in disbelief, his hand slowly going to his throat. Just as slowly as his hand came up, he fell over, landing on top of me and crushing me to the bed. I struggled to free myself from under his dead weight, still unable to catch my breath enough to yell for help. I couldn't get out from under him, but finally managed to roll him off and onto the floor.

Just then, John started banging on the door, screaming my name. I lunged and unlocked it, throwing the door open. John came rushing in, gun in hand, Officer Spence close at his heels.

"*JOHN!!* David found us!" I was shaking all over. "I killed him." I breathed.

I looked at the floor where David lay staring straight up, the hilt of the knife sticking out of the side of his neck, and a pool of blood on the floor. I screamed and jumped back, as if it were the first time seeing him there. I then noticed the blood that was all over me, and started retching.

"Kathryn. Don't look at him," John said, fiercely. He went to the crib, picked up the now crying baby, and ushered me out of the room.

Just then, I noticed that the other cop had been slain by David, along with a nurse, and I cried out again. John took me down the hall to the visitor's lounge, closing the door behind him. He sat down beside me and put his free arm around my shoulders. Charlene sensed who was holding her and stopped crying momentarily. Good baby.

"Kathryn. Baby, it's all over. It's all over," John kept saying over and over again, until finally my choking sobs subsided into soft crying, which lead me to fall asleep from sheer exhaustion and shock against John's warm, solid body.

I woke up with John still there, holding Charlene, but I wasn't leaning against him anymore. My head was on a pillow, and a heavy blanket covered me. I was shaking uncontrollably. John rushed to my side and dropped to his knees on the floor in front of me. I absently noticed that I was in clean clothes. Blood free.

He stroked my head gently, looking more concerned than I thought necessary, but I was grateful just the same. I reached up and stroked his cheek. Just touching him helped with the shakes and after a few moments, I felt OK. Well, as OK as anyone could be, having just killed their husband in self-defense.

"Thank you," I whispered.

John looked truly shocked. "For what? You were almost killed. Again."

"But, I wasn't. And neither was Charlene," I said, and we both started crying.

John leaned over me and held me tight. He kissed every inch of my face and buried his head in my hair. After a while, we thought we should leave while the baby was content. I needed to be home, and John left stern instructions not to disturb us, despite the nurse's protests that I might be suffering from shock.

"We'll be fine. She's better off at home."

And we left.

Chapter Forty Four

Over the next couple of weeks, everything seemed to get back to normal. John and I began smiling and laughing again, without the threat of David coming back. It was quickly determined that I killed him in self defense, and no charges were handed down. The police also discovered that David had been responsible in a series of rapes and murders of some teen girls some eight years ago, and my heart went out to the parents and families of those girls. I couldn't help but feel somewhat responsible for their deaths. But, then again, I was also a rape victim, and couldn't possibly have known what David was up to. I did dream about it frequently and only prayed that the nightmares would end in their own time with the increasing sense of security with which John surrounded me.

Mom and Charles were absolutely smitten with each other, and on a warm, breezy evening, they took Charlene out in the stroller for a walk down to the market. John and I took immediate advantage of the opportunity and bolted for the bedroom the second they left the apartment. We giggled like school kids as John picked me up and tossed me on the bed. He jumped on after me and pinned me down so he could tease me with his soft, full mouth.

It had been five weeks since we had been together, and we were both a little nervous and extremely excited. After all, this was to be the first time that we would be making love without a huge bulge in my belly, and I didn't want there to be any constraints.

John kissed me deeply, and before long, we were overcome with a raw need to join. I ripped off his shirt and stuffed my hand down the front of his pants, holding tight to the hardness I felt there. He gasped as I stroked and squeezed, bringing him to the edge, only to stop and start over again. When he could hold back no more, he took both my wrists in one hand, pinning my hands over my head, so he could play with me some more.

He shifted his weight beside me and unbuttoned my jeans with his free hand, then my shirt. My bra clasp was in the front, so it was easy for him to free my breasts. He took turns, slowly teasing me with his tongue circling and sucking each nipple. After a few minutes, he let go of my hands and traced his tongue down until I arched my hips to get his full attention, crying out at last, in a shock of ecstasy.

"My turn," I said, and pushed him back so he was on his knees.

I pushed his jeans down and cupped him, gently manipulating him in my hands. I then took him in, circling him with my tongue and quickly bringing him to the brink. When we could wait no more, he came down over me. I yelped when his hardness entered me, reaching the top with one powerful thrust.

"Yes!" said John.

My knees came up to give more and I arched my hips, wanting to swallow him up. We rocked with each other, lost to anything but us, until finally, I couldn't hold back.

"John! Oh God, John!" I screamed, not caring if anyone could hear me or not. But, John wasn't finished yet, and he went down on me again, taking me over within seconds, and then plunging deep inside for the final climax.

We lay there, sweating and panting afterward. Never in my life had I ever experienced that kind of physical pleasure, and I had a flurry of butterflies in my stomach. I couldn't stop smiling either, and John couldn't help but to giggle at me.

We fell asleep and woke a while later to make love again. This time, though, John was slow until it drove me crazy and I demanded deep, full thrusts, ending with me on top. We then relaxed, stroking and kissing each other.

"Do you how much you drive me crazy?" he asked.

"No. Do you know I've never experienced anything like this in my life? You're amazing."

"So are you. But, we should get up now. They'll be back soon," John said and rolled off the bed.

I groaned in protest, but got up too. We jumped into the shower and emerged looking and smelling clean. At around that time, Charles and Mom came back, depositing my screaming baby into my arms for her next feeding. She was becoming a plump, little turkey ball, with ham hocks for legs.

We went to bed early, because I had to go see Dr. Smart the next morning. She had been calling every day, getting more and more urgent with her messages, and finally threatened to come over if I didn't call her back by the end of the seventh day. I figured I was still malnourished a bit, and probably had low iron from all the blood loss over the last little while. John was coming with me, and I wanted to make sure Charlene was fed before we left.

"Good morning Kathryn. John." Dr. Smart addressed us each with a nod.

"Good morning," we said in unison.

She sat there looking at us for a few minutes, and I began to feel the flutter of unease deep in my belly.

"Kathryn, I don't know how to tell you this," she began, and John reached over to take my hand. "When we took your blood the last few times, one of the things we've been testing is your white blood cell count. It's very high.

"At first, we thought you were probably fighting off a virus, and with resent stresses, it's not unusual for your body to deal with fatigue and stress this way. But then the pathology report came in from your tests." She paused.

John and I looked at each other, his expression of concern, mirroring my own. "What is it?" John asked.

Dr. Smart sighed heavily and came around to perch herself on her desk, sitting directly across from me.

"Kathryn, you have ovarian cancer, and I'm afraid it has spread."

John squeezed my hand.

Chapter Forty Five

Epilogue

AFTER KATHRYN'S DIAGNOSIS, SHE WENT for chemotherapy, and radiation, but it had already spread too far for her to be saved. I sit here, at the cemetery with our daughter fluttering around chasing butterflies, while I pick leaves and other bits of debris off the ground around the gravesite. All I can think about is our last moments together. It's all I ever think about.

I read aloud, for the thousandth time, the inscription on her headstone. I guess because I still can't believe that she is actually gone.

Kathryn Anne Sullivan
Cherished Wife of John,
Beloved Mother of Nicolas,
Gabrielle, and Charlene.

Above her name read:
"As certain as time, and change in the Weather;
My Heart will be with You, Now and Forever."

Pop and Meredith got married six months before Kathryn succumbed to the disease that took her from us, and we all went up to Muskoka to the cottage where Kathryn and I first fell in love. Kathryn wanted to be in nature when she died. She said she felt closer to God up there.

We were down by the water, and Charlene had just woken up from a nap on her Mommy's shoulder. When I think back, I believe Kathryn knew that those were her last moments with our daughter, because she kissed her puffy, sleepy lips and cheeks and nose, over and over, until giving Charlene up to Meredith and Pop to take for a boat ride.

Kathryn came to sit on my lap sideways, and I cradled her into my chest as if she were a small child. We had made love the night before, and up here in Muskoka, all was right with the world. The scenery was breathtaking, and the soft breezes on the spring air caressed our skin like gentle kisses from God. I couldn't help but to be grateful for the time we had. We promised each other that we would focus on that, although I can't say that I didn't feel bitter now and then. How could I not?

Kathryn and I watched the boat float out of sight, with Pop, Meredith and Charlene waving crazily in the distance before the boat was gone. She turned so she could look up at me and we kissed each other for a few minutes.

"I love you, John," she said weakly, and her eyes began to flutter.

"I love you too, Princess," I said, trying hard to swallow the lump forming in my throat, for I also knew that the time was here.

Her breathing became shallow, and she couldn't stay awake, then suddenly her eyes sprang open and she smiled up at me.

"Thank you." Her whispered words carried on the wings of a butterfly. "You have set me free."